HAMSIKKER 2

RUSS WATTS

SEVERED PRESS
HOBART TASMANIA

HAMSIKKER 2

WWW.SEVEREDPRESS.COM

ISBN: 978-1-925342-04-8

This book is dedicated to our aging heroes, to those who have left us, and to those who still fight on.

"All you need for happiness is a good gun, a good horse, and a good wife."

Daniel Boone.

CHAPTER ONE

"Just breathe, honey, breathe." Jonas wasn't sure who was more nervous. He let Dakota take his hand, and her sweaty fingers gripped his tightly.

"It hurts," Dakota said through gritted teeth. "It really hurts. I think…I think something's wrong."

Jonas knew she was trying not to cry. He was struggling himself. He had lifted her up onto the pool table with Erik's help, and now Erik and Pippa were running around trying to find some fresh water and clean towels. A fluorescent strip light hung above the table, casting a bright yellow light over Dakota. Mrs. Danick was standing at Dakota's feet, trying to help as best she could while Quinn held a sheet over Dakota's legs. The baby had come so soon, almost a month early, and they weren't fully prepared for the birth. Jonas wished they had more drugs, but their meager supplies had been used up over the last few weeks, and now there was nothing left. He had hoped there would be more time, but the baby wasn't waiting, and Dakota was just going to have to fight through the pain. It was coming.

"I know, I know." Jonas wiped his wife's forehead. The sun was beaming in through the window, but it was cold. There was a dusting of snow outside on the ground, and she had been in labor for hours. He had been up with her for hours. The labor had taken them all through the night and into the morning. It seemed like the end was near, though, and he could see the fear in his wife's eyes.

"Honey, look at me, nothing's wrong. Okay? *Nothing is wrong.*" Jonas had no idea if he was telling the truth, but he was praying so. He was no longer certain anyone was listening, but old habits were hard to break. It seemed like only yesterday he had found out he was going to be a father. Now, in a matter of minutes, he would see his child for the first time. He was excited, nervous, and worried. This was no ordinary pregnancy, and certainly no ordinary birth. They had no medical supplies and were relying on Mrs. Danick and Pippa to handle the birth.

"It's almost there," said Mrs. Danick soothingly. "One more push, and…oh."

"Oh? What does *oh* mean?" Dakota looked frantically at Mrs. Danick and squeezed Jonas's hand even harder.

"I'm sure it's fine, Dakota." Jonas winced, convinced she was breaking his fingers. "Isn't it, Mrs. Danick? Everything's fine?"

He looked at her, but she was recoiling from the table, and Quinn looked horrified.

"You did this," said Mrs. Danick, pointing a crooked finger at Jonas. "You did this. You did this!" She began shouting as she continued to back away from Dakota.

"Jonas? Tell me what's going on," pleaded Dakota. "What the…" Dakota screamed and screwed up her face in excruciating pain.

"Quinn?" Jonas could see her eyes wide open, staring between Dakota's legs. Quinn still held the sheet up, but she was shaking her head from side to side. She dropped the sheet and began to walk away too. The bloody sheet slipped down Dakota's legs, and Jonas saw for the first time what was happening. There was so much blood. It was all over the green felt of the table, the floor, and Dakota's legs. It had drained into the corners of the pool table and slopped down between the netting onto the floor, forming small pools at each leg.

"Mrs. Danick, what…?" Jonas looked around the room, but she was nowhere to be seen. "Quinn, help me." He reached out a hand, but Quinn had disappeared too. How could they leave him? How could they abandon Dakota when she needed them most?

Jonas looked around the room, realizing the sunlight had all but gone. A thick rain fell outside, obscuring the light and drenching the room in a foggy grey. He noticed for the first time that the walls were covered in a dark green substance that oozed from the cavities behind, running down them and mixing with the blood on the floor. The walls appeared to be almost black, and the floor was sticky, yet slippery at the same time. He heard footsteps behind him, and turned to face the doorway.

"Erik?"

Erik stepped out of the shadows and into the room, brandishing a baseball bat. His face was expressionless, and his eyes blank, devoid of life. "We have to end this."

Jonas saw another figure emerge from the doorway behind Erik, and Pippa stepped out holding a meat cleaver. "You did this, Hamsikker."

"Wait, what is this?" Jonas backed away from them, noticing more figures behind them. They seemed to be made of swirling mists of grey that formed into human shapes only as they entered the room. He saw Mrs. Danick, Terry, Peter, and even Freya, all holding a variety of sharp instruments designed to maim and kill. All wore the same blank expressions on their faces.

"You did this," they chorused in unison. "*You.*"

As Jonas backed away he bumped into the pool table. He had to help Dakota. Surely they would see sense. Surely his friends were here to help; if not him, then Dakota at least. He turned to face his wife and found himself staring at the thing that had emerged from her belly. Whatever it was had crawled out of its own accord, using its own energy to escape her womb. There was a broken fingernail in one wooden side of the table, and a bloody trail of evidence of where it had clawed its way out of her, dragging itself across the green felt and up onto Dakota's belly. It was gnawing on the umbilical cord, its dead eyes coolly observing Jonas and the growing group of people behind him.

"Dakota?"

Jonas knew he was not going to get an answer. Dakota was unconscious. Her eyes were closed and her lips shut. Her arms hung limply from each side of the table, and her skin was so pale that it looked almost translucent. Blue veins coursed her legs, looking like rivers plotted out on a map, and blood pumped through them lazily. She had lost too much blood, and he knew she was going to die without help.

"Dakota," he whispered. He looked back to the dead baby sat on her belly. It had finished eating the umbilical cord, and was now digging into Dakota's intestines, the baby's tiny hands pulling out stringy lengths of its mother's gut before greedily shoving them into its small, toothless mouth. Jonas's child was a zombie, and now he was being forced to watch it kill Dakota.

"It's time," said a voice from the head of the table. Another figure emerged from the darkness holding a sword above its head. Jonas clenched his hands together, more terrified than he had ever been before. He needed to stop this, to save Dakota, but he was powerless. The green sludge from the walls had reached his feet and was sucking him down into the carpet. He tried to lift a foot up, just one foot, but he couldn't. He was stuck fast.

"You did this," said Cliff. The man's greasy overalls were smeared with oil and dark, crimson blood. His face was battered and bruised, and he spoke through a mouthful of broken teeth; one eye was swollen shut. Cliff raised the sword above Dakota's head. "I'm going to put Dakota out of her misery. Then I'm going to kill your son."

"No, wait," shouted Jonas. "Wait!" As the sword swung down Jonas tried to wrench himself free from the green sludge, but it had slowly crept up his legs to his waist. The whole room was full of it, and it lazily filled the room making the games room appear more like a swimming pool. Steam rose from the surface, and pieces of bodies bobbed on the top of the sludge where a film of grunge had settled like the skin on a bowl of custard. Dismembered arms and legs protruded through the dirty membrane only to sink again into the mire. Jonas tried to close his eyes, not wanting to watch Dakota die, but his eyelids refused to work. The sword came down slowly, its clean, shiny blade slicing through the air as it neared Dakota's throat.

"Wait!" Jonas shouted again, but it was too late to stop it. Cliff had found him, and the others had helped. How could they do this? Jonas wished he had his axe. He wanted to kill them all, and then he would kill Cliff again. It always came back to him.

"Dakota!" Jonas screamed as the sword severed her head from her body, and it fell away, landing in the sludge with a barely audible plopping sound.

"What is it, honey? What is it?"

Jonas felt Dakota rubbing his arm, and he opened his eyes to find her looking at him with fear and concern on her face.

"I think you were dreaming. You've been tossing and turning for a while. I was going to let you be, but then you called out my name. Are you okay?" asked Dakota.

Jonas sat upright. He looked around the room, looking for Cliff, a pool table, or a baby. He looked for his son, but of course, there was nothing there. Jonas still expected to see slime running down the walls, but there was none. The walls were painted a mint green color and adorned with certificates and photographs of Saint Paul's construction. It was still the same room they had gone to bed in hours ago: a basic room full of old pictures of golfing champions and tarnished trophies locked in glass cabinets. A faintly sterile smell hung in the air, emanating from the cleaner's trolley in the corner, still laden with bleach, dirty cloths, and polish. The thin blanket covering them had slipped off, and he drew it up to his chin, shivering as the cool air found his sweaty body. There was no baby. His mind awakened, and he knew there wouldn't be for several months yet.

"Sorry, I didn't mean to wake you," Jonas said as he tried to push the nightmare from his mind. He didn't need to remember it. There were enough horrors in the day to occupy his mind. The last thing he needed was to freak Dakota out with stupid dreams. Jesus, it had only been one night, and already he was having worries about the baby. He was going to have to get a grip on things.

"Okay. Well, we should try to sleep. It'll be dawn soon," said Dakota. She turned away from him and laid her head back on the floor. They had no pillows and had balled up some old drapes they had found earlier to sleep on. It was surprisingly comfortable. Jonas knew they were both shattered and would've slept on a bed of nails, so despite the tightness in his neck and the pain in his shoulder, he wasn't about to start complaining.

There was no going back to sleep now. He was too awake, and Dakota was right. The dawn would be around soon. He didn't feel like laying there when there was so much to do and so much to learn. If things were different he might've taken the opportunity to try it on with Dakota. There was once a time, years ago, when they made love at the drop of a hat. Over time, the lust had faded, but they still loved each other. In the last few months they had found it impossible to get any quality time together, and it was only yesterday Dakota revealed to him she was pregnant. She was still mad at him, too, and it took some convincing on his part to get her to sleep in the same room as him. In the end he won out, and she admitted she would rather be near him than be separated whilst they were sharing the place with strangers. There were still a lot of issues to work through, but at least she was talking to him again.

Jonas slipped out of their bed quietly. Dakota was already asleep, and he dressed as fast as he could. If he was the only one up he could use the time to do a little exploring. They had been so tired yesterday that there was little time for anything else. After some introductions, Gabe and Mara had shown them around the clubhouse. It was a quick tour, just enough so they knew where to find the bathrooms and where they could sleep for the night. They had eaten a light meal and then retired, agreeing to discuss their plans in the morning. Gabe had collected up all their guns and weapons, but he promised to return them when they left. They clearly didn't need them in the golf course, so Gabe told Jonas he would put them somewhere safe. Jonas was concerned about being unarmed, but Gabe seemed trustworthy, and the reality was that they didn't have much choice. If they wanted to stay, they had to accept Gabe was in charge. It irked Jonas that he didn't know where their weapons were, especially his axe. He felt odd without it. It had become like a safety blanket, and his empty hands twitched for something to hold onto.

They hadn't discussed what might happen beyond the night. Nobody was in the mood for making small talk, and thoughts of their recently deceased friends weighed heavily on their minds, Tyler and Randall in particular. Jonas was eager to know more about where they were, and who their hosts were, and now he was up it seemed like the perfect time to do a little private exploring. Aside from the nightmare, he felt better. He had slept, truly slept, and with a good feed, he felt better than he had in a long time. Life wasn't perfect, but they had at least managed to spend the night in safety, away from the world of the zombies outside the fences.

As he closed the door he heard Dakota's soft breathing, and he hoped she wouldn't suffer from the same nightmares as him. He suspected she did, but if so she kept silent about them. They all suffered from painful dreams. Freya was particularly susceptible to them and frequently woke the others in the night with her cries. Jonas walked down the upper corridor; he couldn't hear any sounds, and trusted everyone was asleep. The silence was reassuring. It meant the dead weren't present.

Jonas retraced his steps from last night and found his way back down to the entrance. The key was in the door, and he unlocked it so he could take a look at the golf course. The sun was barely over the horizon, and it was slowly illuminating the greens in a golden haze. Sunlight trickled through the oaks and elms that lined the fairway, and Jonas noticed it reflected off the fence that was still in place, strong and sturdy. He wondered how many of the dead were outside those walls. Were they pressed up against it, trying to get in, or had they found something else to grab their attention? Right in front of the clubhouse was the porch and a swing. Just as Gabe had said, there were two small mounds of dirt indicating where he had buried their two attackers. A man and a woman, Gabe had said, just a couple of drifters who should've known better. Jonas wasn't about to risk crossing Gabe, and whilst they were staying under his roof, it was his rules. How long they stayed depended on a few things, all of which would be discussed later in the day.

Jonas returned inside and checked out the downstairs level. He passed through the bar, a lounge, a library, a couple of meeting rooms, and finally found himself in the kitchen. It was a little dirty which surprised him considering how well kept the place was otherwise. A few empty tins lay on the counter, and the dishes from last night still hadn't been cleaned. Perhaps, with the arrival of new guests, Mara hadn't found time to clean up. Jonas examined the cupboards and discovered a treasure trove of food. There were canned vegetables and fruit, boxes of pasta, jars of herbs, and a host of cooking materials that would satisfy even the most demanding cook. He ran the tap and poured himself a glass of cool water, finishing it instantly. He poured another, and walked over to a set of doors that he guessed might lead to a pantry. It was a huge double door, set into a recess, and when he opened it he was surprised to find that it was a walk-in freezer. The automatic light flicked on as he walked in. There were boxes and boxes stacked up on metal shelves, and he examined the labels: turkey, lamb, chicken pies, sausages, and beef patties. There was enough meat to last them for months as long as the freezer's power held out. Gabe had mentioned something about the generator last night, and Jonas was keen to know more. If he was going to leave the others here whilst he went to get Janey, he wanted to know they were truly safe.

What with Dakota telling him she was pregnant, and with everything that had happened in the last 24 hours, he hadn't thought about Janey much. He doubted that she and her three boys had as much food as this, and with fall rapidly approaching he couldn't leave it any longer. Her supplies would surely be running low, and he had no idea how well off she really was. She had promised to stay at home in Thunder Bay, and he knew he could take her word on it when she said she would wait for him. But how bad was it up there? Was it any better or worse than Kentucky? He hadn't even met his three nephews yet, and he wanted more of a relationship with them than a once-a-year conversation over Skype. That was all he'd ever had, and now he didn't know if he would even see them again. The internet had gone belly-up the same time as everything else, so phone calls and emails were a distant dream. Mike and Chester understood their uncle lived far away, but Ritchie was too young. He was only four, and didn't understand why Uncle Jonas didn't visit. Well, he was going to visit them now, and nothing was going to stop him. Jonas decided that Dakota needn't come with him anymore. It was safer here than out on the roads, and he had all but made up his mind that he was going alone. He could travel faster, and he wouldn't have to worry about looking out for her or his unborn child. If anything, he was more determined than ever to get to Janey now they had found this place. He could bring her back to Saint Paul's; perhaps offer her a fresh start.

A rattling sound interrupted his thoughts, and he carefully peered around the doorway of the freezer. He was still cautious about their new surroundings, and he kept silent as he looked at who was in the kitchen. Jonas watched Gabe open up a jar of coffee and begin spooning it into a white mug. There was an electric kettle boiling, and Gabe unplugged it before pouring the hot water into the mug. The aroma of the fresh coffee struck Jonas, and the smell was heavenly. It reminded Jonas of a life before the dead, when he could get up in the morning and get breakfast without having to worry if he was going to be eaten alive by a zombie.

"Think you could spare an extra mug of that, Gabriel?" he asked Gabe as he approached the counter.

"Shit, Hamsikker, is that you?" asked Javier, dropping the spoon on the counter. The clattering sound echoed throughout the kitchen. "You made me jump."

"Sorry, I was just checking out the place. It's pretty amazing. You've enough food in the freezer to last a good time."

"Yeah, everything you need under one roof, right? Sorry, I wasn't thinking, it's just habit to make myself a cup. I should put the pot on. I dare say the others might want a drink too. And it's Gabe, not Gabriel. Only my mother called me that, and she's with the boss upstairs now."

"Absolutely," said Jonas, as Gabe took a percolator from a cupboard. He took a sip from his mug as he began to spoon more coffee out and fill the percolator. "Damn, that's good coffee. I think even Freya might be tempted."

Jonas chuckled. "I'm sure we can find some milk or juice for her."

"Right, right," said Javier as he pressed the plunger down. He looked at Jonas. "If you don't mind me saying, Hamsikker, you look like shit. You manage to get any sleep at all?"

Jonas shrugged. "Some." The smell of the coffee had brought back memories of real life when he would spend weekends with Dakota, pouring over newspapers during Sunday brunch at their local deli. He would demolish a plate of pancakes in seconds, whilst Dakota would take her time over a bowl of muesli and homemade plum jam. He felt his stomach rumble. Jonas seemed to remember seeing some maple syrup in one of the kitchen cupboards, but it was unlikely they had any eggs. Perhaps the pancakes would have to wait a bit longer, and he pushed away his hunger pangs. It was something he was used to doing now.

Javier handed Jonas a mug of hot coffee and smiled. "What did I tell you? Sweetness and light, right? You don't have to worry anymore, Hamsikker. You're safe. Your family and friends are safe. You can start to relax, okay?"

Jonas raised his mug and chinked it together with Gabe's. Perhaps Gabe was right. Perhaps this was a fresh start. He reassessed his plans in his head as he sipped on the coffee. A day or two to rest up, and he could leave the others here, happy to know they were safe when he went to find Janey.

Javier reclined against a stainless steel counter-top as Quinn and Mrs. Danick entered the kitchen. Jonas pointed out the fresh coffee, and they poured themselves a mug each.

"Couldn't sleep?" asked Jonas.

Quinn yawned. "Not over Mrs. Danick's snoring."

"Keep it up, Quinn, keep it up," said Mrs. Danick. "Actually, we slept pretty good considering. Still, it's hard to let your guard down completely. It's hard to think we finally made it. Of course, some of us didn't. I remember…"

"You got any theories?" asked Javier. He wasn't interested in their sob stories. He knew once they got started they would never end, and he had to get things moving along. "You know, about where it all came from, or why it all started? You know anything?"

Mrs. Danick gave Gabe a stern look but ignored his question and began rummaging through drawers.

Quinn sipped on her coffee. "All I know is that all those debates about carbon emissions, asteroids on a collision course with Earth, and flu viruses without a cure all turned out to be a truckload of bull. In the end, it was good old-fashioned zombies that did for us," said Quinn. "Who, why, and when is all irrelevant now. What's done is done. We'll never know, and quite frankly it doesn't matter. Questions like that don't mean jack now. They're here. We're here. They can be killed. End of."

Javier admired Quinn's response. He noticed her pick up a large kitchen knife, and then she put it back in the drawer where she'd found it. If she was looking for anything specific, she didn't give a clue as to what.

"This doesn't have to be the end," said Mrs. Danick. "There's plenty of life in us yet. Even in an old fart like me. Like Quinn says, they can be killed. So what's your story, Gabe?"

Javier chose to ignore the last question. "Maybe so. But we are vastly outnumbered. You all know what it's like out there beyond that fence. How many of your friends are still out there?"

"We have God on our side, and our faith," said Dakota as she slipped into the room. She headed straight for the coffee.

Jonas hadn't noticed her standing there, and he wondered how long she had been listening. He thought she might sleep in, but evidently everyone was waking up. She didn't look at him, so he stayed where he was, waiting for her to approach him. She never was a morning person, and when she was pissed at him, she knew how to push his buttons. He hated being ignored, and he knew she was deliberately avoiding him.

"We have to think of this as not a curse, but a chance. It's a chance to prove ourselves to Him, a chance to be rescued and taken into His hands. I can't believe we've been abandoned. I *won't* believe it," said Dakota.

"You *still* have faith after all this?" Javier looked at Dakota with large eyes. "You still think someone is looking down on us and looking out for us? Do you honestly believe that someone up there is saving a space for us in Heaven? Darling, we have been screwed. God's not just on vacation. He's packed his bags and moved on."

Dakota appeared to be downcast, and she was only going through the motions. Jonas could see her heart wasn't in it. She spoke of faith and strength, but if she had any left in her it was buried deep. She said nothing to him as she took a mug of coffee and walked back to the door.

"I'm going to see Pippa," Dakota announced. "I'll see if she needs any help with Freya."

"Hold up, dear," said Mrs. Danick. "I'll come with you. I think I'd rather be with you than stuck in here. There's a nasty smell in this kitchen."

As Mrs. Danick and Dakota left, Javier stifled a laugh. He'd apparently touched a nerve and was amused how easily he could wind them up. Dakota could keep her faith. It was useless in this world. It was nothing now but a stick to beat over the heads of others, a tool to make people feel guilty. It didn't provide hope, just a sense of futility. And when you let fate take over, you were just another person lining up to join the dead.

"You find what you're looking for?" asked Javier as Quinn pulled a whisk from a drawer beneath a large stove.

"No, I … ah-ha." Quinn plucked out a small plastic chicken and held it aloft like a trophy. "Perfect."

Javier studied her face for clues, but when she looked at him all he saw was mistrust. Despite letting them in, despite his offer of help, they still had reservations. Clearly he was going to have to do more to get them on side. Some of them were more important than others, more useful, and he was weighing up how much time to spend on Quinn. He had earmarked Mrs. Danick as a troublemaker from the outset. Something about her irked him. It was as if she could see through his lies.

"Is that a timer?" he asked as Quinn turned the head of the chicken around in a circle. "I didn't have you pegged as a cook."

"No?" Quinn smiled as the chicken started ticking.

"No," said Javier. "Something a little more…dangerous? I'm sure you've broken a few rules in your time."

"Actually, I haven't had an alarm clock in a while now. When it's my turn to take watch, I like to know how long I've got left. Once I'm properly dressed I'll go walk around the perimeter, make sure everything's in shape. I used to have an App, but, well, that went south about the same time as the colonel's secret recipe."

"Gabe, you think Mara can help rustle up some breakfast?" asked Jonas. "I'm sure we can help. Quinn, you feel like helping us out before you head out?" Jonas could feel the tension in the kitchen rising, and he couldn't quite explain what it was, but something was off. Gabe was asking some pretty direct questions.

"There's plenty of food to go around. We can sort something out for everyone to eat. Mara's sleeping, but she'll be up soon." Javier whistled and proceeded to walk over to Quinn. "There are certain things you miss, and there are certain things you don't even want to talk about. It's like an itch you can't scratch. I know it was junk, but fried chicken is one of those things. You liked it, too, huh? Don't tell me you worked in one of those greasy places?"

Quinn tossed the ticking chicken from hand to hand as Javier approached her. "Work there? No. I was never much of a fan myself, but my husband couldn't get enough of it. Roger would eat it every day if I let him."

Jonas was curious. Quinn had never told them about her past. He couldn't see her flipping burgers for a living, and this was the first time she'd ever mentioned having a husband. She was a blank canvas, and it seemed that Gabe was pressing her buttons, getting her to open up.

"Roger?" Javier studied Quinn's face, but she gave nothing more away. It was like his name was a keyword, and she shut down.

"He's gone now. Anyway, I should get back to the others."

As Quinn went to the door, Javier held her arm. She twisted it away, but he refused to let her go. "What about the pantry?" he asked. "You want to see all the food we have? I've only shown you half of what we have here. This is…"

"Let go," said Quinn forcefully. She yanked her arm back, and Javier let her free. "Show me later, when the others are here."

Javier started to tell her that there was so much more to the complex she should see and that he would gladly show her around, when the ticking chicken emitted a buzzing sound.

"Time's up," said Quinn, and she left the kitchen.

"You know, she's smart. You shouldn't rile her up like that," said Jonas. "Quinn won't appreciate you messing with her. She's strong."

"Quinn's a big girl, I can see that. I don't doubt she can handle herself. I just like to know who's on my side. We're all under the same roof now, and I don't want any nasty surprises. I'm sure you can understand that."

Jonas nodded.

"Hamsikker, you got a second? I'd like to show you something."

"Sure."

Javier led Jonas back through to the library, and he pulled back the thick velvet drapes. Sunlight came streaming in through the tall windows, and they both put down their coffee mugs. Jonas noticed the library walls were lined from top to bottom with books. Around the window frame were photographs, mostly in black and white, of golfers stood outside the clubhouse. The room was cozy and elegant, with furnishings that wouldn't look out of place in a palace.

Javier sat down on a plush leather chair and unfurled a large map of the US across a desk. He placed a finger over it and looked at Jonas.

"Here's where we are." Javier looked up at Jonas to make sure he had his attention. "And here's where I need to be."

Jonas watched as Javier drew his finger north, up through Illinois, and Wisconsin, before resting over Winnipeg.

"This is the last place my brother was living. He was moving there from Thunder Bay last I heard. I can't stay here forever with Mara, wondering how he is. I need to know. I *need* to get up there and find out."

Jonas waited for Gabe to continue, but the room was filled with silence. He wasn't entirely sure how to respond; whether Gabe was looking for reassurance or information. He had no intention of telling Gabe that Janey lived in Thunder Bay. He wasn't sure yet if it was a good idea to part with that information. "I thought you had settled in here for the long-run," Jonas said. "You said yourself there's enough food to last for months."

"Water too," said Javier. "The irrigation system is working perfectly. We have clean water, power, heating, and fresh vegetables. It's quite safe too. It would take a hundred zombies to get through that fence out there."

"So…" Jonas looked at the map. He was going to be taking a very similar route north, and now the caffeine had worked its way into his system, Jonas was feeling more alert. His brain was already thinking about what lay ahead, about Dakota and the baby, about where he was heading, and how he was going to find Janey.

"So, what do you say you and me take a road trip?" asked Javier as he reclined in his chair. The black leather squeaked as he settled into it. "Mara can take care of this place with the help of the others for a few days. There are plenty of vehicles out front we can take our pick from. They're fully tanked up, and ready to go. I was thinking that maybe you and Erik might accompany me?"

"Why do you need us?" Jonas couldn't help but wonder. Why now? If he didn't want Mara out there with him, then Gabe could just as easily go on his own.

Javier looked at Jonas. The moment that Rose had killed Gabe, things had changed. Javier wanted her more than anything, but she was a liability. He couldn't rely on her anymore. The events of the crash had come back to him, and he'd realized Rose would've left him out there on the roadside to die like Cindy. He needed to change the direction his life was going, and get back on track. Rose had been holding him back. It was time to cut her free. If she wanted to set up home, she could do so without him. Over the last couple of days they had recovered from the crash, eaten and slept well, and yet Rose refused to entertain the idea of leaving and continuing on to Canada. The fences around the golf course seemed secure, and they hadn't seen a single zombie inside, but he really had no idea how secure the place was long-term. Fate had thrown him a bone. Going it alone was an option, but it was more useful to have someone watch his back. When he had seen Erik and the others surface through the storm drain, he had decided to let them in. Rose wanted a little fun, and when she had spotted Freya she had practically forced Javier to go along with her plan, not that there had been much time for discussion. By assuming the identities of Gabe and Mara, Javier thought they could find out what the new group of people might offer. Javier knew Rose only really wanted the girl. But there was something about Erik and Jonas that appealed to him. They had been through a lot out there, probably more than he could imagine. They were fighters. If he could get them on side, they could be useful - to a point.

Javier hadn't told Rose about going solo, about leaving her behind, but he would sell it as only a temporary thing. He would tell her that he'd be gone just long enough to find his brother, and then he would be back. Of course, he had no intention of coming back. With Gabe's identity hanging around his neck, he didn't want to return to it once he was able to shake it off. No way was he going to pretend to be some worthless security guard any longer than he had to. Once he reached the Canadian border, with Erik and Jonas's help, he could shed it, rid himself of this new identity and rid himself of anyone who thought he was Gabe. He wanted to become Javier again. Gabe would die, and so would Gabe's associates.

"I could do with some help out there on the road," said Javier. "You know how difficult it is out there with the dead roaming around. If I give you a couple of days to rest up, perhaps you could talk to Erik, and we could get this done quickly. I just need to get my brother, and then we'll be straight back." Javier didn't know exactly where his brother was. Diego had shacked up with some girl in Lorette, just outside of Winnipeg, and Javier had no reason to believe Diego had moved on. He had been working in Thunder Bay, and been spending a lot of time between the two places. All Javier knew was that he had to find him.

"I'm not so sure," said Jonas. He was thinking about Janey. He was thinking that maybe he could use Javier to get to Canada too. Still, he would be hard pressed to convince Erik that leaving again so soon was a good idea. "I think you'd be better off on your own. My wife is pregnant, and I'm not sure going out again so soon is a good move."

Javier sighed. "Hamsikker, I thought you would understand. I'm offering you a chance here. This isn't for you, or me, but for your family. This is a chance for everyone. If you do this for me, then I see no reason why we can't all stay here. You know how good this place is."

The inference was clear to Jonas. If he didn't help Gabe, the offer to stay was gone. Jonas needed this place for Dakota, for his child; turning down the offer to head north to Canada would undoubtedly lead to trouble. Perhaps he could go with Javier alone and leave Erik behind to look out for everyone.

"Just me," said Jonas. "I'll go with you, and once we find your brother, we're coming straight back. I've a sister, Janey, up in Canada. Maybe I could try to contact her when we're there. I won't take up any of your time though. We get what we want, and then we head on back here, agreed?" Jonas decided that once they reached the border he would split up and go to get Janey on his own. He didn't want to waste time searching for Gabe's brother. They would have to meet back at Saint Paul's independently. Jonas didn't know how much he could trust Gabe, so he wanted to keep the fact that Janey lived in Thunder Bay to himself.

Javier stood up and held out his hand. Hamsikker's sister held no interest for him. The woman was just another zombie. Still, at least Hamsikker was on board now. "I'd appreciate it if you could keep this just between us. Mara's got a lot on her plate, and I'd rather not have her worry about me going out there again. You know, I think we're going to get on like a house on fire, Hamsikker," said Javier, grinning as they shook. "To the future."

CHAPTER TWO

"I miss music. I played the cello. Not professionally, but I was good. The sound of it used to give me shivers. Have you heard much classical music? When you hear the cello you can't help but fall in love. The sound it makes is so rich and sorrowful. Honestly, it's like a piece of me is missing. I doubt I'll ever get another chance to play again."

Jonas never would've guessed Mara to be musical. Not that there was a type, but he was surprised at her honesty, for opening up to him. She had taken him and Erik outside after breakfast so she could show them around whilst Gabe busied himself in the kitchen. She cooked and he washed, that was the deal. Everyone else was washing up, trying to get themselves clean again. The bloodstains were difficult to scrub from their clothes, but at least their bodies were clean at last.

"You might. This can't go on forever. I bet one day you'll get to play again. I'd like to hear you. Are there any pieces of music you really like? Any favorite composers?"

Mara shook her head and looked away. "No, I didn't have any one favorite. It was just a hobby."

"My Peter tried the guitar for a while," said Erik as they walked across to the storm drain. "Freaking useless. I had high hopes he would be the next Springsteen. Turns out he wasn't. Not even close. He has many talents, but music is not one of them. Takes after his father, I guess."

"You don't like music?" asked Mara. They reached the edge of the garden, and she bent down to pick at some weeds.

"Sure, I do. More your old school rock like Springsteen or Hendrix. I didn't get much time for it with the day job anyway. Work and kids soon put paid to any free time I had. I think the last CD I bought was some fluffy pop stuff for Freya."

"A CD? What, had they sold out of old 45's? Erik, I doubt Freya even knows what a CD is. Nobody *buys* music anymore," said Jonas.

"Nobody buys much of anything anymore," said Erik wistfully.

"What did you used to do?" Mara asked Erik. She looked him up and down. "Laborer? Something like that?"

"He was a cop," said Jonas. "A damn good one at that too."

"Oh, right," said Mara bluntly.

Jonas thought he picked up on something in her tone, something that suggested she wasn't too comfortable around a cop, but he dismissed it. Most people felt nervous around a cop, even if they had nothing to hide. Quinn had been like that, too, at first.

Mara cleared her throat. "That's the tool shed over there," she said, pointing to a large brown building. It had a door at either end with heavy looking padlocks and dirty, dark windows. "It's full of crap. There are a lot of hand tools, some gardening equipment, and a couple of ride-on lawnmowers. We used them to keep the course in shape, but we don't tend to bother much anymore. It's just a waste of gas, and there doesn't seem much point really."

"What's that?" asked Jonas pointing to a smaller shed. It was painted a lurid white color, with ivy growing up the walls and clinging to the tin roof.

"Nothing of use, unless you plan on televising the end of the world. The media crew stored their gear in it. You can see the top of the TV tower from here. Gabe goes up there sometimes to look around, make sure the dead aren't getting too close. You can smell them sometimes. It's the smell of death. It just comes over the fence, and you know they're there. You can't see them, but they're there. They're always there." Mara shuddered. "Look, you're welcome to have a walk around the course, but I should go find Gabe. We have a lot to sort out today."

"For sure," said Erik. "We'll take a look around and come help you later."

Mara nodded and smiled, but Jonas felt as if it wasn't sincere. Perhaps her encounter with the two drifters a couple of days back had her on edge, wary of strangers. It was understandable.

"I'm going to take a shower, Hamsikker. I'll see you later." Mara looked at Jonas as she left. He wasn't certain, but she definitely hadn't been comfortable since finding out Erik was a cop.

"If I didn't know better, I'd say she has the hots for you," said Erik.

"That your expert opinion?"

Erik shrugged. "Just thought I picked up on something. Something feels a little different about her. I don't know."

"They seem fine, but we just have to be careful. They must be nervous having a bunch of strangers crashing their private party."

"Don't think I haven't forgotten they took our weapons too. I'll have a word with Gabe about that later. I'd feel a lot better if I knew where they were," said Erik. "Just in case."

Both of them started walking toward the TV tower, away from the clubhouse. Jonas was contemplating climbing it and taking a look over the fence. Would it make him feel any better knowing the dead were gathered there instead of just thinking they were? He decided it could wait. There was a lot to plan, and he needed to go and talk to Dakota. As they walked, Erik began humming a tune.

"What is that?" asked Jonas. "That song you're so badly humming. I think I know it."

"Oh, just a little something by the Boss. I took Pippa to see him last year. Man, he rocked." Erik smiled and continued humming.

"Wonder what he's up to now," mused Jonas. "You think he's a bad-ass zombie killer or six feet under?"

"Ain't no question, Hamsikker. Springsteen is out there somewhere kicking some mother-fucking zombies back to mother-fucking hell."

Jonas laughed, and Erik joined in.

"Shit, I remember listening to Springsteen when we were back in high school. He has longevity, I'll give him that."

Erik nodded as their laughter died down. "What about Slash?"

"You need to ask? Please," said Jonas. "Zombie-killer all day long."

Erik clicked the roof of his mouth with his tongue while he thought. "Okay, I'll go with that. How about the piano-man?"

"Billy? He's toast." Jonas raised his hands in the air and shrugged. "Don't blame me, I didn't waste him."

"The Dixies?" asked Erik. "Those country chicks know how to handle themselves."

"Dead."

"Taylor?"

"Deader."

"Kenny?"

"Even deader. Don't you watch the news, Erik? He went before this whole thing started. Shit, he's probably back shuffling around looking for Dolly so he can take a nasty chunk out of her neck."

Jonas clacked his teeth together and stretched his arms out, mimicking taking a bite out of something. "I can see it now, his eyes all glazed over and his tongue hanging out while Dolly bats him away, still trying to apply some lipstick before he severs her jugular vein."

"Ha." Erik laughed. "I guess the gambler lost in the end. What about all those action heroes? Remember those films we used to love? You ever think what they might be doing now?"

Jonas drew in a breath. "Well, Arnold and Sly undoubtedly are dead. I mean, come on, what are they going to do, defend themselves with their pensions?"

"Oh, tough call," said Erik. "You know, I like to think John McClane is out there, picking off the bad guys, still kicking butt for us."

"You know who is still kicking butt?" asked Jonas.

"Who?"

"Bruce. He's fought off an army of the dead already. This is a walk in the park for him."

"Bruce is indestructible, I'll give you that. So who would win in a fight? Ash or McClane?"

"Seriously?" Jonas rubbed his jaw. "No. There's no way they would fight each other. More likely they would join forces. Imagine that, the two of them side by side armed with a chainsaw and a magnum."

"Yippee-kay-ay," said Erik.

The two men laughed some more, and Jonas noticed the air was cooling as they talked. At one point Pippa came out to check on them, saying that Peter and Freya were having a wash, and she suggested Erik do the same. He shooed her back inside, promising that he was fine, and that they would wash later. It seemed like they finally had a chance to relax. Back when they were hiding in

Erik's place, there was no time for idle chatter or friendly reminiscing. It had been about survival back then. Jonas knew their future was uncertain, that this peace probably wouldn't last forever, but he wanted to enjoy it while he could. For all their talk, they never covered anything serious, and Jonas knew he was going to have to bring it up. There was one thing eating away at him, and the sky was threatening rain. If he didn't speak honestly with Erik now, he might not get time later. They reached a bunker, and Jonas sat down on the grass, inviting Erik to join him.

"So what is it? You're about as hard to read as Freya's pop-up books. I can tell you've something on your mind, so get on with it."

"You're too smart to be a cop, you know that?" Jonas sighed. "I just don't know. It's hard to decide what's right and wrong anymore. I thought life was simple, but now…I've killed people Erik.

"We all have, Hamsikker."

"No, not like you mean."

Erik frowned.

"Back in Jeffersontown," explained Jonas. "At the garage, when we were ambushed. Anna, Mary, and James were killed by the zombies, but Cliff…"

"What about him?"

Jonas looked down. He had to get it out, but he didn't want to see Erik's face when he told him. As much as he felt guilty for killing Cliff, he felt just as ashamed for letting his friend down. He didn't want Erik to hate him or think less of him, but Jonas hated himself for what he'd done. He had to let it go, otherwise it would just eat him up.

"I killed him," said Jonas. As soon as the words were out of his head he couldn't stop, and the rest came rushing out in a torrent of relief. "I was so mad. I was so *fucking* mad at him for setting us up like that. All I could feel was this anger building up inside of me. Then I saw his smug face as he stood over Mary's body. He wasn't sorry for what he did, not one bit. So, I beat him. I beat on him until Tyler pulled me off. I wanted to beat Cliff's face in until he was broken. When his face was smashed in, I took Tyler's gun, and I was going to put a bullet in his brain. I thought I'd better save the bullets though, so I took my axe and…

"Jesus Christ, I killed him, Erik. I mean he was messed up, but he could've lived. He could be with us now. What's been going on since then, well, it screwed me up. That wasn't me. My head was all over the place. You know that, right? At the garage, the things I saw, what happened there, just…"

Jonas remembered his father's body and how it had climbed out of the casket at the funeral. His father had been put down, too, except he was already dead. There was a difference. There was a big difference between taking down a zombie, and killing a man in cold-blood. Jonas wasn't sure he would ever forget it. Somehow he had to forgive himself, though. He had to find a way to move on.

"Get over it, Hamsikker," said Erik plainly. He drew in a deep breath before continuing. "Cliff was a liability from day one. You had to make the call, I understand that. I don't know if I would've done what you did, but you did it, and I'm in no place to pass judgment on you. Only He can do that, and He'll wait until he's good and ready. I for one am pleased you're around."

"That's it?" asked Jonas, unsure if Erik was just waiting to argue, waiting to pull him up and castigate him for cold-blooded murder. "I'm not proud of what I did, you know. I still see Cliff in my dreams. I can picture myself kneeling over him, pounding my fists into his face over and over and over. I see his eyes closing and his nose breaking. I can feel his teeth rattling in his head, and the feel of his skull as it smacked back against the concrete."

There were so many things Jonas wished he could change, but he couldn't. He wished he had bought the velvet-lined coffin for his father. He was starting to realize that, starting to accept that he couldn't control everything. After Cliff had died, he had wanted to take charge of everything. He'd lost his mind for a while there, and now that he was back he was determined not to mess up again. The only way he could start afresh was to be honest, with not just the others, but himself too.

"I don't think I could do that again," said Jonas. "Killing a man is easy in that second right before you pull the trigger. It's the easiest thing in the world, but afterwards? There's no law now.

There's no clear path anymore. What is justice these days? Without Dakota, I…"

Erik pulled a slim piece of licorice out of his pocket and examined it. "This is my last one. I was trying to save it, but seems like I may as well light it up now." He tugged at the end and plucked a piece off. As he chewed on it, he offered a piece to Jonas.

"No, thanks."

"Right and wrong? That'll depend on who you ask. Pippa and I chose a path a few years back. We follow Him and are thankful that we have Him to guide us. We have our prayers, our children, and that is all. I can't say if you should do the same, that's up to you, man, but it works for us. As for Cliff – forget about it. I don't see the need to spill any tears over him, and I sure don't see the need to tell anyone else about this. We've all seen and done some crazy shit. I'd never let anyone get in the way of getting my family to safety, and I know you're the same, Hamsikker. If you hadn't stopped Cliff who's to say where it would've ended? With him getting more of us killed, probably. What's done is done."

Jonas leant back and looked out at the golf course illuminated by the dim light. It was serene and quiet, a world away from what lay beyond the fences. "I could do with a cigarette."

Erik laughed. What started out as a chuckle developed into a full-blown belly laugh. Jonas watched on, bemused, as Erik finally regained control of himself.

"I tried going cold turkey a few years back. It didn't go so well. I was a pain in the ass, and I was horrible to Pippa, just horrible. I hated myself, but we got through it."

Jonas looked at Erik as he took a bite of licorice.

"It tastes like ripe tar on a hot day," said Erik grimacing. "It's foul, absolutely no doubt about it, foul."

"Didn't you develop a taste for it?" asked Jonas.

"Are you kidding, Hamsikker? I'd rather chew on Cliff's bloody bones right now, but it's all I got. I don't miss the cigarettes anymore, and I ain't going back. I'll be pleased when this last one is finished. Then I'm clean."

"You're certifiable, Lansky." Jonas remembered how he had left his father, and his mind presented an image of his father spread out on the stone floor with his brains splattered everywhere. Jonas and Dakota had run out of the church listening to Mrs. Danick shooting the place up. If Erik hadn't stopped then to pick them up, where would they be now? A long time dead, probably. He owed Erik. They had saved each other countless times since then, but he would never forget that. Erik could've driven away. He had his own family to take care of, but he had still stopped to make sure Jonas and Dakota were okay.

"I'm certifiable?" Erik sighed and shivered. "You're in a fit of rage, about to kill a man, and you stop to save the bullets? I don't know how you're wired, Hamsikker, but I can only assume Dakota keeps you grounded, or you'd be floating around in space by now."

"You want to go back inside?" asked Jonas. "It's going to get cold soon. You feel it? I think there might be a storm coming."

Jonas could feel the last rays of sunlight trickling through the trees surrounding the golf course. More and more clouds were appearing overhead, and the temperature was dropping quickly. It could barely be mid-morning, but it was as if the evening was drawing in.

"No, let's stay a while and just sit. We'll go if it starts raining." Erik sucked quietly on his last piece of licorice. "I want to enjoy the peace and quiet for a bit."

Pippa, Peter, and Freya were tucked up safely inside. It had been a long time since Erik could leave them alone and relax, and Jonas knew that. He felt it too. This place was a haven, and they needed it. The zombies were securely locked out behind strong fences, and everyone inside the clubhouse was pulling in the same direction. It seemed the corner had been turned, and they could actually relax. Jeffersontown could burn to the ground for all he cared. All that mattered was that they kept their heads down. He could go with Gabe to Canada, bring back Janey, and leave the killing behind him. Erik would find out soon enough that Jonas was planning a trip back outside, and there was no reason to break the peaceful atmosphere yet. The nightmare was over. He'd talk to Erik later.

Barely half an hour had passed before the first raindrops splattered down, and quickly Jonas and Erik were running back to the clubhouse, laughing like schoolboys. The wind swept the rain into their faces and drenched their clothes.

"Now that's what I call a proper Bluegrass storm," said Erik as they made their way inside. He shook his thick shaggy hair, scattering water over the hallway.

"Guess there's no need for that shower now," said Jonas as they made their way to the bedrooms upstairs. There was no heating, so he wanted to get out of his wet clothes and check on Dakota. They raided the gift shop and found a heap of polo shirts, jeans, and even Saint Paul's branded underwear to change into.

"Good, you're back." Quinn met Jonas and Erik on the staircase. "We need to talk." She followed them into Jonas's room and waited as he changed.

"How was it? You check the fence?" asked Erik.

"Yeah, yeah it's fine," said Quinn. "I'm not sure it's a good idea leaving that TV tower up, it's a hazard if you ask me. Looks like a strong wind could take it down. I'd also recommend we clean up the body that's still out there. We don't want anyone getting sick. Look, I can take you round later, but right now, Erik, I think you need to have a word with Peter."

"Why? What's happened?"

"Nothing really, but that's not how Gabe sees it." Quinn pulled out a chair and sat down. "Pippa let Peter take Freya for a shower."

"Yeah, I know, Pippa told me."

"Well he probably should learn to knock first. He walked in on Mara."

Jonas caught Erik's eye and couldn't help but laugh.

"Can it, Hamsikker," said Quinn. "Gabe wasn't too pleased about it."

Erik began to laugh too. "Look, it was an accident, right? So, no harm done. I'm sure Peter didn't mean anything by it. I'll talk to him, make sure he apologizes. Anything else we missed?"

Quinn shifted in her seat nervously. "Well…"

"Well what?" Jonas dried his hair on a blanket. He wasn't feeling too concerned about the shower incident. Peter had copped an eyeful, and Mara was good-looking, so good for him. It was a lot of fuss over nothing.

"Terry and Mrs. Danick have been checking the place out. Mrs. Danick was looking at the pictures on the walls, reading about the golf club's history and stuff."

"Great," said Erik. "Think we can go to my room now? I need to get changed."

"Hold on. You need to hear this. She said she couldn't find a *single* photo of Gabe anywhere. You've seen this place. They must have a hundred photos on the walls, and yet he's not in any. Mara neither."

"So what are you saying?" asked Jonas. "Did she ask Gabe about it?"

"No, she wanted to wait for you."

"Well, there you are. I'm sure there's an explanation," said Erik. "If that's all you've got to worry about..."

"Come on, Erik." Quinn stood up and walked over to the door. "I'm trying to tell you that things aren't necessarily what they seem. You weren't here when Gabe was shouting at Peter, telling him he was a pervert for spying on Mara in the shower. You should talk to Mrs. Danick. Look, just get changed and come downstairs will you? Both of you. We're all gathering in the library before lunch."

As Quinn slammed the door behind her, Jonas looked at Erik. "We should go talk to her."

"Perhaps we should try and let things blow over. It doesn't sound like much to me." Erik went out into the corridor, and Jonas followed him into Erik's makeshift bedroom.

"I know you have your doubts about Quinn," said Jonas, "but she's got a level head on her."

Erik looked at Jonas with surprise.

"Yeah, I can read you too, and I know when something's on your mind. You've never fully believed in her. What is it?" he asked Erik.

Erik pulled on a tight black polo top emblazoned with the Saint Paul's logo on the chest. "She's fine, but we don't know anything about her. Before she turned up on our doorstep, what was she? Who was she?"

"Does it matter?" asked Jonas. "As far as I'm concerned she's one of us. She's never let us down, she always pulls her weight, and if she thinks something is up we at least ought to listen to her."

"I guess." Erik looked at his reflection in the window as the rain battered against it. "I need a shave," he said rubbing his hands through his untamed red beard.

"Mrs. Danick deserves to be heard too. Come on, Erik, let's just go down and smooth things over. We don't need things going pear-shaped now."

"You're right, Hamsikker. Shit, is this what it feels like?"

"What's that?"

"To be an asshole? I thought you had the rights to that."

"Funny man," said Jonas. "Let's go before things get out of hand."

In the library they found Mrs. Danick studying a photograph on the wall. Quinn was sitting with Terry at the desk where Javier had earlier shown Jonas the map of the country. The map was no longer there, and Javier was stood next to Mrs. Danick pointing out various golf players and long-standing members.

Mrs. Danick saw Erik and Jonas walk into the room. "So I see a lot of staff photos here Gabe, you must be very proud, except…I can't see you in this one either. What gives?"

"This one was from the Christmas party last year. Unfortunately, I had a bout of the flu, so I missed out. Such a shame. It's a good photo."

Mrs. Danick turned to look at Jonas. "Seems you must be very unlucky, Gabe. You missed out on a few. Maye you need to take more vitamins, fight off the bugs."

Javier smiled. "I was wondering, Mrs. Danick, how you survived so long."

"You mean on account of me being a little old lady?"

"Well, to be blunt, yes. I mean, there are not exactly a lot of people like you left." Javier strode over to the window where the rain was steadily beating against it. "I'd say you're the oldest person in Kentucky right now. Living, that is."

Mrs. Danick pulled her handbag tight to her chest. "I carry a .38 special snub-nosed revolver with a two inch barrel. Light enough to carry discreetly in my bag without being too heavy for practical use. A .22 caliber would be too small. When I need to take down one of these motherfuckers, I want to be able to blow its brains out with one shot. And trust me - I've taken down a lot. If you'd like to let me have my gun back, I'd be happy to show you *exactly* how good a shot I am."

Jonas looked at the surprise dawning on Gabe's face, and then he burst out laughing. Erik followed too with a big booming laugh that echoed around the room. Jonas saw Gabe joining in the laughter, but he could tell Gabe had been offended. It was like they were all laughing at him and not sharing the joke.

"I'm sorry," said Jonas. "I don't even know why I'm laughing. Look, Mrs. Danick can handle herself. Believe me, Dakota and I wouldn't be here right now if it wasn't for her."

"I see. Okay, okay. Well good for you, Mrs. Danick. I'm pleased to be in such sharp company. May I know your first name?" asked Javier.

"No. My name is Mrs. Danick, and that's all you need to know, young man. My late husband, God rest his soul, would tear a strip off you for being so impertinent. If he were here now…"

Jonas stifled another laugh. "Mrs. Danick, leave him alone. Gabe, why don't you…"

"No, no, let her speak. If we are to live under one roof together, we need to be honest with each other. I think Mrs. Danick has a problem with me, so let's hear it."

"Can I suggest we save the chat for another time," said Terry. "I'm worried about this weather. Have you been through many storms here, Gabe? Are the fences strong? Quinn thinks they're good, but we've only had a brief look. Is there anything we need to do to make sure?"

"And I thought Mrs. Danick was the old woman of the group," said Javier sighing. "It's Terry, right? Look, you have nothing to worry about. We've been through plenty of storms before, and I'm sure we'll roll right through this one too." Javier had no idea how Gabe had looked after the place, but was happy to assume that everything was in order.

A rolling thunder boomed out and rattled the windowpane. A few seconds later, and a flash of lightening lit up the room.

"The storm's getting close," said Erik. "I think we should…"

Everyone in the room shook as a tearing sound filled the air followed by a tremendous crashing and booming noise from outside. It sounded like the earth itself was being torn apart, and Jonas raced to the window.

"What is it? The fence?" asked Mrs. Danick.

"The TV tower is down. It's fallen on one of the fence panels. "Oh shit. The dead…" Jonas turned and stared at Erik, his eyes wide open with panic. "They're in."

CHAPTER THREE

"We need to get to the weapons before they cut us off. I stashed them out in the workrooms behind the garden. Hamsikker, Quinn, you come with me," ordered Javier. "Erik, can you…"

"I have to find my family," said Erik as he backed out of the room. "Get me my gun, Hamsikker. I'll meet you on the front porch in five."

Without waiting for an answer, Erik charged out of the room with Mrs. Danick chasing after him. Jonas heard her promise to help find Dakota too.

"Shit, look at them all," said Terry. He was peering through the window as a succession of grey figures stumbled onto the golf course. "The TV tower brought down a good section of the fence. We're not getting that back up in a hurry."

"Terry, forget it, and come help us," shouted Jonas as he followed Javier out of the room. "We need to hold them back until the others are safe."

The three men ran from the library, through the clubhouse, and headed to the back entrance. Their feet pounded against the wooden floorboards, and the noise ricocheted around the building, clamoring for attention alongside the thunderstorm raging outside. Javier flung open the door, and they were all immediately hit by a wall of rain. The storm was right overhead, and the sky was so dark that it could have passed for night.

Cold pricks of water hit Jonas in the face as they charged outside, heading for the gardens and the storage sheds. He knew Dakota was safe for now, somewhere inside the clubhouse, but for how long? He looked south at the fallen TV tower. The earth had softened with the rain and caused it to fall right on top of the fence. A stretch had come down, about twenty feet of it, and he could see the zombies coming through. There was nothing to stop them, no barrier at all, and he managed to count a dozen before they reached the workshop. So they had been there all along, packed up against the wall, just waiting for an opportunity to get in.

Javier opened the door, and reached down to the pile of weapons he had left on the floor.

"Terry, take these," said Javier, thrusting a couple of guns at him.

"I'll take Erik's Glock and give it to him," said Jonas picking it up. He trusted Erik to come help, and wanted him to use a gun he was familiar with.

"I'll leave the door open in case we need more." Javier pointed out the rows of shovels and hand tools as he stuffed ammo into his pocket. "If things don't work out, we're gonna need to get to the white van and the SUV parked out back. I loaded them up in case of an emergency with food, water, and weapons. There's a hammer, a nail gun, even a hand-held chainsaw. All sorts of stuff we can use."

"Don't even think about it," said Terry. "We are *not* losing this place. We only just got here, for Christ's sake."

Jonas picked up his axe. It was still bloody, but when he felt the weight of it in his hand, he knew it was all he needed. He wasn't a very good shot with a gun, but he never missed with the axe in his hands. The head was strong and sharp, and the blade never seemed to dull despite the numerous skulls it had crushed. As he took it, he relished the feel of it, enjoying the coarseness of the helve. He ran his fingers across the smooth oak from which it had been fashioned, and he felt stronger immediately. He could do this. They could do this together, and beat them back. The zombies stood no chance.

"Runner!" shouted Terry.

A gunshot rang out, and Terry took the first one down before it reached them.

"Follow me," shouted Javier. He led them back to the clubhouse, and positioned himself beside a water barrel. He told Jonas and Terry to line up beside him underneath the back porch where they had shelter from the rain. Javier began shooting with Terry, trying to take down the front of the pack. Runners came splintering away from the group, but they were hard to pick off as they ran in a zigzag, bumbling their way through the horde.

Through the rain and the bullets Javier picked his targets carefully. He didn't want to get caught in the crossfire, and ducked under a tall elm, ready to take down any runners that evaded the gunfire.

"There're a lot of zombies coming through that gap in the fence," shouted Terry over the gunfire. "Mostly stumblers, but we can't let them keep coming." Terry continued firing at the faster ones. As Terry shot at the dead, he could tell that they were only just managing to stay on top of them. All the time, he could see more and more zombies piling in where the fence was down. Gabe was a good shot, but the numbers were not in their favor.

"Shit!" Jonas yelled as the first of the stumblers reached him. A woman appeared almost from nowhere. The rain was blinding, and as if emerging from a waterfall, the woman reached out for him.

Jonas gritted his teeth and sunk his axe into the woman's neck. He sidestepped to the left, and let the woman fall to the ground where he hit her again, smashing in her skull. Another figure emerged from the rain, a dead body ambling toward him menacingly. Whether it was male or female he couldn't tell, and he didn't wait to find out. He swung the axe sharply across the figure's face, and the skull split apart instantly as the axe wrenched the person's head from the body. The exposed bone was shiny and white, and Jonas watched as the zombie staggered forward before dropping to its knees. Rainwater pooled at Jonas's feet, and it turned red as the zombie's innards began spewing out onto the ground. Once he was sure it was dead, he had no time to react as another zombie reached him. It was a runner, and it was fast.

Jonas saw the zombie almost too late. There was a crack of thunder, a flash of lightening, and then he saw it coming from the corner of his eye. A young boy, probably no more than eleven or twelve, still fully clothed, and still with all his limbs, ran to Jonas emitting a horrifying groaning sound. The boy ran with his arms outstretched, as if desperate for a hug. Jonas saw the angry red face of a bird on the boy's shirt and recognized the boy wore a Cardinals shirt, the same sort of one that he had worn at that age. Amazingly the boy still wore a Cardinals cap, too, and for a second Jonas wondered if he was mistaken. Perhaps the boy just needed help and was running *away* from the dead instead of with them. In his heart, Jonas knew there was no way the boy could still be alive, and when he got closer, Jonas could see the dead boy's face. His jaw had been gnawed away to the bone, exposing two rows of teeth. Maggots filled his cheeks, and the skin was a dark gray color. The boy's eyes were a deep brown, ringed by tiny freckles, and almost looked alive. Reluctantly, Jonas swung his axe once more, letting the blade slice through the boy's head. The Cardinals cap flew through the air, landing at Jonas's feet. The zombie fell to the ground, and Jonas turned to face the house. The poor kid didn't deserve that. He had been somebody's child, and now he was just another zombie, another dead body on the ground with a lost soul and a mangled face. Jonas sighed. How many more was he going to have to kill? Where were the others? Amidst the noise of the storm, he had lost track of how many shots Gabe and Terry had taken. He could see bodies scattered throughout the drive where the runners had fallen, but they were still coming.

"Terry? Gabe? Where are they? We can't keep this up much longer." Jonas watched as Terry took down another two runners, and then reloaded his gun. He watched Gabe do the same, and then he saw Erik run from the house.

"Over here!"

Erik ran up to Jonas, and he handed him his Glock. Erik fired off two shots without hesitating, and he took down a couple of stumblers. "Everyone else is inside. Quinn's going to see if she can get one of the trucks over to the fence, and block off the hole."

Jonas heard the rumble of an engine behind him and saw Quinn moving one of the trucks across the garden. She was peering through the windows trying to see clearly, and he hoped she could do it. If they could somehow find a way to block the gap in the fence, they might just be able to save the course.

"Dakota…is she?"

Erik put a hand on Jonas's shoulder. "She's fine. She's with the others waiting in the lobby. If things go sour, they're ready to go."

Jonas nodded. "We should try to clear a path for Quinn. It's hard enough driving in this weather, but any zombies in her way are only going to slow her down. If we don't get that hole patched up, we're going to lose this place."

Erik said something in agreement, although quite what he said Jonas didn't know. Erik's voice was lost in the cacophony of the storm. Jonas darted over to Terry just as Erik began shooting.

"Gabe, Terry - concentrate your fire on the zombies that are headed for the house. I'm going to take Erik and clear a way for Quinn." Jonas didn't wait for a reply but headed straight back to Erik.

"Come on," said Jonas as they left the shelter of the tree and made for the slow-moving truck.

Jonas stayed in front of Erik and used his axe to take down any zombies that got close enough while Erik shot at any who looked like they were about to get in front of the truck. Jonas could see Quinn struggling to keep the truck moving, and as it veered over the fairway, it began to lose traction. The truck was heavy, loaded with supplies, and it gradually began to move slower. Jonas watched as two zombies fell under it, and their bodies helped the rear wheels gain some grip. It lurched forward, and Erik dropped more right in front of Quinn. The dark sky above opened up, and lightning coursed through the clouds again, illuminating the golf course fully. Jonas saw Quinn heading for the TV tower, but he also saw what lay beyond. Further down the fairway, to the south, another stretch of fence had gone down. It might have been the storm, the winds, or even the sheer weight of the dead pressed against it, but whatever had caused it to collapse was irrelevant. The golf course was covered in zombies. Hundreds of them were scattered over it, all walking or running to the sound of the gunfire. Jonas thought there could be a hundred or more. Their numbers were insurmountable, and he knew they had to go. They could fight them back, try and repel them, but eventually they would run out of ammo, and then they would be reduced to fighting by hand. It was too dangerous to stand and fight. The golf course was lost. They had been so close, and now it was gone.

"Erik, we have to go," shouted Jonas as he killed a zombie, whirling his axe around him like a baton. As the dead body fell at his feet, Erik stopped firing and looked at him.

"No way; we *can't* lose this place, not now." Erik resumed firing, picking off the zombies nearest to Quinn. He managed to get off headshots nearly every time, and Jonas was impressed. But Erik was wasting his time and bullets.

"Erik," said Jonas pulling on his friend's arm, "you have to stop. You know what I'm saying. It's too late."

Erik looked at Jonas and the swarming dead around him. His eyes sank to the ground. "But we can't lose this, we can't. It isn't fair. My kids are shattered. Pippa was finally beginning to think we had a future again. I was. I…"

"I know," said Jonas, "but we have no choice."

Erik looked up. The dead were coming at them from all angles. The wind was tearing up branches and leaves, whirling them around and sending them tearing through the air like darts. The rain hadn't eased up either, and another boom of thunder rolled across the Kentucky plains.

"Fuck," said Erik plainly. "Just…fuck."

Jonas began waving at Quinn to stop, but she had already stopped. The truck had become stuck by a sandpit, and the wheels were spinning uselessly, kicking up sand and water.

"You go back," shouted Jonas. He had to make sure Erik heard the plan, as the storm was not abating. The zombies were closing in on them, and the sounds of the moaning dead were increasing too. "Get Gabe and Terry, and tell them that we're evacuating. Gabe said there were two vehicles prepped and ready. A white van and an SUV, I think. Get everyone inside them and ready to go. I assume Gabe will take one, so let him take the van. I want you behind the wheel of the SUV. Come and get me as soon as you can."

"What the hell, Hamsikker? We're not going without you. If you're off on one of your suicide missions again…"

"Erik, we don't have time to argue. For the record, no, I'm not off on a suicide mission. Quinn needs help. There's no point us both going over there. Make sure your family is okay. I'm counting on you, so get going." Jonas practically pushed Erik away, and he turned to face the van Quinn was driving.

Gunshots rang out around him, and Erik ran back toward the clubhouse. Jonas started forward to go and fetch Quinn. She was still trying to get the van free of the sandpit, but the falling rain was only making it harder to get out. Three zombies had surrounded the cab, and he was going to have to take them out before Quinn could get out safely. There were runners coming in, too, and he was going to have to be smart to avoid them.. He sliced his axe through a dead woman as he ran to Quinn, and then slipped behind a huge oak tree. Its trunk was thick, and it hid him briefly from the view of the dead. Jonas counted to five slowly, and then spun around, knowing the runners would be there. This time he was surprising them, and he split their skulls open before they even knew where he was. Particles of brain splattered him, and he brought the axe down upon them on the ground, making sure they couldn't get back up again. He left the shelter of the tree and sprinted over to the van.

"Quinn!" he shouted, but she wasn't paying attention to him. He could make her face out through the front windshield, but she was looking out the passenger windows, at the zombies trying to get in. They were hammering on the doors, pounding their hands against the side of the cab, and she looked scared. Was she thinking that they would leave her? If Jonas didn't think he could do it, he might have done just that. He had to make his own family a priority, but things would have to be seriously dire for him to leave anyone behind. However small a chance there was, if he could save someone he would. Quinn had plenty of life left in her yet.

Jonas summoned up all his energy. Breakfast had been cold ham and coffee, and he could feel his arms tiring already. The axe was a brutal weapon, but it left him feeling exhausted, and with the storm swirling around them, he knew he was starting to tire. With the zombies' attention on Quinn, Jonas had little trouble picking them off. One by one he cut them, slicing through their necks and shoulders, severing their heads from their bodies, pressing them down into the dirt when necessary so he could finish them off. When they were dead, the passenger door swung open, and he climbed up inside.

"Hamsikker, am I pleased to see you," said Quinn. "The damn truck's stuck. I can't free it."

"Leave it," said Jonas. "We're going. Come with me."

"Wait, what? Leaving?"

"Quinn, have you seen what it's like out there? They're everywhere. Maybe on another day, if we can get more ammo, we can come back and try to retake this place. Today, though, right now, we have no choice but to leave. There's more of the fence down on the south side. Probably the storm. I guess it wasn't as secure as Gabe thought. Maybe he missed something, I don't know. Look, Erik and Gabe are coming to pick us up. I know it's not what we wanted, but this way we get to fight another day."

Jonas could see the disappointment in Quinn's eyes, but he also saw acceptance there. She was not just strong, but intelligent too.

Quinn turned off the engine, and they sat in the cab silently for a moment, listening to the wind and the rain batter the truck.

"Fine. Let's go," agreed Quinn. "I don't have anything though. Did Gabe at least give you the weapons back?"

Jonas nodded and looked in the mirror. "I can't see for the rain. Can you see if they're coming?"

Quinn shook her head. "Can't see shit."

"Right." Jonas put his hand on the door handle. "Let's start making our own way back. We hang around here much longer, and we'll get surrounded again. Plus, I don't want the others to get stuck like you did. Just stay behind me. We can outrun them. I'll take care of any that get too close. Okay, let's go. *Now.*"

Jonas jumped out of the cab, making sure Quinn followed him. He ran around to join her and instantly put his axe to use. An old black man dressed in crimson shorts and a turquoise polo ran up to him, the man's eyes white and his face bloody. As the runner let out a low moaning sound, Jonas cleaved off its jaw, and the zombie crashed to the ground. It floundered in the sandpit, trying to find Jonas, but another swift blow to the head, and the man was still.

"This way," said Jonas. He led Quinn back toward the clubhouse, aware that there were more runners behind them. Quinn ran beside him, and neither of them looked back. Unless he felt something grab him, Jonas wasn't about to waste time looking behind him. Instead, he focused his attention up ahead, and he tried to see through the falling rain where the others were. He spotted a white van moving slowly away from the work sheds, but he couldn't tell who was driving. A figure ran from the clubhouse and jumped up into the passenger side of the van, after which it picked up speed. Jonas wondered where it was heading when it turned back toward the house; then he realized the main driveway that led back to the road was on the other side of the house. He had assumed that they were going to have to punch a hole through the dead and drive out through the fence, but as long as Gabe had the keys, they could go out of the main entrance.

"That our ride?" Quinn pointed out the brown SUV coming up behind the van. It was accelerating quickly, and the wipers were swishing back and forth rapidly.

"That's it," shouted Jonas. He saw the SUV plow through the vegetable patch, churning up dirt and mangling the crop as it did so. It was the most direct route to them, and Jonas was sure Erik was driving. Jonas batted away the rain from his face, and saw Erik. It looked like the passenger seat was empty, and as the SUV pulled up beside them, the door flew open.

"Get in," shouted Erik. "Get the hell in, *now*!"

Jonas shuddered as he experienced a startling moment of déjà vu. When this had all started, back at the church for his father's funeral, Erik had said exactly the same thing. Erik had picked him up and rescued him from the dead then too, and here he was doing it all over again. The setting was different, and instead of an achingly hot sun, the sky was full of thunder and rain, but it didn't escape Jonas's attention that they were repeating something they had done once before. All the effort they had gone to, and yet they were still on the run, still having to escape the zombies' attacks.

Jonas jumped into the vehicle and made sure Quinn was in, too, before shouting at Erik to move it. Jonas snapped his belt in quickly, and saw Quinn had settled into the back seat next to Terry and Dakota.

"Everyone okay? Everyone out?" asked Jonas as the SUV spun to his left and began to catch up to the white van.

"All accounted for," said Erik.

He was gripping the wheel so tightly that Jonas thought he might yank it out completely. The SUV tried to spin out of control on the dirt, but Erik managed to bring it under control and get them back onto the driveway. Jonas was grateful that his friend was a cop. All of Erik's knowledge and experience had saved them

39

countless times. If Erik had ended up a computer programmer or a desk clerk, who knew what state they might all be in right now?

"Gabe has the van. Mara's sat up front with him. Pippa and Mrs. Danick took Peter and Freya into the back with them. It's packed full of supplies so it ain't gonna be comfortable in there for them, but it seemed the best thing to do."

"They'll be fine," said Jonas, hoping that Gabe was as good a driver as Erik. As they skirted the fringe of the fairway, Jonas looked back at the course. The dead were everywhere. There had to be a hundred of them staggering beneath the gloomy sky, soaking wet, and all now heading for the van and the SUV. They began to slow down, and Jonas instinctively grabbed his axe.

"Gabe's got to open the gate," said Erik. "He has the keys, but it'll take him a minute. Hamsikker, we're low on ammo. It took everything we had getting everyone safely in the van. I think Gabe has a couple of rounds left. Me, too, but with Mrs. D's, that's about it."

The SUV pulled up to a stop behind the white van. Through the windshield everything was blurry and grey. Gabe was hidden behind the raindrops and the wind that carried leaves and dirt, and Jonas could hardly see what was going on. The engine rumbled idly as they waited, and every second that passed felt like a year. He stared ahead at the back of the van, willing it to move, wanting it to race away out onto the open road and away from the dead.

"Hamsikker, this is taking too long," said Terry from the back. "What if he grabbed the wrong keys? What if he got attacked?"

"They're getting close," said Erik quietly. His side window had fogged up, and he wiped it with his forearm. "The runners are…"

"I got it," said Jonas jumping out of the car.

"Jonas, don't you…"

Dakota's words were lost as Jonas slammed the door behind him and began advancing on the white van with his axe raised. If something had gone wrong, if Gabe had been attacked, he was going to have to get the others out of there. The SUV would be a squash with everyone packed in, but there was no way he was leaving anyone behind.

Jonas crept around the side of the van to the driver's door and saw that it was open. Up ahead, a figure was crouched beside the fence. Huge wrought iron gates were sandwiched between two posts, and Jonas saw a sign through the railings hanging from an ornate lamppost. The road itself was clear, and he guessed the zombies had all been drawn to the opening in the fence further down the course. They would be lucky to find the road empty, but he could hope. As Jonas passed the van's open door he glanced inside and saw Mara. She was sat perfectly still, with her feet up on the dashboard. The visor was pulled down, and she was examining herself in the small mirror. She was too preoccupied applying some lipstick and didn't notice Jonas, so he continued on to see if Gabe needed any help.

"Fucking thing," said Javier as he punched in the numbers to open the door.

"Everything okay?" asked Jonas.

Javier straightened up, and there was a clanking sound as the two gates began to open slowly. "Yeah, I just had to get the code in. I lost the piece of paper I had it written down on, so it took me a while to remember it. We're good to go now."

"Okay, let's get the hell out of here," said Jonas grimacing. "We should…"

Suddenly Jonas pushed Javier to the side, sending him sprawling to the floor. Directly where Javier had been standing was a zombie. A tall, thin man with spectacles and spindly arms was inches away, and Jonas quickly brought the axe up, catching the man under the chin, and smashing open his jaw.

"Get back," shouted Jonas, as Javier got to his feet. "Stay behind me."

Jonas wrenched his axe free and lifted it up to strike again and end the man's undead life. Holding his axe aloft, Jonas heard a cracking sound, and the man's head exploded. Jonas turned away to avoid being covered in gore and blood. He still held his axe in his hands and was unsure what had happened to the man.

"You can thank me later," said Javier as he holstered his gun.

"Sure," said Jonas slowly as he lowered his axe. "I had it under control, but sure."

Javier ran back to the van, leaving Jonas standing beside the dead body. The gates were now fully open, and Jonas waited for the van to pass. Erik pulled the SUV up, and Jonas ran around it to climb back in the front.

"What was that about?" asked Erik. "You good, man?"

"Yeah, I'm good. Let's just get out of here." Jonas dropped the axe in the footwell and wondered why Gabe had shot the zombie. There really hadn't been any need to. Surely he could see that? Perhaps he was nervous. Perhaps Gabe just wanted to prove he still had it, could still shoot straight. Jonas shrugged it off. They were away from the course. The dead could go to hell. He looked back at Quinn and Terry and then at Dakota.

"You all right?" He reached back for Dakota's hand, and she squeezed his hand back. She smiled and nodded, but then withdrew her hand from his.

Jonas let it go and told Erik to keep following Gabe. Wherever they were headed, it had to be better than the golf course. Right now he had to trust that Gabe knew where he was going.

"So where now, honey?" asked Rose.

Javier reached for the glove compartment by Rose's knees and pulled out a crumpled up map. "You tell me. I'm driving, you do the directions."

Rose took the map and studied it for a moment. "Oh, I see. I know." She rolled down her window, letting in a flurry of rain, and threw the map out.

"What the fuck are you doing?" asked Javier.

"Me?" asked Rose as she wound the closed the window. "Why ask me? I'm just the pretty little housewife, right? I cook and I clean, and I fuck when I'm told to, but I really don't know how to do anything more than that."

Javier looked at Rose. She was smirking, as if she knew the answer to everything. If he wasn't driving he would've wiped that cute smirk from her face, but as it was he had to keep both hands on the wheel. The road was smooth and straight, but the storm was making it difficult, and he was trying to monitor the road ahead for stumblers.

"How about, what the fuck are *you* doing?" Rose put a hand upon Javier's thigh. "We had it all, you know. Now it's all fucked. We could've made something of that place, but you had to get all buddy-buddy with them. If it was just us two we might have been able to deal with it, but with so many of them dumb fucks running around, we had no chance. I don't know what's got into you, Javier."

"Keep your God damn voice down," said Javier. "Don't blow our cover now. They hear you talking like that, and we'll find ourselves facing a mutiny. I don't want to stop this van and open up the back door to find a gun in my face. You?"

"Do you know anything? Jesus, *Gabe*, the redhead, Erik, he's a fucking cop. *A cop*! We should just off them now."

Javier swerved the van around a corner and narrowly missed crashing into a stationary tractor that had been left halfway out of a ditch.

"I don't care what he was before. He's nothing. All of them. I'm in charge now. They follow me. If we play this right, then they follow us. Get it? You want to get out there, get your hands dirty? Be my guest. Otherwise, listen up. Forgetting the little girl, we have eight people running with us now. That's a lot of people to watch our backs. Remember the trouble we had getting out of Jeffersontown? Remember Cindy?"

"Yeah, so what?"

"We were forcing it. This is much easier. These people need us. They want us. We string them along just enough to keep them interested, and we have an easy ride. I'm telling you, *Mara*, that with their help we can get to Canada and start over. Set up home. Really make a go of it."

"Really?"

Javier could see the hope in Rose's eyes. By the time they got to Canada and found his brother he intended to be flying solo again. He would use them along the way and dump them when he was tired of them or they became useless. Until then, everyone was going to be at his disposal, and that included Rose. All he had to do was make the right noises, say what they wanted to hear, and he could get people to do whatever he wanted.

"You know," said Javier quietly. "There's no reason we can't keep the girl. You can do the parents. Start with the cop if you want."

Rose bit her lip. "You're my eagle. Forever. I'm sorry I doubted you. I just wanted you to fill me in. I thought something must be going on, but it was confusing, and…"

"Never mind that now," said Javier. "Just look out for a road sign. We need to get out of this storm, some place safe and warm, preferably somewhere without a pack of ravenous zombies on our asses."

Rose smiled. "On it."

Javier knew what she was thinking about. She would already be planning who to kill first. He had had to rein her in lately, but as long as she took her time, she could have some fun. He was going to have some fun too. Just for a short while. Once they had regrouped and thrashed out a plan, he could get on the road north. In a couple of days they would be in Canada, and he could free himself of the others. Hamsikker would be the last to go. He was useful, certainly. Back at the gate, if he hadn't shown up when he did, Javier knew he might have a death sentence or worse right now, but Hamsikker had saved him with that damn axe of his. He would save Hamsikker for last, have some fun with Dakota, and then enjoy watching the life drain from their bodies.

CHAPTER FOUR

"Pull up behind Gabe, but keep the engine running. I'll have a quick word with him. If we're stopping, I'll give you the nod. Stay alert."

Jonas asked Erik if they knew where they were, but he had to admit he was lost. He didn't recognize any features on the land, and the town names meant nothing. From that, they took it they were heading out of Kentucky. They had been driving for just over an hour, and they were getting nervous the further they drove. With no way of contacting Gabe, Jonas and Erik had followed, hoping he was leading them away from Jeffersontown. They had no wish to go back there, and Jonas couldn't think why they would. There was nothing there for them anymore, nothing but the dead.

They had taken small back roads for a while, skirting past towns and villages, keeping their distance from the main developments and built-up areas. It felt like they were heading north, but the storm had taken a while to die down, and the sun was hidden behind a bank of dark, grey cloud for a long time. Even now, the sky was a hazy shade of blue, and the air was cool.

Jonas jumped out of the SUV and scuffed his boots into the ground. The earth was soft and salty, but almost dry. Evidently the storm had largely avoided this area. For the last few minutes they had driven very slowly, and there was no sign of the dead. Erik had followed the white van down a small side street on the outskirts of a small rural town, and eventually they had pulled up next to a soccer field. The nets were still up, and the lines across the pitch painted white, but they were mostly hidden by overgrown grass. Jonas looked around. He had to admit it felt like a safe enough place to stop. Other than the rumbling engines of the van and the SUV, there were no other sounds present. There were no voices, no birdsong or dogs, and no groaning sounds indicative of the dead. He saw no movement, and, therefore, no reason to panic. He approached the driver's side of the white van and looked into the cab.

"How you holding up, Hamsikker?" asked Javier with a slight grin. "I think we're in the clear now."

Jonas rested his axe on his shoulder and looked back at the SUV. A mere nod of the head told Erik all he needed to know, and the engine stopped. Jonas watched as Quinn, Terry and Dakota got out, and they all began stretching their legs.

"Let's just take five minutes. Seems clear. You did good, Gabe. Thanks. I bet your passengers need a break."

"You got that right," said Peter.

"How's everyone inside?" asked Jonas as he watched Peter climb out of the back of the van. He held open the rear doors, and out came Pippa with Freya hanging onto her anxiously. Mrs. Danick got out slowly, and Peter helped her out.

"No windows, just a sunroof to let the air in. It's no fun, I can tell you that much," said Mrs. Danick as she rubbed her legs. "You want to trade places, Hamsikker? Jump on in, and try sitting on a box of Gatorade for the next hour. I'll go sit up front of that nice SUV you got there. Honestly, I don't mind."

Jonas rubbed Mrs. Danick's back as he watched Gabe and Mara get out of the van. "How's the ankle? Better? I'm thinking we can stop here a while, so maybe walk around on it, and get the blood flowing."

"You can ride in the SUV," said Terry as he approached the van. "I'll swap with you, Mrs. Danick."

"Thanks," said Mrs. Danick. "I thought we were through with running. It never gets any easier, does it?"

"Hey, be careful will you?" Erik called out to Peter who was taking Freya to see the soccer goals. "Don't go too far. Yell out if you see anything, and haul ass."

Javier grabbed a box of snack bars from the back of the van and ripped the top open. He took a handful out and held them towards Quinn. "Here, take these, and pass them around."

Quinn took them and handed them out. "I'll go take these last two to Peter and Freya."

"Thanks," said Pippa. "I'll come with you. I need to stretch my legs."

"You have any idea where we are, Gabe? I appreciate you taking the lead back there, but we can't keep driving in circles. We need to formulate a plan before it gets too late, or we'll end up in the middle of nowhere. Where do we go now?" asked Erik. "It seems like we have a lot of options, but they all come with a lot of questions attached."

"Options?" Dakota rubbed her eyes. "Surely, we're going back? Why would we even think about going anywhere else?"

"Why would we go back?" asked Rose. "We only just got the hell out of dodge as it is. Saint Paul's is gone. Louisville is just down the road, and you're looking at close to a million zombies when you factor in Jeffersontown, St Matthews, and New Albany. Hell, I think we should leave Kentucky far behind. We've got a van full of gas, plenty of food for now, and more water than you can shake a stick at. I'm sure we can find somewhere better."

Jonas looked at Dakota, his eyes wide as if to suggest she was crazy. "What's the appeal in staying here, in going back to that hell? We need to move on."

"Are we really giving up that easily?" asked Dakota. "Are *you*?"

"We're not giving up," explained Jonas. "We'll keep away for a while, and perhaps we can go back when they've dispersed. If we can get the fences up again, we could still make it work. There's a lot to consider though, Dakota." Why did it feel like every conversation he had with her had to turn into a battle? Jonas wanted her to be on his side for once, but it seemed like they wanted different things these days.

"I understand where you're coming from, Jonas," said Dakota, "and maybe you've had your fill of being on the road. We all have." Dakota poked the tip of her tongue out between gritted teeth and rubbed her eyes once more. "Look, I'm tired, and Kentucky is no better or worse than any other state really. Where would we go? I seem to remember back at the golf course there were plenty of gassed up trucks ready to go whenever we needed. What's the rush in leaving so soon? I looked around the place when we got there, and I've got to tell you, that place could be nirvana. We should go back."

"*Could be*, Dakota, could be. Truth is, it isn't right now, and we're not equipped to make it happen." Jonas reached for his wife, but she turned away. "I'm not sure about going back, not now, and maybe not ever."

"It's true," said Erik. "Maybe you didn't see it, but I sure did. There were hundreds of them things all over the place. The fence was coming down, and no way could we deal with them all. We can find something better, something…"

"Gabe, surely you're with me? Come on," said Dakota. "Tell 'em. Tell us about how you made it so good. You lived there for a long time, right?"

Javier leant back against the van and looked at Dakota. He could see the desperation in her eyes, but he couldn't lie to her. He couldn't afford to let her convince the others to go back. "The golf course has an impressive irrigation system that we turned to our advantage. Rainwater collects in several drums and stations that are situated discreetly throughout the property, and it's channeled into a tank and a series of pipes. The greens and lawns are kept pristine even in summer. There are sprinklers spread over the grounds which we turned off to preserve our supply. There's a recycling system that purifies the wastewater, and it feeds into the showers and kitchens. The whole place is pretty self-reliant and runs without much interference. Subject to enough rain, we potentially have a never-ending supply of water. The solar power would keep us going a while, and we have gas and a back-up generator running just fine. As long as we were careful, we could live there for months, if not longer."

"See?" Dakota let out a triumphant smile.

"But…" Javier shook his head. "But…"

Dakota's smile began to fade, and Javier sighed, purposefully making a big deal of it. It felt good to crush the woman's hopes. He could derive a good deal of pleasure from someone else's pain. He didn't always need to use his fists. "The fairway was actually still in good condition, considering we didn't maintain it over summer. The grass was green, just thinning in patches where it had turned brown and sour. The cedars smelt beautiful, and the outside world, as horrible as it was, was hidden from us by the trees, and, of course, the fence. A twelve-foot high perimeter fence extended all the way around the course – until this morning. And *that* is your problem. I was remiss not to check it, and I never thought the

TV tower would come down like it did. I'm sorry about that, truly I am. Patching up the fence with those zombies around is not going to happen, no matter how much we want it to. With all the commotion, there will be even more of them back there now. There are millions of them out there. How many do you think are behind us, right now?"

Javier watched as Dakota looked at Mara for backup.

"Don't look at me. I'm with Gabe on this."

"*Millions*, Dakota. We need to keep moving forward. Right, Hamsikker?" Javier knew he had done enough. He planned on letting Jonas explain to his wife why they were doing the exact opposite of what she wanted.

"Dakota, have you forgotten about Janey? Have you…"

"Have you forgotten I'm pregnant? I felt sick enough this morning, but riding around in the car for the last hour hasn't exactly helped me feel any better. You…" Dakota blinked back tears. "Never mind. Just do what you want to do."

"Dakota?" Jonas felt helpless as she walked away. He couldn't put her attitude down to the pregnancy. There was a small part of him that wanted to go back too. It had seemed so good.

"Leave her be." Erik shoved half of his uneaten snack bar into his pocket. "She'll hammer it out with Pippa, that's what she does, and she'll come around. We're making the right decision here. We can't go back."

"So where do we go?" asked Javier. He knew the answer, but he didn't want to spell it out for them. He had already planted the seed in Jonas's mind earlier. Javier slipped an arm around Rose's waist. "I've got my Mara to think about. We've all got family to take care of."

"And the rest," said Mrs. Danick suddenly.

"The rest?" Javier had forgotten about Mrs. Danick. She had been walking around the van, trying to shake off the pins and needles in her legs, listening to the conversation, but saying nothing.

"I might have fifty years on you, young man, but I'm not senile yet. What about the rest? That place was a paradise compared to what's out here. Yet you're happy to give up on it, just like that. Tell me, where were the bankers and the lawyers? Hm? Where were the golf nuts, the corporates, the sleazebags, and all those rich types that frequent those places? You telling me that they forgot about their wonderful golf course? You telling me hardly any of them showed up asking for help? This all seems a little too… contrived to me. Why are you so quick to move on?"

"Mrs. Danick, I hardly think…"

"Shut up, Erik, you big oaf. You're smart, but even you can't see the bigger picture here."

"Listen, now is not the time to start arguing amongst ourselves," said Jonas. "Why don't we take five to…?"

"You need to clean your ears out, too, Hamsikker." Mrs. Danick frowned as she spoke. "I heard these two arguing about something on the way out of the golf course. I don't know what, but they're not the loving, peaceful, tree-hugging couple they're trying to make us believe they are. Not everyone is up front and honest like you, or have you forgotten about Cliff already? I know he was a bad egg, and he led us into trouble with that garage. It got some of us killed, and we need to be more careful now than ever. We don't need some asshole like that messing with us again."

"I don't know what's gotten into you, Mrs. Danick, but I can assure you we're all *friends* here." Javier shrugged his shoulders nonchalantly and smiled at her. "We weren't arguing. We were just worried about everyone. As for the golf course, well, of course it's upsetting to leave it behind, but as I explained, there's no safe way of getting it back. As for all the members, well, maybe they all got in their private jets and are living it up in Bora Bora. How the hell should I know where they are?"

Mrs. Danick stared at Javier as if waiting for a further explanation.

"All right, Mrs. Danick, let's just focus on what really matters right now," said Jonas. He looked around the field, noticing that Dakota was deep in conversation with Pippa. Peter and Freya had found a deflated soccer ball, but they were still kicking it around the long grass as best they could. Quinn was sat on the sidelines, just watching patiently, nibbling on her snack, keeping a lookout for them. "Look, Mrs. Danick, do you think you could go talk to Quinn? Make sure she's okay?"

"That's right," muttered Mrs. Danick. "Get rid of the old woman."

Jonas could see she was still brooding over something, but he didn't want to get into anything else right now. She was picking up on something that wasn't there, and their main concern right now was to find somewhere else to stay.

With a click of her heels, Mrs. Danick turned about and grunted. She headed across the soccer field, walking briskly and wrapping her shawl around her tightly. If he wasn't wound up so tight, Jonas would've laughed at the sight of her. She still held onto that shawl, day and night. It was probably the first thing she'd grabbed when they'd had to leave Saint Paul's.

"Here's the thing," said Jonas. "Kentucky was my home once, but it hasn't been for a long time. Truth is, I don't know what is home anymore. We need to keep moving. North is my best advice." Jonas looked at Gabe, wondering if he was going to chip in. From the silence Jonas guessed that Gabe hadn't told Mara yet about heading north. Or maybe that's what they had been arguing about earlier.

"Anywhere that's not here," said Erik. "North is good with me. Let's keep on trucking until we find somewhere to stay the night."

"We could take the I65, head past Indianapolis, and then right on past Chicago, up the I90 into Wisconsin." Jonas started tracing his finger up the door of the van as if drawing out a route on an imaginary map. "If we stay east of Minneapolis and avoid the city completely, we could get around the edge of Lake Superior. That way…"

"Whoa, hold your horses, Hamsikker. I thought we were just vaguely heading north, looking for a safe place to bed down for the night. Sounds to me like you've thought this through. You're not making this up on the spot." Erik glared at Jonas through his bushy eyebrows and gave him a withering look. "Care to share?"

"I suspect what he was trying to suggest is a way north that avoids the major cities. Right, Hamsikker?" Javier looked from Erik to Jonas and back again. "Seems that the safest places are well away from the large cities. Places like Columbus and Chicago are big no-nos. I mean, personally, I've never been north of

Indiana. Never found the need. You guys will know a lot more about this than me."

"Yeah, I was just spitballing, trying to figure out where we were headed. I guess I got a bit carried away." Jonas glanced at Erik, and his answer seemed to placate the man who was relaxing again. He didn't really want to tell him about Janey just yet. He wanted to do it in his own time, to talk to him about it, and explain why he needed to go her. Jonas didn't want to have to explain everything in front of Gabe and Mara.

"Well, wherever we go," said Erik, "the chance of finding an easy path is slim. Thousands and thousands of people took to their cars when this shit started, and the roads are likely to be clogged. We've been lucky up until now, keeping to the smaller roads. Once we hit an interstate, I'm not sure we'll have as much luck."

"You know, I think you told me that your sister lives in Canada, Hamsikker," said Javier. "We could make a rough plan to get to her place, perhaps. Her house might be safe. What was her name again? Jenny?"

"Janey?" Erik glared at Jonas again. "This all about her?"

Jonas began talking, hoping that Erik wouldn't put two and two together and make seven. There was no conspiracy, but if Erik found out he and Gabe had been making plans without him, it might look bad, as if he was deserting them. "Erik, you traveled around a bit after college, right? I heard you took some time off before college. If the major highways are clogged with vehicles, we'll need a good navigator. I know the main arteries, but we go off the beaten track, and I'm clueless. Chicago is a day's drive easily, probably two. Let's not even think about what happens after tonight. Erik, switch with me. I'll drive the SUV, you navigate. Gabe, you can bring the van after us. What do you say Erik? Think you can find somewhere for us to go tonight?"

"Yeah, Erik," said Rose. "You're the smartest one here. You can figure this out. You were a cop, so it's only natural you take the lead now. You *were* a cop, weren't you?"

Jonas could feel the tension rising, and wondered what the hell was going on. There were so many lies, so many things not being said, that he was getting lost. They should be thankful they had all made it out of Saint Paul's in one piece, but instead, they were taking shots at each other.

"Erik. Please? We can talk later, I promise," said Jonas, "but right now we need to move. Who knows where the hell we are. We don't want to get stuck in a dead-end town with nothing but the dead for company, the sun over our heads, and a prayer to keep us safe."

"Round everyone up," said Erik. He folded his arms and looked up at the sun. It was burning away the clouds, and the light made Erik's beard seem redder than ever. "I think I can figure a way back to the Ohio River. From there I'll find a way across it. If we stay out of trouble, we can be somewhere safe tonight. Maybe a house, or it could be anything. Right now we don't have the choice to be fussy. As long as we have a roof over our heads and four solid walls around us, I'll take it."

"Thanks, buddy." Jonas knew Erik wasn't stupid. He had figured out something was going on when Gabe had mentioned Janey. Why had Gabe done it? Was he trying to stir things up? He seemed so sincere that he probably hadn't even realized what he was saying. Jonas would talk to Erik later and smooth things over. He would talk to Dakota first though. She was the most important person in his life, and now that she was carrying his baby, he needed her on his side more than ever.

"How are you for gas?" asked Erik. "I think we have enough left for today."

"The van was half empty. We're down to nearly a quarter of a tank," said Javier. "We might need to stop soon and get more. If there's no gas station, don't worry; any vehicle will do. I can siphon it out."

Erik nodded. Jonas could tell he was surprised that Gabe knew how to siphon gas, but he said nothing about it. "Let's roll."

As they regrouped, Jonas got behind the wheel, and Erik got into the passenger seat.

"Hamsikker, I don't need to know what's going on in your head all the time. Shit, I don't think even God knows what goes on in your head half the time. But while you're behind that wheel, you've got me and my family's lives in your hands, so don't fuck up."

"No sweat," said Jonas as he clipped in his seatbelt. "You tell me where to point this thing, and I'll take it there."

"We good?" asked Erik.

Jonas looked into Erik's sparkling blue eyes. "We're good."

Quinn and Dakota nestled themselves into the back, and then Terry joined them.

"I thought you were switching with Mrs. Danick? She okay?" asked Jonas.

"Yeah, she changed her mind. Said she preferred to stay with Freya and keep an eye on her. Suits me. I'd rather be squashed in the back with two beautiful women than the back of a van any day."

Jonas saw Dakota and Quinn smiling, and they all groaned as Terry winked at them. Jonas suspected Mrs. Danick changed her mind more so that she could keep an eye on Gabe and Mara, but he chose to keep his thoughts to himself.

"Buckle up," said Erik.

"Sir, yes, sir!" Quinn and Dakota giggled, and then Quinn held up her hands in surrender. "Sorry, must be all that fresh air."

"Or that sugary snack," muttered Erik.

"Maybe you're just glad to be alive?" Jonas put the SUV into drive, and took them out of the field and back onto the road. He couldn't catch Dakota's eye in the rear view mirror, but he was pleased to see she was smiling. Being with Pippa and the kids was good for her. He didn't want her stressed any more than she had to be. It was going to be difficult enough with the baby, and worrying about where they were spending the night, how many zombies were waiting for them, or where their next meal was coming from was something he wanted to take care of for her.

A couple of hours passed, and they drove cautiously. Jonas kept checking the mirror to make sure Gabe was still with them. Erik eventually found the river, and they followed it a while before coming to a bridge where they could cross over into Indiana. From there, Erik tried to hug the Interstate, although it was difficult. A few times they came across a blockage that they couldn't get past, and they were forced to turn around. Jonas wanted to get at least as far as Indianapolis by nightfall, but they lost a lot of time going over their tracks. It was mid-afternoon when Jonas noticed the headlights flashing in the mirror.

"That's Gabe. I think he wants to stop." Jonas pulled the car over to the side of the road, and Erik jumped out. They were in between towns, surrounded by a few abandoned vehicles and not much else. There was a signpost indicating they were coming up on Greenwood in ten miles, but as far as Jonas was concerned, they could be on Mars. Erik reassured him he knew where they were going, but driving blind was unnerving. Now and again they saw zombies. Occasionally the dead would stray into the road and sometimes give chase, but they never caught up with them. Jonas was relieved that the zombies were always in the distance, never close enough to do any damage. He wasn't reassured, though, by the fact that they hadn't seen anyone else alive. There hadn't even been a single trace of anyone else living. No moving cars, no lights, no signs for help; it was as if the whole world was dead.

"I'll go see what he needs." Erik cocked his gun. "I know. Be careful." With that, he jogged back to see the others.

"Hey, Erik, we've been coasting on fumes for the last ten minutes," said Javier. "I was hoping we'd come across a gas station, but it looks like we've run out of time."

Erik nodded and looked at the road ahead of them. "There's a town a couple miles ahead, and I'm sure we'll find a gas station. Gotta be worth trying. Think you can make it?"

"I guess so. I'll flash again if we have to stop." Gabe banged on the panel behind his head. "We're stopping in a minute folks," he shouted. "Just hold on a few more minutes."

Erik looked at the van, puzzled.

"They're not too happy back there," Javier explained. "Fair enough, really. Can't be too pleasant being cooped up in there."

"Let's be quick then," said Erik, and he returned to the SUV, leaving Javier and Rose alone.

"We stopping?" asked Quinn as Erik got into the car.

"No," said Erik. "They're running on fumes, but we're going to try to make the next town, see if we can't find a gas station there. When we stop, we need to switch over vehicles too. They're cramped up in the back of the van, and it's no fun for any of them."

Jonas cruised the next few miles with little trouble, and finally came upon a road sign welcoming them to Westport, Indiana, population 1663. The town border was desolate and dusty, and the welcome sign was riddled with bullet-holes. A lone crow picked at something red and fleshy which Jonas hoped was just road-kill. The bird abruptly flew up and settled onto a telegraph pole when they drove past, watching them from a distance. As the number of buildings began to increase, Jonas began to hope they would find a gas station soon. Driving down the main street, nobody came out to see them. Nobody from Westport came out to welcome them, but nobody came out to attack them either. Jonas really didn't want to get sucked into the town center where there was more risk of being attacked.

"Looks deserted," said Erik.

"Think there's anyone around?" Dakota leant forward. "Anyone living here?"

"Doesn't look much like it." Jonas eased off on the gas. He wanted their arrival to be discreet. It was best to get in and out quietly and quickly.

"It's not the living I'm worried about," said Quinn as she scanned the empty streets.

"There," said Erik, "pull up by that campervan."

Jonas stopped a few feet short of the van, which was parked underneath a billboard offering 'tomorrow's real estate at yesterday's prices.' The gas station was offering two for one soda, and Jonas scanned the forecourt. Everything was still. As they watched the white van pull in and park by the nearest tank, nobody came out of the small store attached to the garage.

"I'll go help," said Jonas.

"I'm going to check out that store," announced Terry. "They may have some gear we can use."

"I'll come with you," said Dakota yawning. "I'm feeling a bit car sick, so I could do with stretching my legs."

"Me too." Quinn opened the car door. "I'm not waiting in here; I'll come with you."

"Okay everyone, just be careful, and don't go too far." Erik wound down his window and reclined his seat. "I'm going to close my eyes for a minute. I'm exhausted. Yell if you need me."

"You take it easy. We'll be back in five." Jonas picked up his axe and turned off the engine. He jumped out of the car and strolled over to the van where he could see Gabe trying the pumps. He watched Terry, Dakota, and Quinn head over to the store. It was small and appeared to be deserted. The large window offered a pretty good view inside, and all he could see were a few empty shelves and an open cash register. They might come back with a few Hershey's bars, but he doubted they would find much of real value, like medication or water.

"Anything?" Jonas approached Gabe who was thrusting the nozzle of the final pump back into its slot.

"Nothing. All empty." Javier looked at Jonas and wondered what it would be like watching him die. Right then he wanted nothing more than to pull his gun out and shoot him between the eyes. Progress was slow, too slow, and maybe his idea of having help wasn't going to work out. They were all too casual, too carefree. What were the others doing going into the store? And it looked like Erik was having a nap. He was going to need to shake them out of their comfort zone. Maybe when they realized they hadn't any gas they would realize the severity of the situation.

"How much you got left in the tank?" asked Jonas as he opened the back doors of the van.

"Squat," said Javier. "Unless you want to push us all the way to Canada, we are not going anywhere."

Jonas watched Peter, Freya, Pippa, and Mrs. Danick clamber out of the van. They all looked tired too. Their night at the golf course seemed like an age ago. Before and since then, they had been fighting and traveling, and one night's rest wasn't enough.

Jonas watched as Pippa, Freya and Peter went over to see Erik. Freya was twirling the keychain in her hand as she walked, and it reminded Jonas of what they were doing. The keychain from Fort William was a reminder that Janey and his nephews were still out there waiting for him, relying on him, and he couldn't afford to get slowed down by anything. "Can you siphon some out of another vehicle? We shouldn't hang around here too long."

"You think?" Javier sighed. He looked back at the street. There were a couple of cars parked close by. "I guess. I'll get Mara to help me. We'll go check out those cars first of all, then…"

Two screams simultaneously filled the air, causing Jonas to spin his head, firstly in the direction of the store, and then in the direction of the road. Someone inside the store was in trouble, but he couldn't see who or what was happening. The second scream was from Pippa. The door to the campervan they had pulled up beside was now open, and a man was stepping out. He practically fell out, and stumbled towards Pippa who managed to push Freya away. The man's face was peppered with scratches, and as he got to his feet Jonas knew the man was dead. Peter charged at him, not waiting for the zombie to attack, and then Jonas heard another scream from inside the store. This time he knew who it was: Dakota. The scream was definitely one of terror, and it ended abruptly, the echoes of it ringing in his ears, leaving scars across his worried mind. He sprang to life, and sprinted for the store, hoping he wasn't too late.

CHAPTER FIVE

A bell tinkled as Jonas pushed open the door and entered the store. The air smelt warm and stale, and he saw Terry straight away. He was stood in an aisle with his back to Jonas. He held a large knife above his head and was walking backwards slowly.

"Terry, what the fuck is going on?" Jonas gripped the axe in his hands, looking for Dakota and Quinn.

Terry whirled around. "Hamsikiker? I think...I think she's..."

Jonas saw Terry's eyes dart to a door at the back of the store. "What is it? Are they in there? What's through that door?"

Jonas walked past Terry who wasn't answering. The man looked petrified, and Jonas couldn't afford to waste any more time. If Dakota was in trouble, Terry would just have to take care of himself. Jonas put his hand on the blue door. It was cold, and it creaked as he opened it. Beyond lay a narrow corridor, and Jonas could feel the air get cooler with every step he took on the tiled floor. Another door to the left was closed, and Jonas called out softly. "Dakota?" There was no answer, and he tried the door, but it was locked. Up ahead lay another blue door, and he heard noises on the other side. Voices. They were faint, but he wasn't imagining them, and he hoped it was Dakota and Quinn. They were too muffled to be heard clearly.

He pushed the door open slowly. "Dakota?"

As the door opened and revealed the room beyond, Jonas was taken aback. He stepped forward into a large garage with a roller door to one side and walls with metal shelves surrounding him loaded with tools, cans of oil, dirty cloths, and spare tires. A large A-frame ladder rested by one wall, and a car stripped of parts lay in the center of the garage like a rusted dinosaur with nothing left of its body but bones. In the middle of the garage were Quinn and Dakota. All around them, suspended from the ceiling, hung dead bodies, all of them naked. Jonas counted five in all. Four of the bodies were twitching, their legs and arms jerking spasmodically. This wasn't the last desperate attempt of a family trying to avoid becoming part of the undead, but a cynical murder. Someone had forced them up there and hung them, leaving them to forever hang in suspense, never able to free themselves. The four twitching bodies belonged to men; some old, some young. The fifth body, the one not moving, was a woman, and it looked like she had a bullet hole in her forehead.

There were a few bloodstains on the ground which Jonas tried to avoid as he approached Dakota. "Are you hurt? What happened?"

Dakota flung her arms around her husband as she sobbed. Jonas looked to Quinn for answers, searching her face for clues as to how these people had ended up like that.

"They were all like this when we found them. Dakota came in here first and got quite a shock. I'm guessing you heard her scream." Quinn looked shaken. Jonas couldn't recall the last time he had seen her looking so upset, so tired - so beaten. "Who would do such a thing? They must've pissed someone off. Who would kill these people and just… Jesus, just when you think you've seen everything."

Jonas had to admit, he couldn't understand why anyone would hang four men and leave them to die and then to return. Stripping them naked just seemed malicious. It was as if the murderer wanted them not only to die, but to be humiliated too. He couldn't fathom as to why the woman had been spared the ignominy of returning as a zombie. She had been hung, but shot in the head. What was the point? Perhaps Jonas was wrong to feel sorry for them. Perhaps they deserved it. Who was he to know what those four men had done? Perhaps they were the evil ones, and they deserved what they got. The smell of the oil and the blood took Jonas back to Jeffersontown, to the day when he had gone into a garage with five other people but had only come out with one other man still alive. The smell forced him to remember Cliff. Was what had happened to these men really any worse than what he'd done? He had killed Cliff and left him to rot. The method was different, but the result was basically the same.

"I heard two screams," said Jonas. The coolness and stillness of the garage was unrelenting, and he found himself wanting to leave. The bodies above were uttering faint moans, and the movement of their bodies caused the rope to make groaning, squeaking sounds.

"Me again," said Dakota as she pulled away from Jonas. "There's a body over there in the corner."

Jonas looked and saw an old man dressed in dungarees and a red and white striped shirt. The top of his head was caved in, and blood streaked his face.

"He wasn't like that when we found him," said Quinn. She held up a bloody crowbar. "The first scream must've alerted him to our presence. He was dead and came out of nowhere. We figured he must've been trapped in here. You would've heard Dakota's second scream when he jumped her."

Dakota wiped her eyes. She had stopped crying, although Jonas could see she was still shaken. "I just saw him come out of the shadows at me. Thank God that Quinn was around."

As opposed to me, thought Jonas. "Thank God you were," he said.

Quinn shrugged. "Let's get the hell out of here. This place is horrible."

"Shouldn't we do something," asked Dakota feebly, "about, you know, them?" She looked down at the ground, but pointed above her head.

"It's too risky," said Jonas. "We shoot, and we risk bringing more of them here. It may not feel right, but this is not our argument."

They made their way back through to the store. Dakota and Quinn continued outside whilst Jonas checked on Terry.

"So I take it you didn't find anything useful in here?"

Terry looked disconsolate. "No. The place has been turned over, but there's nothing. I'm sorry, Hamsikker. Truly, I am."

Jonas looked outside. The zombie that had been attacking Pippa was lying on the floor, and the others were crowded around the campervan. He would have to check on the situation, but right now Terry needed help. The man's usual demeanor had been replaced by a look of weariness that Jonas was beginning to see all too much of.

"What is it, Terry?"

"I can't do this anymore. After we lost Randal, I didn't know what we would do. Then when we came across Saint Paul's, I thought we'd be able to survive this. Today, right now, I'm not so sure anymore. I heard Dakota screaming, and I froze. I'm ashamed to say that I let Quinn run in there after her, and I stayed here. I'm a coward, Hamsikker. I left a pregnant woman alone. The thought of seeing just one more zombie…"

"I don't think you're a coward, Terry. You've done more than enough to prove to me that you're anything but." Jonas remembered how he had been the first one to try and help Randal when he was attacked. Terry had certainly changed though. He used to help look after Freya, but now he kept his distance. It was as if Terry was cutting himself off from the group.

"I just can't face being responsible for other people's lives. I couldn't help Randal or Tyler, and the rest of you are so good that… Look, I've been thinking about it a while, and I think it's best if I leave."

Jonas stepped forward and opened the store's door. The voices of the other's talking became clearer, and Jonas held it open. "Terry, those people need you. I need you. We're a team, and any talk of leaving is just crazy. So you froze up, so what? We've all been there. You think I don't get scared? You think you're any worse than Erik or Quinn? There's nothing to worry about, Terry, we're all with you, we'll all help you. Come on, let's get back to the others and see if we can't get on the road again."

Terry joined Jonas at the door and looked outside at the rest of the group. "No. I'm leaving, Hamsikker. I've always thought we should head for the coast."

"Terry, not that again. You know how hard it will be to…"

"Don't, okay? Just don't." Terry took a step outside, and Jonas followed him, letting the door close. "I know you think I'm mad, but it's all I've ever wanted to do. I kept going along with everything, but I have to go. I need to. If I stay with you I'm just going to end up driving myself mad or do something worse, and someone will end up getting hurt. I'll go tonight. I don't want any long good bye. I just want to slip away, so do me a favor, and don't tell anyone else about this, please. I need to be on my own, and this is what I want to do. Honestly. I'm going to get myself to the east coast, find myself a boat, and take it from there."

"Sure." Jonas didn't know what else he could say. He knew it had been on Terry's mind for a while about trying for the coast, and it seemed like the man had made his mind up. "Just do me a favor, Terry, and don't disappear before I get a chance to say goodbye. I'll sort you out a few supplies, enough to last you a few days at least on your own. Deal?"

"Deal."

As they walked back towards the others, Jonas wondered if there was anything he could say to convince Terry to stay. He couldn't blame the man for freezing back there, nor could he blame him for wanting to try to make it on his own. It wasn't easy being thrown together with a bunch of strangers and putting your life on the line every day with them. He doubted Terry would change his mind, but he would give him every chance to reconsider.

"Everyone good?" asked Jonas as he approached Gabe.

"We're fine. Pippa got a bit of a fright, but no harm done. This guy came off worse." Javier pointed to the zombie that had emerged from the campervan. Prostrate on the ground, his head was nothing but a pile of red and white gore, his brain mashed into the sidewalk. "Peter was quite the hero."

"He sure was," said Rose. "Very dashing."

It seemed almost as if Rose and Gabe were enjoying the action. Jonas noticed they were the only ones smiling. "Did you manage to get any gas?"

"No, not yet," said Javier. "What with all the excitement, we got a little sidetracked."

"I was going to ask you about that." Mrs. Danick nudged Jonas's arm. "I think we should ditch the van and take this camper."

Javier laughed. "Yeah, sure, and we'll stop for a picnic lunch later while I write the postcards." He looked at Jonas and rolled his eyes.

"Actually, that's not a bad idea," said Hamsikker, ignoring Gabe's sarcastic comments. "There's still plenty of room for the supplies, and the windows and seats will make traveling a lot more comfortable for those in back." It was smaller than the white van, but would provide a lot more comfort for traveling. Jonas was sure that Gabe would understand.

"Hamsikker, can I remind you that time is not on our side?" Javier was fed up of the distractions and eager to get moving. Hamsikker was too easily swayed by the others. Javier was beginning to doubt he'd made the right decision in letting the others tag along. Instead of inheriting a small army, it felt like he'd inherited a group of children, constantly demanding attention.

"It won't take us long to transfer the gear if we all help," said Mrs. Danick. "Plus, I checked the gas, and it's near full. There's a bit of a funky smell in there, thanks to our dear departed friend, but a few minutes on the road with the windows down should sort that out." Mrs. Danick smiled at Gabe triumphantly.

"Fine, let's do it then." Javier bit his tongue and resisted the urge to slap Mrs. Danick in the face. "Then we really need to get going. I want to be much further north by sundown."

It took them a further ten minutes to get everything organized, and they resumed their seats when everything was transferred into the campervan. Jonas returned to driving the SUV, while Javier took the camper. After a quick bite to eat, Erik got them back on track, and they spent the afternoon hours navigating their way north. The sun never managed to fully break through the cloud, and by early evening a drizzle had settled in, making progress slow. They avoided any more confrontation with the dead, and as they neared Indianapolis Jonas realized they were going to have to find somewhere to stop for the night. In the gloomy dusk, the dead were harder to spot, and he had to swerve around several at the last moment. Erik was struggling to navigate in the darkness, and when they passed a sign that stated Indianapolis was thirty miles away, Jonas called it.

"Erik, we need to quit while we're ahead. Let's get somewhere safe tonight, and call it a day. I'm straining to see much in this damn weather, and if we keep going into the night, we're liable to hit something on the road."

"Sounds like a plan to me." Erik shuffled around in his seat. "That all right with you guys?"

Dakota, Quinn, and Terry all concurred, and they decided that Gabe would follow them wherever they stopped. The others would surely see it was too dangerous driving at night.

"There's a town up ahead. Martinsville, I think," announced Erik. "Commuter town for Indianapolis. We're on the fringes now, so everyone keep a look out for somewhere to stay. We don't want to go right into the center, that's way too risky. I know we'd all like a decent bed for the night, but I'm inclined to say we take somewhere that's likely to be empty. Maybe a warehouse or…"

"Or a factory?" asked Quinn. "Look over there to the right. There's a small business park. I doubt we'd find much company in there, dead or alive."

"Please let there be a mattress factory," said Dakota as they turned into the side road toward the park, "my back is killing me."

They slowed down to a crawl and monitored the buildings as they drove past warehouse after warehouse. Nothing moved, nothing came crawling out of the shadows, and nothing stirred when Jonas pulled up outside a textile factory. They sat in the car waiting for the camper to stop behind them and watched the building. It had a small brick office at the front, with two square windows and a lime green door that was wide open. Surrounding it was the hub of the factory, a huge oblong shaped building with a forklift parked up beside what appeared to be a delivery bay. A gantry ran up one wall where a signpost was being erected. Evidently the work had been stopped before completion, and the letters above the door only read 'C.R.Lew', before abruptly stopping.

"It looks quiet." Jonas turned off the engine and waited. "The door's open which makes getting in easier. What do you think? We could scope it out, and if it's a go, we could bring the vehicles right up to that delivery bay. No one would even know we're here."

"Well, I would feel happier if we assessed the security situation first. Someone should go in there," said Erik, unbuckling his seatbelt. "I'm happy to go, but I need someone to watch my back."

"If I'm going to spend the night here, I want to know nothing's going to go *bump* in the night. I am *so* coming with you," said Quinn.

"Me too," said Jonas.

"No," said Erik firmly as he opened his door. "You stay here. If there's any trouble you need to get your wife out of here, and let

Gabe know too. Anyone but Quinn or me come out, get the hell out of here. It'll be faster if there's just the two of us anyway."

Jonas opened his mouth to protest, but Erik gave him a glare, and he knew there was no point arguing. It did make sense. As Erik and Quinn jumped out of the cab, Jonas felt beneath his seat for his axe. He knew it was there, but he couldn't help it. He had to touch it, to feel it, to truly know he wasn't defenseless. The firmness of it made him feel better. It made no sense, he knew that, but logic went out of the window the day the dead started walking.

"Terry, you mind running back to Gabe and letting him know what's happening?" asked Jonas.

"Sure. Honk if anything happens." Terry got out, leaving Jonas alone in the car with Dakota.

"How're you feeling, honey?" Jonas turned around in his seat so he could see her. He expected her to brush him off or to ignore him, but she actually looked directly at him and reached for his hand.

She stroked his hand and spoke in a low voice. "I've felt better. I suppose the stress isn't good for the baby, but it's hard to shrug it off. I keep feeling sick, and all I can think about is how this is affecting her."

"Her?"

"Well, I don't know." Dakota smiled. "It's just a feeling."

Jonas looked at his wife, feeling more proud of her then than he ever had before. "I love you, Dakota. I'm going to sort this out. Get everything sorted out so we can be safe, once and for all. It doesn't matter to me if it's a boy or a girl, as long as it's safe. I promise we'll get through this. I'm going to do whatever it takes to make sure of that, you know that, don't you?"

"Hm." Dakota sighed. "Jonas, I apologize if I'm a little distant, but I've a lot on my mind at the moment."

"I know, what with the baby, and…"

"No, just shut up for a minute will you? It's not just the baby. I mean, I'm worried about it, but we've got a long time to figure out how we're going to manage living with a child to look after. I'm worried about you too. The things you do, the way you are, the things you've done; you can't do it again, Jonas. You can't kill someone and just *decide* to take their life away." Dakota didn't speak accusingly or angrily, but softly, as if chiding a child for sneaking an extra biscuit from the meal table. "Jonas, I want you to promise me that you'll never do that again. Ever. There's no going back from that. Despite all this shit around us, we have to be better than that. When Tyler told me what you did to Cliff..."

"I get it, I do. I'm not going to go into what went on in that garage, but I hear you, Dakota." Jonas knew that explaining it to her was pointless. She had her views, and she wasn't about to change them.

"Killing zombies is one thing. Cliff was *alive*. He still had something to offer, and whatever he did, you took away any chance he had at redemption. You shouldn't have done it. I can't reconcile what you did with the man I married."

"I'm not sure I can either. But I can't undo it. I did what I thought was right at the time. I can assure you it wasn't easy, and I won't be doing anything like it again. I was out there, not in control, trying to deal with too much. I know I was acting like an idiot, but...what happened at the garage really got to me. Seeing what happened to Anna and Mary. What happened to Cliff was..."

"Promise me," said Dakota. "Promise me you won't do anything like that again."

"I do. I promise."

The door next to Dakota swung open, and Terry jumped inside. "Gabe's happy enough here. Mara seemed a bit sniffy, but I suppose she's used to living in luxury after being in that golf club place for so long. The others are just happy to get out of the van. I've gotta say, it still stinks a bit in there."

They waited in the increasing darkness, listening to the patter of the rain on the roof of the SUV. Jonas found it soothing, although he couldn't fully relax until Erik was back and they were all tucked up safely for the night inside. It took a minute more before he saw movement. Quinn came running out of the open office door and ran up to them. Jonas opened the door for her, and she jumped in, beaming.

"We're good to go," she said. "The place is deserted. We couldn't get any power on, so we'll park up close by. There's plenty of room inside, and a vending machine still stocked up with crap. If anyone's got a hankering for a Hershey's, you're in luck."

"Pregnant ladies first," said Dakota.

Jonas moved the SUV closer to the office door and let the others go inside. He waited for Gabe to pull up alongside, and then the rest went inside carrying a box of food and drink each.

"Thanks," said Jonas. He and Gabe were the last ones outside, and he held out his hand to shake. "We sure appreciate your help, Gabe. I'm not sure that anyone else would've welcomed us as much as you and Mara have. We owe you. I just wanted you to know that." He noticed Gabe hesitated in taking his hand, but when he did it was a firm handshake. The man was probably a little intimidated by them. Seven people had just turned up on his doorstep demanding sanctuary, and less than a day later they were back on the road. It was perfectly understandable that he might keep his guard up for a while. Jonas would've done exactly the same thing if the roles were reversed. He remembered the house in Jeffersontown they had been staying in, and when Randall and Quinn had showed up. It had taken a few days for them to be accepted into the group. They had surrendered their weapons and been so weak that they couldn't possibly have posed any danger. Yet living on edge all the time kept you on your toes, and Jonas wasn't about to accept anyone into their lives easily. Trust had to be won these days, and blind naiveté led you down a dangerous path. Gabe was right to be careful. He had a wife to think about.

"Don't mention it," said Javier. "What did I tell you? I'm all sweetness and light."

Jonas picked up a pile of blankets from the campervan, and brushed past Mara coming back out as he entered the building. "Don't be too long," said Jonas, "we'll want to close up soon. Best not to stay outside too long in case we draw attention to ourselves."

"Thanks, Hamsikker," said Rose. She watched Jonas disappear inside and turned to face Javier.

"Let's leave them. Let's take the van, and get out of here. I'm sick of them already. I thought I could do this, but their whining is driving me insane. What happened to you and me? What happened to you, Javier? The girl, Freya, she's cool. I *love* how freaking quiet she is. We could keep her, but the rest of them? Let's just go, or get rid of the others now, please? Especially that cop and his goody-two-shoes wife. I want them gone."

"*Be patient*," said Javier, making sure that no one was listening. "I know it's difficult, but we have our own little army now. You won't need to get involved in any dirty work with the zombies any more, we can send our minions out to do it for us. If they happen to run into trouble, perhaps get bitten, well bad luck for them. Until we don't need them anymore, just wait and go with it. I'll keep them in line. If anyone gets out of order, I'll see to them. The cop's nothing but a big pussycat. He looks tough, but he's a softy. Hamsikker's the one to watch. He likes to make out he's a nobody, but he's a threat, for sure. I've noticed he doesn't back down when the going gets tough, but if he starts making waves with you and me, he'll soon find himself on the end of something sharp and pointy."

"You promise?" asked Rose.

"Promise. These people will only be around as long as they are still useful to us. Once we hit the border, they cease to be of any use."

Rose laughed, and in the silent gloom of the office, Jonas stopped dead in his tracks. He was going back to help bring in more supplies, and he paused before stepping outside. He wondered what Mara could possibly find to laugh about in their predicament. Seeing Gabe and Mara stood at the back of the campervan, he decided to stay in the shadows for a moment and try to hear what they were talking about.

"I just think we can do better than this, you know? Look at us, squirrelling away food and water, playing Mom and Dad, and driving around in a damn campervan. When did we turn into the Brady bunch? I want to be with you, not a bunch of strangers. I'm cold and wet, and…"

"I don't need to hear another litany of complaints, *Mara*. Just remember who's in charge. You don't need to tell me what needs doing, or what I should be saying or feeling. I've got it covered. We'll get a fire going inside and get warm. Just learn when to keep your God damn mouth shut. Got that?"

Jonas noticed that Gabe's hands were down by his side as he spoke, but they were curled up into fists and trembling. If he struck

Mara, then Jonas was going to have to confront him. It seemed so out of character, though, that he felt he must be reading the situation wrong. He had never seen a man actually hit a woman, forgetting the endless procession of violent Hollywood movies that he'd watched, and he wasn't sure if he needed to get ready to intervene. Gabe had been nothing but, well, sweetness and light, so to hear their raised voices was concerning. Gabe spoke quite forcefully to Mara in a tone that was not reassuring to Jonas at all.

"What's up, Hamsikker? You coming inside or what?" Peter brushed past Jonas as he went out to the van. "Freya's cold, so I thought I'd grab some extra blankets. I'm glad you prepared for an emergency, Gabriel, you're a lifesaver. If you hadn't pre-loaded this van, we'd have nothing right now."

As Peter lifted a box from the back of the van, Javier watched as Jonas stepped out into the rain.

"I was…just coming to help," said Jonas. He grabbed a random box from the campervan, and followed Peter back inside. Jonas could feel Gabe's eyes burning into his back as he walked and hoped Gabe didn't suspect he had been eavesdropping on him. It was the truth, but he didn't want to upset Gabe now, not when they were just starting to get to know each other.

"You think they heard?" Rose pressed herself up against Javier. "You think…"

"I doubt they heard much. If they did, they would've said or done something about it. Still, we can't be too careful." Javier wasn't convinced they were in the clear, but he didn't want to take any chances and wake to find a knife at his throat in the middle of the night. "I'll speak to Hamsikker."

"I wish we could find some private time tonight. It's been too long," said Rose. She licked her lips and rubbed Javier's back.

"What about the boy?" Javier looked at her. "We need to contain this first, make sure the group is still on our side. Why don't you play a little game with Peter? Get him to take watch with you or something."

"A game?" Rose ignored the rain dripping down her back and suddenly felt warm again.

"What's that game you like to play?" asked Javier playfully, knowing full well what it was. He curled Rose's hair around his fingers. "Stick, or twist? Im sure Peter would love it if you played with him."

Rose reached up to kiss Javier, and he grabbed her, cupping her face in his hand. "Just be *discreet*. Make it look like an accident. If it works, you can do the cop next."

Rose twisted herself free from Javier's grip, and grinned. "I can't wait."

CHAPTER SIX

"So come with me. Come with us to Canada. I should've been honest with you from the start, I get that, but Gabe asked me not to say anything until he had spoken to Mara."

Erik continued stroking Pippa's hair as she lay beside him.

"I don't waste time holding grudges, Hamsikker. I always suspected you would try to help Janey at some point. I haven't been sitting around with my finger up my ass, you know. I'm always thinking about Pippa and my kids; what I can do for them and where I can take them that's safe. I thought Saint Paul's was going to be that place, but it didn't work out. Since then, I've been trying to decide what to do. Canada? Maybe. I've thought about Terry's plan, too, heading for the coast, but I'm not sure it's for me. It just doesn't feel right."

"I think he'll make it. Don't ask me how, but he's made it this far. He's tough."

After securing the building they had set about creating separate areas to sleep in. The office was cold, but the blankets they had with them helped, and they managed to start a fire in a waste paper basket that gave them a little warmth. It was burning now beneath an open window that sucked the smoke out. The warehouse had a staircase leading to a series of ladders and rails that crisscrossed the floor, suspended high above the machines that lay silent below. The front door was secured behind a large filing cabinet, and the only windows in the place were high up, well away from any prying eyes or curious zombies. They ate and then moved to their own private areas to rest. They decided to leave at first light, so an early night was called for. Terry indicated to Jonas that he still wanted to leave, and Jonas had even gotten as far as filling a backpack for him with a little food and water, but when it came time to say goodbye, Terry hesitated. Jonas was so sure he was going to leave, but they talked, and eventually Terry decided he would wait another day. He told Jonas he wanted to make sure they were safe, on their way north, but Jonas thought it was more likely that Terry was scared. Going it alone wasn't a prospect to savor, and Terry was going to need a bit more time to summon up the courage he needed to make it on his own.

Jonas asked Erik to help him with a chore after supper, and he told him everything about Terry's plan to leave. Jonas knew he could trust Erik to be discreet, and it was a relief to share it with someone else. Erik was perfectly suited to being a cop. He just had that natural confidence about him, like he was your best friend and protector rolled into one. Jonas knew it was only because of Erik that he was still alive, and just as when they were growing up, they still relied on each other.

The fire crackled and popped, and the flames splashed across Erik's face. Jonas looked at Pippa, who was fast asleep, and then across at Dakota. Her eyes were closed, but he wondered if she was pretending to sleep so she could listen in.

"For now, we'll come with you. It'd be good to see Janey again."

"Great. I'm so relieved, Erik. I really didn't want us to split up. I'm telling you, things will be better up there. Once we find Janey we can make a real go of it. We can find somewhere safe, somewhere away from people, just us, and…"

"Hold on, Hamsikker, I said for now." Erik yawned and lay down beside Pippa, careful not to wake her. "Once we find Janey, and she's okay, I can't promise what we'll do next."

"Okay, okay. I hope you're not thinking of going back," said Jonas. "Kentucky is a dangerous place now. There's nothing back there for you, nothing but memories and graves. Saint Paul's is gone. Your home is gone."

"I know, I know." Erik yawned again, but Freya began to stir, and she began crying in her sleep. "Hold on," said Erik as he got up to attend to his daughter who was sleeping nearby.

Jonas listened in the dark as Erik tried to comfort Freya. She didn't really wake from whatever nightmare she was having, but as Erik soothed her, she stopped crying.

"I know, I know," whispered Erik repeatedly.

Jonas had never seen Erik cry, but it sounded like the man's voice was breaking. It must be killing him that he couldn't help his family.

"Close your eyes, and pretend we're in Hawaii. Picture that sandy beach, and try to feel the warmth of the sun on your skin. Remember when we were there last year? Go back there, honey, go back. Just go to sleep, and dream about those pretty Hula girls and how good it was. We'll go back one day, honey, but just sleep now. I'm here. I'll always be right here beside you. I love you."

Freya's crying had stopped, and Jonas guessed she was probably fast asleep already. Despite her restless sleep, she was exhausted, and nightmares or not, she needed rest.

"I love you, Freya."

Jonas felt guilty for listening, but it was soothing. The events of the day kept running around his mind, and dark images populated his thoughts. Restless, he turned over, but there was little he could do to force himself to sleep. He'd always been a poor sleeper, whereas Dakota could sleep through an earthquake. In fact, only a couple of years ago she had done just that when a large one had hit the west coast. He looked at her now, sleeping so peacefully. The blanket had slipped down, and as he carefully pulled the blanket up to her chin, he draped an arm over her. She was warm, and though he wanted to snuggle up to her, he didn't want her to wake. She was tired like everyone else.

Erik returned, and Jonas gave up on the idea of sleeping before he took watch.

"Peter took Freya to the bathroom at the clubhouse yesterday and let her take a shower," said Erik. "Peter told me it was the first time in weeks he'd seen her smile, like *genuinely* smile. My daughter doesn't do enough of that anymore. She's been scarred by all of this. I just hope it's not permanent."

"Kids are resilient," said Jonas, trying to reassure his old friend. "She's still here isn't she? She's tougher than you think. She'll come round."

Erik raised his eyebrows. "Resilient?"

"So I hear. Okay, so I don't know anything about kids," said Jonas, "but she's kept it together this long, hasn't she? Peter is amazing for her. Pippa, too, but Peter's what, seventeen? He's taken on so much, and I never hear him complain."

"True. I'd do anything for my boy. He's going to be an amazing man one day. I'm proud as hell of both of my kids, and that's why

I'm not ruling anything out *or* in. I just need to make sure I do what's best for my family. When we get to Janey in a couple of days, then I'll decide. *We'll* decide." Erik let out another yawn. "Let's get some sleep. Gabe's on watch, right?"

"Yeah, I'll go switch with him shortly. Get some rest, Erik."

Jonas made sure Dakota was warm and then took a look around the warehouse that was their home for the night. Using the blankets they had brought and some carpet samples they had found, everyone had a bed of sorts to call their own. Even though they had spent much of the day driving, it was still tiring. Jonas hoped Terry's impending departure didn't inspire a similar idea in Erik. In the morning Jonas intended to lay out his plans very clearly. There would be no more hiding or messing around. Gabe would have time to talk to Mara, and when they were all up, Jonas was going to make it clear that their best chance of survival was to head north to Canada.

He trudged to the now open vending machine with its front panel smashed in and pulled out a packet of chips. Jonas figured he may as well go up early and relieve Gabe of his shift on watch, as he didn't feel like sleeping yet.

"Hamsikker, you got a second?" Quinn was making her bed for the night, laying out a blanket in a dark corner, and he had almost trodden on her in the dark.

"Sure. What's up?" Jonas always had time for Quinn. He wasn't in the mood to chat, and Quinn rarely wasted her breath on idle gossip, so he assumed it was important. "You know I never properly thanked you for earlier. Dakota freaked out, but you stepped up. I appreciate that."

"No problem. That's what we do, right? Watch each other's backs?" Quinn looked around the room, but Gabe was off doing his rounds, and it seemed like everyone else was asleep. "I wanted to talk to you. How are you doing?" She struggled to find the right words. "I'm sorry about how things went down. These last couple of days have been hell. With everything that's happened lately nobody would be surprised if you needed some time to, you know...*adjust*."

"Adjust?" He knew Quinn was being polite. "You're talking about the garage? What happened inside is my issue, not yours. If that's all you want to talk about, then forget it."

As he went to leave, Quinn grabbed his arm. "No. Look, I know it affected you, and I just wanted you to know that I understand. Seeing your friends die like that... Sorry, Hamsikker, but I wanted to talk to you about something else too. Please, just sit with me a minute."

Quinn sat on the makeshift bed and drew her knees up to her chin. The way she was looking at Jonas was unusual, and he couldn't work out what she wanted.

"Sorry, I didn't mean to snap," he said as he sat down beside her. The floor beneath the blanket was hard, but the room was warm and quiet. They were all exhausted, and he doubted she would have much trouble sleeping tonight.

"It's nothing. For what it's worth, I'm truly sorry. Anna and Mary were fun to have around. I don't think Freya's handling it too well, losing her friend. This whole thing has got her scared. We've lost some good people lately. Sometimes I still turn around to talk to Tyler, and I forget he's gone. I know, I know, you don't want to get into anything now, and that's fine. If you ever do want to talk though, then I'm here."

"Thanks, Quinn." Jonas wanted to tell her about Terry's plan to leave, but the less people who knew the better. It would be best to clear the air in the morning, make a fresh start as a group. "It's not easy. Sometimes I lose sight of what we're doing, where we're going. I need to be doing something, though, and bumbling along doesn't suit me. Before all this I used to plan and organize my life, but now it's a mess. I wake up in the morning, and I don't even know where to start."

"Motivation, is that what you want?" asked Quinn. "How about living. I mean, you don't need to save up for that condo in Florida anymore. The two-week vacation in Bora Bora is off the menu, and the only thing you're likely to pick up at Penny's is a bad case of dead. Look, you're alive; that's it. There doesn't have to be anything else or any more to life. All we do now is get by. That's how we stay alive. We look out for each other. That's our life now."

Jonas knew Quinn meant well, but she was young and didn't have the responsibilities that he did. "It's funny. I used to be wired differently." Jonas offered Quinn some chips, and they munched on them as they talked. "When I was a kid all I wanted to do was leave home, and get as far away from my father as I possibly could. Once I'd achieved that, I tried to make my fortune. My early twenties were a succession of dead-end jobs and bad choices in women. Don't get me wrong, for a while there I loved it, but after a time you realize you need something more out of life. I finally got a good job, I met Dakota, and my life changed. I had a reason to live, not just a selfish one, but a *real* reason. Dakota made me happy, and I wanted to give her everything. I worked my butt off, and until a few months ago, I didn't think life would change. I saw no reason to change anything, but then of course, it was forced on all of us. My father died, then he un-died, then he died again. My world was turned upside down, but you don't need me to tell you that. You must have lost someone you love?"

"You don't have a monopoly on guilt, Hamsikker. I saw my parents killed right in front of me," said Quinn. "I saw my husband kill them, and there was nothing I could do about it. You talk of love. What I had with Roger… What's past is past, right? Forget it and move on?" Quinn looked at Jonas accusingly with bitterness and anger in her eyes.

"I'm sorry." Jonas instantly knew he should never have brought it up. Quinn was a private person, and he felt bad for making her open up to him.

"Don't be. Just accept that life deals you a shitty hand sometimes, and there's nothing you can do about it but grab what you can, while you can. I used to run with a bad crowd. I'm not proud of it, but that's who I am. I've been hiding it, and I admit I'm not sure how Erik would take it, but the truth is I was part of a gang. At first it was all about hanging with the cool kids, then it progressed into a few muggings, and by the end we were holding up liquor stores at gunpoint. Roger was in on it too. I thought we were invincible. I thought we were *bad motherfuckers*, but we were just kids playing a role. In the end…"

Quinn trailed off into silence, and Jonas could see why she didn't talk about herself much. "So you got out?"

Quinn laughed, but there was nothing funny about what she said, and her laughter was tinged with sadness. "Got out? No. On our last job, Roger got bitten. We thought it was some crazy drunk, and we put a bullet in his head. I got Roger home to my parents. We couldn't exactly go to the cops about it, you know? I drank a bottle of bourbon, fell asleep, and when I woke up in the morning... well, that was when the world changed. Like you said, we've all lost someone."

Quinn trailed off into silence again, and Jonas waited for her to continue, but she didn't. "Like you said, what's past is past. We've all done things we're not proud of." Jonas had no intention of telling anyone else about Cliff, but the man's battered face would haunt him forever. "Was there anything else, Quinn, as I really should go up and relieve Gabe?"

"What do you think about our two new friends?" Quinn stared at the floor as she spoke. It was as if she was regressing to her childhood. Now she wasn't out in the battlefield, she could let her guard down and relax. Maybe it was the talk of her old life that had her looking so dejected.

"Gabe and Mara? They seem like nice enough people, don't you think?" asked Jonas. "And this place is just what we were looking for. Gabe was decent enough to take first watch. It's warm and secure, so I don't see why we shouldn't be safe enough tonight. If it wasn't for Gabe having the foresight to pack up that van, we would be half starving by now. Look, if we hadn't found them when we had, then God knows what would have happened to us. Chances are we'd be out there getting our asses kicked. I think Gabe and Mara came along at just the right time." Jonas was pleased the conversation had taken a more upbeat tone. He didn't want Quinn dwelling on dark thoughts. He knew from experience that churning up old memories usually led to depression or anger, neither of which were useful in a world full of the walking dead.

"I guess so..." Quinn sighed. "It's just that Mrs. Danick was talking to me earlier. She isn't convinced that they're so sweet. She thinks the innocence and sweetness is all a show. She swears they were arguing earlier. She says they're hiding something."

Jonas snorted. "Sorry, but come again? What is she basing this on? Did she elaborate on anything 'cause it seems to me that they're just about the nicest damn people we've met in a long time. They let us in and asked for nothing in return. *Nothing.* You know how rare that is in this world. What do *you* think?"

"They were perfectly pleasant, I have to admit, but…"

"But what? Other than a senile old lady's theories, I don't see the problem. Mrs. Danick might be a sharp shooter, but sometimes she's not on the same planet as us. Two weeks ago she thought she saw Elvis. Remember? Did you believe her then?"

"That was different," said Quinn. "She gets confused sometimes, you know that. Mara hasn't said much, but Gabe can be a little blunt, if I'm honest. Mrs. Danick said he wasn't in any of the photos back at Saint Paul's, and I think…"

"I think," said Jonas, "that you need to remember the only reason you're alive right now is because Gabe and Mara let us in. I think you need to show a little more gratitude, and stop listening to Mrs. Danick's crazy stories." Jonas stood up and left Quinn staring up at him. She looked like a lost young girl as her brown eyes looked at his. "Get some rest, Quinn, you're on watch in a couple of hours."

Jonas hated leaving Quinn on bad terms, but she had dealt with far worse than a telling off from him. Tomorrow was going to be a fresh start for everyone. They had navigated their way out of Kentucky and managed to avoid coming into contact with many dead since leaving Saint Paul's. Jonas slowly climbed the metal steps to the upper gantry to find Gabe. He vowed that he wouldn't run away anymore. He wasn't going to keep hiding, but he would confront things head on. Dakota was slowly coming around, and Erik would too. As long as Gabe played ball, there was no need for any more issues. If Mrs. Danick kept her head, then who knows, they could even make Canada by nightfall the next day. If they stayed clear of trouble, perhaps he could get Freya to open up too. His promise to Dakota was solid, but there was one thing he had to promise himself.

"I'm going to get us out of here, and then I'm going to find Janey." He had to say it out loud to make it real. He couldn't bottle it up anymore. Jonas stepped up onto the catwalk, and he saw Gabe at the far end of the warehouse. Now that Erik knew about Canada, Jonas's resolve had been strengthened, and the last part of the jigsaw was Gabe. Mrs. Danick didn't suffer fools gladly, and if she had convinced Quinn, then something might be up. There was no reason they couldn't all get along. It was time to find out what Gabe wanted and who he really was.

CHAPTER SEVEN

They wanted to go into the office to look outside, so together they dragged the filing cabinet to one side, pushed back the flimsy wooden door, and entered the office. Satisfied there were no zombies around and that their vehicles were still parked up close by, Peter checked the other door that led outside. The key hung in it loosely, and he kicked a sheaf of papers underneath the reception desk.

"It's locked, but it wouldn't take much to get it open if a few of them came across us. We should get back inside before we're spotted," he whispered. The rain still fell and almost drowned out his soft voice.

Rose took Peter's hand. Saying nothing, she pulled him to her and brushed her lips gently over his. She knew that she smelt good, clean and fresh, with a hint of perfume. In the clubhouse lockers she had found a discarded gym bag with a half-empty bottle of fragrance inside, and she was putting it to good use. It was eerily quiet in the warehouse, and she had offered to take watch with Peter before dawn. With Peter being so young, it had sounded like a good idea to Erik, and he had practically encouraged the two of them to do the night watch together. The others were asleep, and now that they had reached the office, Rose pulled him close to her and let her lips rest on Peter's. She pulled him closer, sensing what he wanted.

"Mara, stop, what are you doing?" Peter let go of her, confused. "We're supposed to be on watch, what are you doing? Jesus."

Rose smiled and maintained eye contact with Peter. He was making the right noises, but she knew how men worked, and she knew when their body was disagreeing with what they were saying. Most men wanted her, or at least used to, and she could deal with that. She used it to her advantage, and usually got what she wanted. Now that she was with Javier, she had decided to stop playing around and had taken up a different sort of game.

"Peter, don't worry so much. I know what you want." Rose slipped off her polo shirt and let the cold night air wrap around her body. The boy was scared, but excited. She was half-tempted to let him have her, but then the thought of anyone else inside her apart from Javier brought her senses sharply to the fore. She shivered at the thought of Peter laying a finger on her, let alone anything else. She would rather disembowel herself with a rusty nail than let a pig's offspring touch her.

"Are you cold?" Rose asked. She could see Peter admiring her breasts through her bra, and knowing how desperately he wanted to touch her made her want to laugh. He wanted her so much, yet he was so afraid. It occurred to her then that he might be a virgin.

"We don't have to do this," said Peter timidly. "We *shouldn't* do this. You're married, and…"

"And I saw how you looked at me in the shower yesterday," said Rose as she approached Peter. "I want it too. I need it Peter. I was Gabe's sweetheart at school, and I've never been with anyone else. I need a man. I need *you*." Rose stifled a giggle as Peter's mouth fell open. With reactions like that, he *had* to be a virgin. Any other man would have long since given up resisting her, and dropped his pants in seconds.

"Mara, I think you're beautiful, but I…I'm…"

Rose pressed her finger to his lips. "Shush," she whispered. "Just relax. We're completely alone. We can do *anything* we want."

Rose kneeled down before Peter, and unbuckled his belt. She waited a moment, wondering if he would grab her head and thrust himself into her like most men. Instead, he placed his hands on her shoulders, and she thought she heard him whisper something about wanting to make love to her.

"Sit down," she instructed Peter forcefully, and she pushed him back into a swivel chair. "Now close your eyes."

Peter closed his eyes instantly. Rose shook her head at how easy it was. She reached into her pocket and pulled out some industrial cable ties that she had found earlier, maneuvered herself around the back of the chair discreetly, and then tied Peter's hand together, binding his wrists tightly.

"Hey, I'm not sure about this. Do you…"

"Be quiet," Rose whispered in his ear, "or I won't let you fuck me."

Rose made sure Peter couldn't escape his ties, and then unlocked the front door, letting the moon light up the room. Warm rain dripped inside from the roof, and Rose had to admit that she was turning herself on. If only Javier were sat in that chair instead of Peter. He was such a typical, obnoxious American college boy. Rose imagined that Peter was the sort of person who probably helped his Mom bake apple pie before offering to cut the grass and prepare for his exams by taking on extra homework. Undoubtedly, the closest he'd ever gotten to a woman was taking the girl next door to the cinema to see some God-awful romantic movie before buying her an ice cream, giving her a peck on the cheek, and getting her home to her parents by ten p.m. Where were the real men? Rose knew Javier hated much of America, and she thought that sometimes she did too. It wasn't so much the place as the people that she despised. Then again, she wasn't fussy who she killed. Most people, whether they were American, Korean, or from the North Pole, were scum. They all bled the same in the end.

Rose was tempted to put a blindfold on Peter, but she was beginning to tire of the game she was playing, and was eager to get back inside to Javier.

"You think you're the first man I've met since this whole thing started who wanted to fuck me?" Rose laughed as she straddled Peter. "You're not even a man. I don't think you'd even know what to do with it." She didn't try to hide the contempt in her voice, and waited for Peter to open his eyes. In the moonlight, they shone brightly, and she could see his father in those piercing blue eyes.

Confusion and embarrassment spread over Peter's face. "What is this? I thought…"

Rose laughed again, and her shrill laugh scared him more than anything. Suddenly Peter wanted out; he wanted to be back inside, back at Saint Paul's, back at home, even back in the campervan - anywhere but here. He pulled at the ties around his wrists, but she had secured them well, and as much as he struggled, he could not free himself. "Let me go. This is bullshit. You're insane."

Rose got off Peter and stood over him. She picked up her polo shirt, and put it back on. Yawning, she took a large knife out of her boot and watched as Peter's face turned to fear. She yawned and let the reality of what was happening to him gradually sink in. The bulge in his jeans had gone, and he was probably about to piss himself. Rose laughed again, imagining Peter pissing himself in the chair where he thought he was finally about to lose his virginity.

"What are you? Who *are* you, Mara?" he asked quietly. He wanted to cry, but how would he explain this to his parents? "Look, just let me go, and I won't say anything. I won't tell Gabe what happened, okay? I know you're just messing with me."

"You still think you're getting out of this, don't you?" Rose shook her head. She enjoyed the teasing most of all. Javier was always in charge, and rarely did she get the chance to take the lead. Now she had the power, and she wasn't going to waste it by killing him quickly. "You know how many men I've fucked?" she asked.

"What? I don't know. I don't care." Peter pulled at his ties, but they only seemed to get tighter as he pulled. It was nearly impossible to get up out of the chair with his hands tied behind his back, and with Mara holding a knife over him, he wasn't sure he wanted to try.

Rose could see Peter straining to free himself, and tiny beads of sweat were beginning to show on the boy's forehead. She leant over him and placed the tip of the sharp knife over his crotch.

"I would appreciate it," she said calmly, "if you could sit still for a minute."

Peter nodded. A bead of sweat ran down his nose and dripped off the end. He swallowed nervously. His throat was so dry that it felt like he was trying to swallow a brick. If only someone would come check on them. If only Freya would have one of her nightmares and wake up his father. Erik would know what to do in this situation. He always knew what to do.

Rose looked at Peter expectantly. "Well?"

"Well...what?" Peter asked. All he could think of was the knife perched above his crotch.

"Answer the fucking question!" screamed Rose. She instantly regretted losing her temper. The shouting might wake the others.

She couldn't afford to get caught, Javier had made her quite aware of that, so she was going to have to finish this quicker now. She leant in closer to Peter, so her lips were only an inch from his. "Answer the fucking question, Peter." Her cheeks were flushed with rage, and her hands holding the knife trembled.

Peter froze, and looked down in terror. Mara was pressing the knife down on him, and he could feel the pressure above his groin. Any further, and she would break through his pants. He didn't want to think what would happen after that.

"Okay, okay, I apologize. Um, look, I'm not really…three? Four?"

Rose drew the blade slowly up over Peter's belly, up his chest until it rested against his neck. The coldness of the blade made him shiver. She thought that his eyes, so full of fear, were beautiful. Such a waste.

Rose smiled, and her voice returned to a normal level. "My father was the first one to fuck me. He was hard and quick at first, and I felt raw afterwards for days. But then he began to take his time. Enjoy it. Enjoy me. I wouldn't say *I* enjoyed it, but…"

"I'm sorry," whispered Peter.

"Don't be." Mara pushed the blade against Peter's neck until the tip of the knife nicked his skin, and tiny droplets of bright red blood appeared.

Peter tried to pull away, but there was nowhere to go. She had him pinned against the chair, and his hands were wrapped up tightly. Christ, why wasn't someone coming? He had taken on the night watch with Mara and knew it would be some time before anyone else came along. This was like a bad dream, except he couldn't wake up. Mara had gone insane. He pulled at the ties more, but there was no way out.

Rose leaned in against Peter's bleeding neck and whispered into his ear. "You could still have me, you know? All you have to do is kill Gabriel. Take my knife and kill him. He's sleeping now. Slit his throat before he gets the chance to wake."

"You're crazy," said Peter. "Mara, just stop this. Just stop this and… and…"

"And what?" Rose laughed, and a high-pitched giggle burst from her mouth. "So, is that a no? I didn't think you would."

She sighed and looked so disappointed that Peter wanted to tell her that he would do it. He wanted to tell her to smile, because she looked so beautiful when she smiled, but he kept his mouth closed. There was nothing he could say to convince her of anything, he was quite sure of that. He certainly wasn't about to kill Gabe. Mara had lost the plot. He didn't know what had made her flip out, but he had to keep talking to her. He realized the best way out of this was to keep her talking. His father had taught him to always try to avoid confrontation, and most situations could be resolved without the need for it to descend into physically fighting. Perhaps someone would come looking for them if he kept Mara talking long enough.

"Mara," he said quietly as she stared at him. "Mara, tell me what you want. I can help. You can stay with us. Leave Gabe, if that's what you want. My parents will look after you. It doesn't have to be like this. I don't know what you've gone through, but..."

Her face turned upward, and Rose sighed. Peter hoped someone would come soon, as he was struggling to hold onto hope. Was there any point in still hoping? Yes, he had to. Freya at least needed him. There was nothing more important in the world to him than Freya. Perhaps Mara needed a dose of reality. Had she gone so far that she couldn't come back? Was this some twisted sex game that he just didn't understand? Those eyes of hers that were once so real, so pretty, suddenly seemed hard and black and cold. This was no game. There was no way this woman was the cozy housewife she'd made herself out to be.

"Mara, who are you really?"

"Me? I'm Mara. Mrs. Gabriel." Rose brought the blade back to his throat.

"What's your name, your *real* name?" asked Peter. He felt the blade press against his neck drawing more blood. He found himself thinking of Freya, praying that she was safe, wishing he could get through this to see her one more time.

"My name?" Rose leered at Peter. The moon glinted in her eyes as she spoke. "I couldn't tell you. I lost it around the same time as I lost my virginity. My father fucked them both out of me when I was thirteen. I always liked flowers, though, so I picked myself a name. You can call me Rose."

Rose drew the blade swiftly through Peter's neck, and his warm blood gushed out. He spluttered and coughed, but was powerless to stop it. Rose stepped back, making sure none of the blood got on her clothes. That would be hard to explain in the morning. Peter kicked out, but his feet found nothing but the corner of the desk, and the chair spun back towards the door. Rose could see him trying to speak, trying to breathe, but he was already turning pale. The gaping hole in his neck gushed blood. His eyes were glassing over, and the spasms that coursed through his body slowly dissipated as the life drained out of him.

"Stick," said Rose. She looked at Peter's lifeless body with curiosity. Would Erik go as easily? She felt more like her old self again. Killing Cindy hadn't really sated her, and Peter had been much more fun. She wiped the knife on Peter's shirt, and tucked it out of sight into her boots. Then she wheeled Peter's body outside, pushing the chair out of sight across the road, and left it behind a dumpster. She severed the ties that held his hands, and checked again to make sure there was no blood on her.

"Enjoy being dead, Peter," she said as she re-entered the warehouse, and locked the door behind her. She made sure the office was the same as earlier, and pushed the filing cabinet back into place. "So fucking easy," she said to herself as she made her way back to her bed with Javier. She was supposed to be on watch for another hour, until Pippa and Dakota replaced her and Peter, but she saw no reason to stay up any longer. There were clearly no zombies outside, and who was going to come looking for them in the middle of nowhere?

* * *

Barely fifteen minutes later, and Erik woke up. He looked at Pippa next to him, still asleep, and couldn't make out what had woken him. He saw Freya's bare feet sticking out and pulled down her blanket. Peter's bed was empty, so he must still be on watch. The noises almost sounded like screams, and he sat up, concerned. As he listened, he realized he was listening to the furious sounds of fucking from above. Cries and groans accompanied the clattering of some metal railings, and it sounded more like fighting than lovemaking. Erik turned over and put his hands over his ears. It was clearly Gabe and Mara. They didn't sound like a married couple at all. Even honeymooners wouldn't make such a racket. He was surprised they had the energy or desire at a time like this. He looked across at Dakota and Hamsikker who were sound asleep. How had they found time to get pregnant in all of this? Erik closed his eyes and shut out the noise from above, forcing himself to sleep. It would be sunrise soon, and then there would be no rest for any of them.

* * *

Javier traced his fingers down Rose's back as he admired the tattoo she had between her shoulder blades. It was a red rose, surrounded by small stars. Anyone else like her would have got a skull or a snake, but Rose had to be different. She had come back from watch and practically jumped him. Not that he minded. It had been a while since they had been together, and it was always good with Rose. No one else he had been with could summon up as much energy as her, and rarely had he found a woman who would willingly submit to all his demands. Faint moonlight came in from a window, highlighting Rose's nakedness, and he imagined that they might even do it again while they had the chance. Killing Peter had got Rose worked up, and he had to admit he was turned on too. Knowing she had taken someone's life only minutes earlier excited him, and it hadn't taken either of them long to get into it.

They decided to make their bed away from the others on the upper floor in the corner of the catwalk. They all decided it would be safer in case of attack, and nobody suspected Javier chose it because he wanted to be able to keep an eye on them.

After they'd fucked, Rose fetched a bottle of water, and when she came back she told him that she'd bumped into Pippa. The woman suspected nothing and believed Rose when she'd said Peter had gone back to bed. Javier looked at Rose as she stared down at the sleeping form of Freya.

Rose smiled. "You think we'll find your brother soon? If he's got a safe place, we could stay there. No more running. No more scavenging and looking for a bed for the night. It'd be good for Freya too. She needs a home. Look at her. Her brother is dead, her mother is weak, and her father is a cop. What chance does she have?"

Javier knew that Rose had hardly spoken to Pippa, certainly not enough to make a judgment on her. She just wanted Freya to herself, and that was probably why she wanted the girl's family gone first. "Hamsikker tried talking to me earlier. He said some of the others were a little uncomfortable with us, what with not really knowing who we were. They've been together a long time, so it's natural to be wary of strangers."

"What did you tell him?" asked Rose.

"Nothing. I told him we were just looking to find a way through this nightmare like everyone else, and that we would do whatever it took to protect the group. I said you were upset at losing the clubhouse, and I was concerned I wouldn't be able to protect you. Then I started to choke up."

"You didn't? Really?" Rose looked at Javier with amazement. Had he really been that worried about her?

"No, not really. I faked it. Made him feel guilty, and he let me be. I was through being buddies with him. I didn't want him asking too many questions. Besides, he thinks we're on his side. It's the others we have to watch out for. That old woman and the cop are the ones who we need to win over."

"I hate that pig," said Rose. She looked down longingly at Freya.

"You know, we could do with checking the ammo situation. Before they realize that Peter's missing, why don't you ask Erik to help you take a checklist of everything we've got in the van?" asked Javier. "I'm sure he'd understand that I wouldn't send Mara out there alone to do such an important job. It's not safe out there."

"Why do I have to go?" asked Rose. "With him?" She lay back down beside Javier and kissed his sweaty chest.

"Rose, *listen* to me." Javier sometimes wondered if he was speaking in a foreign language. Was she not getting it on purpose or trying to wind him up? "It's not safe out there. Anything could happen. The dead are everywhere. If, say, one of those dead, nasty motherfuckers sneaked up on you and Erik whilst you were out there, well..."

Rose looked deep into Javier's eyes, reached up and kissed him. "So if only one of us were to come back…"

"It's just an idea. You be careful, Rose. He's not as dumb as his boy." Javier kissed Rose and cupped her ass. It wouldn't be difficult getting Pippa on her own, and he would kill her while Rose took care of Erik. Javier wanted to slim down the little traveling party he had got together, and Erik was expendable. He was just too dangerous to keep around, especially now his son was gone. With Peter gone, and Erik and Pippa on the way out, the next one on Javier's list would be Mrs. Danick. Terry was annoying, but he could be useful up to a point. The old woman was a serious pain in the ass. She never quit haranguing him, and it was as if she knew he wasn't who he said he was. All those questions at the clubhouse about the photographs, and all the insinuations and snide comments she made had to stop. She needed to be made to stay silent, forever. Old people could suffer from any number of things. Heart attacks, for one. They died in their sleep. Perhaps it was time for Mrs. Danick to meet her maker after all.

Javier had originally planned to only have Erik and Hamsikker go with him to Canada, and now it was time to tweak that plan. If it kept Rose happy, Freya could tag along too. He knew Rose too well though. She would get fixated on something and want it so much that she would do anything to get it. Ultimately, she would tire of her new toy, and when she was bored, it usually ended up with him having to get rid of it. So he'd let her have the girl for a while, until she decided she'd had enough, and then he had no doubt who would have to finish her. He had no compunction in killing children; it was just another part of life that he had forced himself to get used to long ago.

"How long have we got?" asked Rose. "Maybe I can take Erik out later. Literally," she giggled.

"He can wait. We've got long enough," said Javier smiling. Apart from Hamsikker's axe and the gun under his pillow, Javier knew all the weapons were in the campervan. Erik and Mrs. Danick held onto their guns, but Javier was sure they were empty. Hamsikker and his idiot friends could wait. "Long enough," Javier said again as he caressed Rose's neck, and their bodies began to intertwine.

* * *

Hamsikker was woken an hour later by Dakota.

"Honey, you awake?" she asked him as she rubbed his back.

"Sure," he said groggily. "What is it?"

"I'm supposed to go on watch with Pippa now, but…"

Jonas sat up. Pippa was stood waiting, and he felt shattered. The blankets kept them warm, but the ground was rock hard, and it felt like someone had been walking up and down his spine all night.

"Could you go with her? I feel so sick, I don't think I can do it," said Dakota rubbing her belly. "Every time I get up I get a head-rush, and then I get all dizzy, and…"

"It's okay," said Jonas as he got up. "I'll go. Get some rest." He kissed Dakota as she lay back down and walked over to Pippa. "You seen Peter and Mara? Anything going on out there?"

"I think Peter's in bed, but I haven't seen him. I saw Mara earlier. She said everything was quiet, and she was just getting some water. Said she was exhausted, and all the walking around had made her thirsty."

"Right, well, let's go then, the sun will be up soon so we may as well check things over and get ready. It's going to be a long day."

Jonas and Pippa began walking around the warehouse, listening to the others slowly wake. Jonas doubted anyone had gotten much sleep, but some was better than none. He chatted amiably to Pippa, but all he could think about was how they were going to fare as they journeyed north. He remembered when they left Erik's place and how that day had turned out. They had spent hours running around Jeffersontown, not knowing where to turn. Some of them had died in the process, and he could sense it happening again. He was going to lay everything out on the table once they were all up. They needed a plan, something to hold onto; something to help drive them forward. Running around like headless chickens was a sure fire way to get killed. Everyone needed a clear plan, and if everyone was pulling in the same direction, it would be so much easier. They wouldn't make the same mistakes as before. They would have a clear and defined path. It was time to get to Janey and to get everyone to safety.

"I understand," said Pippa as they approached the office at the entrance of the warehouse. "Erik mentioned to me about heading for Canada. About Janey? We'll come with you."

Jonas rested his arms on top of the cold filing cabinet and looked at Pippa. "I should've known the big guy couldn't keep his mouth shut."

Pippa smiled. "Don't worry. I think it's a good idea. We can't keep hanging around here. Sounds like a good idea to me. You think Janey's got a place for us to stay?"

Jonas began tugging on the filing cabinet as Pippa pushed, and they slowly moved it out of the doorway. "I hope so. She lives in a small town surrounded by forest and a lake to the east. There wouldn't be as many of the dead up there. Who knows, we might be able to settle down, and..."

As Jonas pushed open the door, he heard a knocking sound. It was coming from outside but was unmistakable. "Pippa, stay behind me. There may be someone out there." Jonas gripped his axe firmly and stepped into the small office. Through the small window in the door, he saw the head of someone.

"You think they need help?" asked Pippa. She crossed the room behind Jonas full of fear. "You think we should let them in?"

Before Jonas could answer there was a bang as the body threw itself against the door. "I think it's one of them. I just hope it's alone, or..."

Another crash against the side of the office indicated the zombie was not alone. Jonas rushed to the side and looked out of the dirty window. He swept back the beige blinds, and he shivered with fear. Across the yard, in the street, were at least dozen zombies, all heading for the office. What had brought them here? He looked down at the body that was throwing itself against the office. It had fallen to the ground and was slowly standing. As it got to its feet, Jonas stared at the thin figure of a young man. The man still had his backpack on, strapped over a scrawny frame, with bite marks all down his arms. His face had been ravaged, and there was a large black, bloody hole in his neck.

"Shit."

Jonas let the blinds close and stepped back into the office, unable to believe what he was seeing. How had they gotten so close? There hadn't been any zombies around earlier, yet now their number was growing. If they didn't leave soon they were going to be trapped here. They were going to need every weapon they had just to get out as it was, and…

"Shit," said Jonas again, and he raced to the door. What few weapons they had were in the campervan. He looked out through the tiny square window in the door. The van was still there. With his axe and Gabe's gun they might just be able to reach it, but he wasn't sure if anyone else had brought their weapons in with them. The dead body outside threw itself against the door, and Jonas flinched. He looked out of the window at the zombie by the door, and then he realized he knew who it was. Fear was replaced by confusion. He hoped he was wrong, but something inside of him told him he wasn't. What had the boy done? Erik and Pippa would be crushed. Jonas needed to make sure Pippa didn't look outside.

"Pippa, we need to get the others up, quickly. There are more of them out there. Don't ask me how they got here, but we need to move fast." Jonas went to the doorway and stepped into the warehouse. He would help Pippa get the others and make sure they armed themselves with whatever they could lay their hands on.

"Hamsikker, what is it?" Pippa looked terrified, and she approached the tiny square window. "You're not telling me something. I can see it in your eyes."

"Pippa, just…"

It was too late. She stretched herself up onto her toes and peered outside. Jonas knew she had recognized Peter the second she opened her mouth. His heart sank, and Pippa's scream reverberated around the building. Jonas looked at his feet. "Pippa, I'm so sorry. I don't know what happened, but we'll find out. I'm…"

Jonas heard the jangling of keys and looked up. He was expecting to find Pippa crying, perhaps slumped to the floor, perhaps running to him, running to Erik, running away from her dead son, but instead, she was fumbling with the keys in the door, frantically tugging on the handle.

"Pippa, what are you doing? Stop!" Jonas charged across the floor to grab her, to bring her back inside and away from the door, but she was too quick for him. The door flung open, and Pippa opened her arms.

"Peter, honey, come here," she said.

Her voice wavered as she spoke, and Jonas watched as Peter did just as his mother asked. He fell into his crying mother's open arms, his pale skin damp and glistening. Peter's mouth opened revealing bloodstained teeth, and Jonas shouted for help as he raised his axe.

"Pippa, no!"

CHAPTER EIGHT

There was a moment when Jonas thought he was too late. Peter and Pippa were wrestling in the office, and he could practically hear Pippa's flesh being torn from her body. He could sense every one of Peter's teeth sinking into Pippa's neck, slicing through the pale skin before clenching onto the soft succulent meat that protected her windpipe. Jonas could see Pippa's bright red blood begin pumping out of her, spurting out over her dead son's face like a torrential swollen river bursting its banks. Pippa's eyes were glazed, confused, the irises too large, the white of her eyes snaked with broken red capillaries.

With a nauseating crunch, the axe smashed into the back of Peter's head, and Pippa was instantly free.

"Hamsikker, what have you done? My God, Peter… What have you done to my Peter, my…"

Jonas didn't wait to see if Peter was getting back up or to see who was following him through the open doorway. Jonas grabbed Pippa by the scruff of her neck and threw her toward the warehouse. She had somehow escaped being bitten by Peter, but Jonas knew he wouldn't be able to protect them both in the close confines of the office.

"Get Erik," he barked at her. "Get inside, and tell everyone we're under attack. *Go!*"

Pippa looked at the prostrate body of her son at Jonas's feet, Peter's brains oozing slowly from the massive crack in the back of his skull. Thick, dark blood seeped out and curdled around Peter's shoulders. Pippa raised a hand to her mouth.

"Go now, Pippa." Jonas couldn't afford for her to freak out now. She had to warn the others, and prepare them to fight or flee. He heard a scuffle behind him and knew the others were outside, at his back, and would follow Peter inside the building any moment. "Fucking move!"

Turning his back on Pippa as she disappeared into the warehouse, he felt a bead of sweat trickle down his back. It was happening again. It seemed as if the dead followed them everywhere. There was so much killing still to be done. Peter was dead, but there were still dozens more zombies out there standing between him and Janey.

Before he could reach the door to lock it, a woman appeared in the doorway and charged at him. All he saw was a flash of blue and white as the woman's summer dress flew around her like a superhero's cape. The woman's face was hideously disfigured, as if she had been tortured before her death. Her ears had been gnawed away to nothing but stumps, and her hair was cut short, revealing a tattoo of a scorpion on her left temple. There was nothing behind her eyes, just death, and Jonas brought his axe up to meet the rushing woman. The axe head buried itself into the woman's chest, smashing through her ribcage, sending splinters of bone into the air which rained down on Jonas like brittle confetti. Jonas pushed her back, keeping both hands on the axe, and fought to push her down to the ground. Wedged in the doorway, Jonas put his boot on the woman's neck and dislodged the axe from her chest. He swung it down, smashing it into her head, and the woman went limp.

Another figure appeared in the doorway, and Jonas looked straight up into the eyes of the backpacker. There had been times in the past, when faced with other demons, Jonas had wanted to give up. It had left him feeling defeated, deflated, and unable to convince himself that he could carry on. But looking into the dead man's eyes, Jonas didn't feel like that now. He felt angry. He was pissed off that his friends were dying around him, and he couldn't do anything about it. Why Peter? Was this the zombie that had killed him?

Fuck You, thought Jonas as he ran at the dead man, fuck You for doing this to us, and for making me do this. Dakota's wrong. You're not on our side. You've made a pact with the devil. You might have abandoned us, but we're not going easy.

Jonas whirled the axe above his head and lopped off the backpacker's head with one blow. The body crumpled, and Jonas jumped over it to the outside. He slammed the door behind him and wondered how long it would be before Pippa brought reinforcements. The yard was full of them, and he wasn't sure how long he would be able to hold them off. The early morning air was dry, and the sky was a deep blue. There were still a few stars twinkling in the clear sky, and the rising sun was dressing the dead in costumes of grey shadows.

With his back to the door, Jonas let them come to him. He didn't need to go looking for them. They were heading right for him anyway. If things turned bad, he had the door behind him to retreat through. He hoped it wouldn't come to that though. If he was forced back inside, they would be trapped. As the dead neared, his heart beat faster, and he made sure he kept the anger inside him burning. The desire to kill each and every last one of the dead burned so strongly that he couldn't wait to get started. It didn't matter that the odds were against him. He had the edge on them, and he knew it. He had his family behind him to protect, and he had plenty of motivation to take down every last one of them. Jonas was determined that none of them would get past him into the building.

Two zombies reached him at the same time, their four arms twisting and groping through the air to get to him first. Jonas sliced off their hands, severing them all at the wrist, and he was rewarded with four bloody stumps flying at his face. He managed to deflect the first zombie by kicking its feet out from under it, and he ducked as the other tried to take a bite out of his shoulder. The axe did the rest of the work, and he took off both their heads. Another zombie came up to him, an overweight man with a bald head and two heavily tattooed arms. Jonas aimed for the man's head, but his thick arms knocked Jonas off course, and the axe lodged itself in the man's shoulder. Wrenching it free, Jonas brought the axe around again and carved out a hole in the man's side. A stinking, slithering pile of intestines spilled out, still pink and rubbery, and Jonas felt a wave of nausea grip him. There was no time to feel sorry for himself, though, and he heaved the axe one last time. This time the zombie caught the full force of the axe, and the man's bald head split open with an audible crack. Jonas pushed the body away and made a break for the van. He remembered they had left it unlocked in case of a problem just like this, and he needed more than his axe to defeat them all. There were close to twenty or thirty now, and Jonas could only guess they were coming from the town. They had been drawn here, summoned, and nothing was going to stop them. They kept coming, drawn by the noise, or their hunger, or whatever it was that made the dead walk.

He slid back the van door and reached under the seat for the weapon stash. The first thing his hands found was Erik's Glock. He spun around and took aim, firing off round after round at the advancing dead. They fell where they stood, and Jonas managed to kill half a dozen before the chamber clicked empty. He looked at the warehouse, at the entrance, but nobody was coming. Surely Pippa had raised the alarm? Surely someone had heard the gunshots?

Frustrated, he threw the gun back into the van and reached inside for something else. Pulling back a blanket, he uncovered their small arsenal. A hammer, a couple of knives, and a heavy looking wrench were amongst other hand tools that Gabe must've thrown in the van back at Saint Paul's. Jonas noticed a row of metal teeth attached to a shiny black handle protruding out from underneath the seat. He grabbed it and stood as he admired the handheld chainsaw. Finally, something he could use. It must've been used to trim the hedges and bushes around the course. Jonas intended to use it to trim more than just leaves, and he pressed on a small red button, checking the status of the rechargeable battery. It was half charged, but that was all the power he needed. He quietly thanked Gabe for throwing it in the van and then turned back to the yard. He saw that the zombies had converged on his position and were pushed together. They were barely fifteen feet from him, and he dropped his axe in the van.

The chainsaw roared into life, and Jonas stepped forward. There was no going back from what he was about to do. He accepted there was a good chance this was going to end badly for him, but he simply couldn't see any other way.

"Go!"

Suddenly Quinn raced out of the office with Erik and Gabe behind her, and they sprinted for the van. Knowing that he wasn't on his own gave him the boost he needed, and he faced the dead with confidence.

"Kill the dead!" Jonas screamed. Gripping the chainsaw with both hands, he ran into the crowd of zombies. The first to fall was a child, and Jonas swept the chainsaw's blade through the top of its head. He had little time to aim, as the next zombie fell upon him instantly. Hands tried to grab him, but he spun the saw around and around, cutting a way through anything that tried to get near him. Gallons of blood spewed into the air, thick droplets splattering Jonas's face as the whirling blade slashed off body parts, severing arms and hands and heads.

"Hamsikker, watch your back!"

Jonas thought he heard Quinn's voice, but over the thrumming din of the chainsaw, he wasn't sure. He had no time to turn and look either, as the zombies kept coming for him. He wasn't finished yet. Jonas pushed his way into the dense crowd wielding his chainsaw like a crusader's sword. The weight of the closely packed zombies made progress hard as he stumbled over dismembered limbs, and the bodies pressed in on him like a thick blanket. Decapitated arms tried to trip him up, but he could not stop, *would* not stop. He scythed his way through the undead men, women and children, faces twisted by hate, bodies rotting and reanimated by God knows what. More and more hands and arms dropped at his feet as he whirled the chainsaw in front of him. The dead tried to surround him, to attack from all angles, and Jonas swung the weapon to the front and back, and from side to side, not caring who or what he hit. The chainsaw's teeth were beginning to slow, chunks of flesh clogging up the machinery, and the sheer number of dead it had carved through was beginning to draw on its fading power. The stench was disgusting, and blood sprayed over him, drenching him in death.

Kicking away a head, its jaws still snapping at his ankles, Jonas heard a faint scream above the clamor and moan of the zombies. He pushed on, refusing to buckle, knowing he had to continue. Time meant nothing anymore, and it took as long as it took. He heard gunshots, but couldn't be sure who was firing, and until the dead were gone, they weren't safe. Dakota was relying on him. The chainsaw was heavy, and his arms ached. Muscles that hadn't been used in months were pulled taut. His brain was screaming at him to stop, but he refused to listen, only obeying his heart which told him to go on. His head swam, sweat poured down his back, and then suddenly she was there. A slight gap in the zombies opened up, and he saw Quinn standing before him. A mixture of blood and sweat had formed over him, forcing him to look at everything through a red mist, as if viewing the world through a tinted camera lens. He had made it. Through a wave of undead, he had come through it. Quinn held his axe in her hands. It only took a second, but he took it all in.

She was swaying unsteadily, her eyes closed, blood pouring from her head. Jonas was elated. Quinn must have took his axe from the van, circled around the other side of the crowd, and fought them off. He went to hug her, but then Quinn opened her eyes, and Jonas felt the familiar storm clouds gather once again. The clouds that he had long dispelled grew quickly. Quinn's eyes had clouded over, and her arms hung loose at her sides. The axe clattered to the floor as her hand dropped it. As she slowly raised her arms, he saw the chunks missing from her shoulders, the skin that had been flayed from her hands and arms, and the blood that continued to pour from her head. She took a step toward him and almost fell. One foot had been bent backward a full 180 degrees, and it was then that he noticed the blood covering her body too. Her jeans were torn, and blood poured from the ripped holes. Tornados of doubt surged through him, and darkness engulfed his core. His heart skipped a beat, and then the darkness fell. It was pointless fighting it. The darkness was so overwhelming that he could hardly breathe. His body told him to stop – stop fighting, stop running, just stop and wait for the inevitable. He couldn't protect them. The gunshots had stopped. Would the others fare any better than him? What was the point in trying to close the gates to Hell when there was no lock?

A furious wind abruptly swept through the yard, cool air carrying dying leaves with it, and they slapped against Jonas' face as he stood there staring at Quinn. A hand gripped his shoulder, and he looked up at the sky. It was lighter blue now, suggesting it was going to be a beautiful sunny day. As Jonas looked up into the sweet sky another hand wrapped itself around his leg. He could feel cold fingers grasp his knee, but he couldn't bring himself to do anything about it. There were so many. Quinn was with them now, Dakota probably too. Quinn, Peter, Tyler – all of them. Was he the last one?

He felt the hand on his shoulder grip him fiercely, the fingernails starting to pinch his skin and pull at his shirt. The red mist parted slightly, and he looked at Quinn again. She was shouting at him to move, to come to her. The blood pouring from her head was real, but she was moving freely, and her face was full of energy. Her skin was smooth, like a dark pebble, and she was using his axe to beat in the head of a zombie. The silence of the dead was replaced with a rushing blood in his ears, and the tumultuous storm that had appeared in his head vanished. Like a light switch clicking off, he realized he wasn't the last one alive, and he was never going to give in. Through the red mist he had let himself be tricked, letting the weak part of his mind fool him into thinking Quinn was dead. He shut that part of his brain down, forcing himself to look at Quinn. She was real, and the dead were inches away from him, ready to bite.

He shook off the hand on his shoulder, kicked out at the hands grabbing his legs, and bolted toward Quinn. The chainsaw was useless now, its power drained, its blades dulled and the saw too sluggish to be of any use.

"Here, take this," said Quinn, thrusting the axe into Jonas's hands.

She pulled a gun from her back and began shooting as Jonas laid into the zombie that had been crawling over the ground to them. He obliterated its face with a mixture of revulsion and pleasure. He felt more in control with the axe and wasn't sorry to see the back of the chainsaw. A dead man dressed in a postal uniform came running toward them, and Jonas slugged it with the back of the axe head. Quinn stood at Jonas's back, firing, and Jonas finished off a runner with a quick blow to the side of the head. The zombie dropped down dead at his feet, and Jonas heard Quinn gasp. He turned to face her.

"I'm out," she said.

Five zombies were circling them, crawling over the mountain of dead, stumbling over rotten bodies and filth and gore. Beyond them were more. From the street they were coming, dozens and dozens more of them, incessant, like an army forever marching to their goal. Jonas saw movement around the van, and it looked like the others were getting ready to leave. He had to buy them more time and keep the zombies' attention away from the campervan, so he called out.

"Come and get it, dinner's ready you dead fuckers," he shouted. "Quinn, get out of here. Get the others in the van. I'll hold them off."

Quinn pushed her way through the circling zombies, and Jonas wished he had something more than willpower and a small handheld axe to battle with. He scoured the ground, looking for a gun, a knife, anything that could help defend them. Something hard and long stuck out from underneath a body, and he recognized it as the shaft of some kind of tool. Pulling on it, he expected it to come out easily, thinking it was probably a piece of metal. Instead it had weight to it, and he had to yank it out of the body. It wasn't just pinned underneath, but stuck in it, and whatever was on the other end of the handle was dug into the body well. He pulled again, and with a sucking sound, the weapon revealed itself. He freed it and wiped away the blood, admiring the Pulaski. It was slightly larger than the axe he carried, with a steel blade, a tough fiberglass handle, and an adze on the axe head perpendicular to the handle. Jonas knew the tool was intended for chopping wood, but it was still as sharp as the day it was made. A smile crept across his face, and he let his arms drop. In each hand he now held an axe, each one sharp and lethal, each able to sever, maim, and kill. The dead were going down. He looked up slowly, drawing in a deep breath as he gripped the axes in each hand tighter.

Jonas yelled and launched himself back into the melee. The circle around him had grown, and the road ahead was full of zombies. Jonas swung with both arms, not aiming for the head, not aiming for anything in particular, just wanting to inflict as much damage to the zombies as he could, and knowing that every blow counted. It slowed them down, and though the dead threatened to engulf him, he didn't care. A variety of zombies attacked him, and he caught sight of office workers, baristas, schoolgirls and schoolboys, soccer moms, farmers, and even tourists with huge cameras swinging around their broken necks. It felt like the whole world was against him, yet he didn't care. The faces of the dead began to blur into one, and he kept going until he finally heard the yelling.

Gradually Jonas was forced back by the sheer number of the dead, and he caught sight of Erik near the van. Erik beckoned him over, and he heard Quinn shouting, calling his name. He knew he hadn't finished them all off, but they were incapacitated, and that was enough. There were so many bodies lying on the road that they slowed down the other zombies who were still trying to get to the fight. Instead of picking a careful path around, they tried to walk through the mass of corpses that Jonas and Quinn had left, and invariably ended up tripping over them. Jonas charged through the last of the zombies, wiping the blood from his eyes as he ran.

"Dakota?" he asked as he approached Erik.

"I'm here." Dakota leant forward from the rear seat in the van and Jonas leant in, grasping her hand. "Everyone okay?"

Even as the words came out of his mouth, he knew it was a redundant question. He looked around the interior of the van, and could see they were terrified. Dakota and Pippa were in back with a comatose Freya beside them. The young girl was clutching the keychain he had given her, squeezing it in her hands like a stress squeezer, as if it were a comforter. Mrs. Danick was clutching her bag to her chest, and he had never seen her look so scared. Terry sat silently next to her as Quinn and Erik clambered into the van.

"We've used up all the ammo we had. I borrowed Gabe's gun, but short of making our own bullets, it's useless."

"Unfortunately true," said Javier, lying. "It's empty."

Erik held a hammer in his hands, covered in blood. He had knocked back a few zombies as he had helped the others get to the van. "Let's roll, Hamsikker," said Erik gruffly. He sat down beside Quinn and cleared a space for Jonas to sit down next to him.

Jonas got in and swung the van door closed just as a runner reached them. It started battering on the door, and Dakota screamed.

"Gabe, punch it," said Jonas. He noticed Gabe was looking surprisingly calm as he caught his eye in the rear-view mirror. Mara was sat in the passenger seat, looking a little more concerned, but Jonas paid no attention to them. The van was reversing quickly out of the yard, and several bumps on the side of the van told him they were not in the clear yet.

"I think most of them are coming from town," said Jonas. "Martinsville is fucked. Try and take us around it if you can, Gabe."

"Doing my best here," grunted Javier as he swerved the van from left to right, trying to avoid the dead that had filled the road. He didn't need advice and didn't ask for any. Javier concentrated on what lay ahead.

"I feel sick already," said Dakota.

The van lurched from side to side, and Jonas had no doubt that Gabe was doing his best. He also didn't doubt that they were still hitting a lot of zombies, and the van wasn't built to take the damage that it was suffering. He wished they still had the SUV, but he found himself wishing for a lot of things these days. One day He might listen, but Jonas doubted that anyone upstairs was listening to anyone anymore.

"I think we're through the worst of it," said Javier.

Jonas looked at the receding town, and the zombies that continued to follow them down the road, stumbling over body parts as the van left them behind. What had drawn them in? All it took was a noise, a smell, and they closed in like a school of hungry piranha. Aside from a crying coming from Freya at the back of the van, nobody spoke, and Jonas slowly became aware of a tapping noise. It was consistently there, regular like clockwork, and he looked down for the source of the noise. He still held the axes in both hands, and they were clattering together as his hands shook. He dropped the axes at his feet and held his hands up. Whilst the noise had stopped, the shaking in his hands hadn't, and he looked at them bemused, as if watching a television show. His hands were covered in blood, and not an inch of his own pale skin was visible beneath the crimson veil that covered them. He told himself to get a grip, to stop shaking, but his body wasn't listening. Both hands shook, no matter how much he tried to stop, so he sat on them, pressing them beneath his thighs into the seat, hoping nobody would notice.

They rode on in silence for a while, and Jonas lost track of time. He kept replaying over in his mind what had just happened. Peter was gone. How he had ended up outside, he couldn't guess. Had he made a stupid mistake, perhaps gone outside for some air? Perhaps he was going to retrieve something from the van for Freya. Either way he had paid the ultimate price. Jonas knew that if he found out anyone had been involved in Peter's death, he would kill them. Peter was so kind and generous, and it was hard to believe he was gone. The thought of killing made Jonas remember his promise to Dakota. No more killing. He couldn't afford to let himself get caught up in things like that anymore. Besides, he trusted everyone in the van, and whatever had killed Peter was probably just a stupid accident, and he pushed the dark thoughts from his head.

As they drove, Jonas watched the sky as the stars fizzled out to be replaced by the sunlit sky. They passed numerous small towns with no living souls anywhere. He wondered if they might find other survivors, but there were none. The roads were by and large clear, and they kept to the smaller roads, knowing the Interstates were likely to be clogged. Traffic had snarled up causing huge traffic congestion at the start of the outbreak, and there was no one around to clear the roads.

Jonas saw a church coming up ahead, set back behind a small white fence. A lemon tree stooped low before the main gates, its branches bending under the weight of its fruit. Outside the church gates, a billboard with black lettering on a white background proclaimed 'Repent, seek His forgiveness.' There were three bodies lying beneath the billboard, their skin and flesh torn from their bones, and their faces blank, their eyes dead. The bodies tried to get up when the truck drove past, but before they were on their feet the van had passed the church and the town was behind them. Jonas looked in the rear view mirror at the sign that once said 'Romney – Thank you for visiting.' Somebody had taken a can of black paint and changed it.

"Romney - What would Jesus do?" said Jonas quietly as he read the new sign aloud.

"What's that, Hamsikker?" asked Terry.

"Nothing. Just a stupid sign."

"Hamsikker, take this and wipe yourself down," said Mrs. Danick quietly. She handed a cloth over to him, and he took it. His face was caked in gore, and he wiped as much off as he could. He stank of death, but there was nothing he could do about that. He discarded the cloth and looked across at Quinn and Erik. They were silent, their heads bowed, their grief all too obvious. He glanced back at the others, but nobody returned his look. His heart ached when he saw Freya holding onto her mother. Pippa looked as though someone had ripped her heart out. It was difficult when a loved one died, but seeing them turn, seeing them as a zombie, made it all the more harder. Jonas still remembered his father's funeral as fresh in his mind as if it had been only yesterday. Getting through the moments after one of their own had died was even harder than killing or taking out the dead up close and personal.

Jonas thought of asking Mara for a map from the glove box, but he didn't need a map for what he needed to do next.

"I'm going to make this quick. We're heading north, up to Canada. The further we get away from the cities the better chance we have of making it." He could see Quinn frowning and wanted to cut her off before she started. "I know Kentucky is our home, *was* our home, but we have to accept that it's gone. We can't go back. So we keep going. My sister, Janey, lives near Fort William. She has a small, red wooden house by the lake. The city she lives in is relatively tiny compared to what we're used to, and I think the area should be clear of the dead. That's what we need. That's where we're going. That's where we'll be *safe*."

"Then let's get going," said Erik. "We have more of a chance there than here. Honey?" He looked back at Pippa, but she wasn't there. In body she was sat right behind him, but her mind was elsewhere. The loss of Peter had hit her hard, and she had succumbed to a silent grief, lost in her own thoughts. Erik hadn't really expected an answer. He just wanted to look at her and Freya, to be reassured that he still had part of his family with him.

"Let's do it," said Javier. "I like a good road trip."

"It's a long way to go," said Quinn. "You think we can make it in this rust bucket?"

"I do," said Jonas. "We avoid the major cities, stay clear of trouble, and we could be there within a couple of days. I vote we keep away from any built up areas from now on. We can sleep in shifts, and spend the nights in woods or on high ground, anywhere away from people. I'm not saying this is going to be easy, but it *is* our best option. What are the alternatives?"

"As long as we do this right – I'm in," Mrs. Danick said, and then she sighed. "I don't exactly know what went wrong back there this morning, but I know we lost some good people. Peter didn't deserve that. We have to be more careful. Watch our backs. There's good people and bad people in this world; always was, always will be."

"So we're going to do this?" asked Jonas. He looked around, and even Terry was nodding in agreement. He probably didn't want to stir up the others with talk of his leaving, and Jonas appreciated that.

"I've just one question," said Mrs. Danick. "Why was Peter outside? Who was on watch when they attacked? I thought we had the place covered." Mrs. Danick looked at Mara, her eyes questioning, her face full of disdain. "Mara, weren't you and Peter supposed to be on watch? What did you see? What happened to…?"

"Look, you old bag, what's your problem? You're alive aren't you?" Rose was drumming her fingers on the dashboard impatiently. "It happened when we switched shifts. It wasn't anyone's fault, so don't start with your shit again."

Mrs. Danick laughed. "If you think I'm scared of you Mara, you can think again. That attitude won't win you any friends. All I'm saying is if you were on watch, then what happened? *If* you were on watch, that is."

"I've just about had enough of your accusations," said Mara. "You've never given us a chance. Gabe didn't have to let you in. We could've turned you away, but we helped you. All I hear coming out of your mouth, Mrs. Danick, is complaints. You…"

"All right, enough." Erik sighed. "Jesus, this isn't helping. Both of you just quit, okay? Pointing fingers after the fact won't get us anywhere," said Erik. "My boy's gone. I'd give my life for him, but I can't change places with him, so I have to keep going for my wife and for my daughter. I have to."

Jonas glanced back at Dakota. Freya was curled up next to her, squashed in between her and Pippa. Freya wasn't sleeping, her eyes were open, but she looked almost catatonic. Jonas still couldn't believe Peter had gone. Pippa was dealing with it in her own private way, but she was unable to look after herself and certainly couldn't take care of her daughter. Dakota was good with Freya, and she was softly stroking the girl's hair. She was going to be a great mother, Jonas knew that, but first he had to get them all to safety. Erik was right about having to go on. Giving up would be an affront to the memory of those who had died. Peter hadn't died just for them all to give in now.

"Mara, we're just talking here, okay?" Jonas looked at her. "Bear in mind we just lost someone. Peter was a real hero, the way he looked after his sister. I only hope we do him proud and get Freya through this."

Erik slapped Jonas on the back. "We will, Hamsikker, we will."

"You know, I think there's a little food and water still in the back," said Javier. "Not much, but enough for a day, maybe two. Apart from bathroom breaks, there's no reason we can't keep going until we run out of gas. I think getting to your sister is a great idea." Javier was enjoying the show. Erik and Pippa looked as if they were about to break down, and even Mrs. Danick sounded beaten. Rose had really let her have it. When Mrs. Danick had brought up Rose being on watch with Peter, she hadn't even had the guts to follow up with a decent accusation.

Wherever they ended up camping for the night, Javier intended to make sure their numbers thinned out some more. Time had overtaken them at the warehouse, so he was going to have to reassess things. The water would soon disappear with so many thirsty mouths, and he didn't need them all. Rose had her fun with Peter, and now it was time for Javier to get some action. Pippa was like a zombie now that her son was dead, and she was useless. She could be the first to go. If he made it look like suicide, nobody would be surprised. Mrs. Danick was pushing all his buttons, too, and he was itching to be rid of her. It was definitely time to cull the herd.

"Ain't nothing more important than your kin," said Javier seriously. "I never had the chance to have kids before, but I have a brother. He's up north, in Canada, close to where this Janey lives. I mean to get to him, and it seems like we can help each other out, you know? Between us we can share the driving, and like Mrs. Danick says, we can watch each other's backs."

Mrs. Danick snorted, but said nothing.

"We don't have time for this dicking around. Let's get going," snapped Rose.

Javier could see the way Rose looked at Mrs. Danick, and he felt the same way. The old woman suspected foul play, and she was staring at Rose's back as if her eyes were throwing mini daggers at her. Javier was feeling impatient, but he knew he had to be smart about it and wait.

Jonas looked around the cramped campervan at everyone. It seemed as if a little hope had been raised in a few faces. Not all of them by any means, but certainly Quinn and Dakota were at least holding their heads up now. He wasn't sure how Erik and Pippa were going to get through this, but he would do everything he could to make things right. Jonas turned back to the front and looked up into the rear view mirror. His eyes met Gabe's, and Jonas thought he saw a whisper of a smile disappear when their eyes met. "Gabe, get us the hell out of here. Keep pointing north. We don't stop 'til sundown."

CHAPTER NINE

"It's as good a place as any."

The van idled to a stop, and Jonas breathed a sigh of relief. As he peered out at the spread of trees before him that slept silently beneath the sinking sun, he estimated that there was an hour until sunset, and he wanted to make sure they were set up long before it got dark.

They had been driving all day, circumnavigating their way around the towns that seemed to spring up every few miles and keeping well away from Indianapolis after the disaster that was Martinsville. They had refueled down a narrow country lane, with Gabe siphoning off the gas from an old Buick. Jonas wanted to give Gabe a break from the driving and took over behind the wheel mid-afternoon. From then on Erik had joined Jonas up front to help navigate, and he had sent Mara with Gabe into the back seats. There was a frosty atmosphere between Mara and Mrs. Danick that no amount of small talk could banish.

"How's it looking?" asked Javier, stretching. "Safe and sound?"

Jonas didn't even know what that meant anymore. Every time he thought they were safe, something bad happened, or someone died. "Seems to be, but let's check it out. Any sign that we're not alone, and we'll move on."

Jonas jumped out of the van. They were in a small clearing surrounded by lines of grape vines. A thin wire fence surrounded the vines, and the van was parked up beneath a withered old oak tree. The area appeared to be quiet, and they were looking down over a hill, affording them a good view of the valley beneath. The oak tree gave them some protection, and they were far enough away from any roads that they were unlikely to encounter any unwanted visitors. The surrounding trees hid them well, and it looked like a safe enough place to stay. Jonas looked at the van. It was beat up badly. There were countless dents and scratches on the side, and the front headlamps were cracked. They had lost one side mirror, and blood was streaked down both sides as if someone had made a crude attempt with red paint to put stripes on it; all evidence of their difficult escape from Martinsville earlier in the morning.

"I think this should work," said Erik as he walked around the van. "Some of us can sleep in the van, and the rest out under this tree with what few blankets we have left."

Jonas watched as Erik went to Pippa, and he held her to him. Freya clung to her mother's side, and Dakota walked across to Jonas.

"I don't know if it's the baby or being cooped up in that van all day, but I feel like crap."

Jonas let Dakota rest her head on his shoulder, and he put his arms around her waist. He hadn't held her in so long that it felt odd, as if he was holding a stranger. The last person he had embraced this close was a dead woman back in Martinsville. He had decapitated her, and he shuddered at the memory.

"You all right?" asked Dakota.

Jonas just nodded. He didn't want to talk about how hard it was; about what he was thinking or feeling or imagining. Now he had stopped driving, he wanted to just eat and get some rest. Talking about all the bad things that happened wouldn't help anyone, and he didn't need any help in dredging up terrible memories.

Dakota smiled feebly. "I'm going to help Quinn and Mrs. Danick. They mentioned something about collecting firewood so we can heat something up for dinner."

Jonas nodded again, watching Gabe and Mara close up the van. He suddenly felt useless, as if his part was done. He wandered over to the wire fence, and looked upon the valley, at the overflowing vines. There were grapes growing that they could collect and would make a refreshing change from the usual tinned food. At the far end of the valley were some discreet, low-rise buildings indicating the edge of the town they had bypassed.

"Just another shit-hole town, Hamsikker." Javier joined Jonas at the fence. "Nothing there but a bunch of dead people. We'll give it a wide berth in the morning, just to be sure."

Jonas yawned. His body ached, demanding rest, but his mind was full of thoughts. "I'm having trouble figuring how to do this with a pregnant wife, you know? I'm not even thinking much beyond that."

Rose walked up to them and smiled at Jonas as she patted her belly. "I know I'm not showing yet, but I can't keep it in any longer. Just hearing you say it out loud gets me excited about bringing life into this world. There's too much death. It's like that's all we talk about these days. When our little baby girl pops out, I'm going to spoil her rotten."

Javier patted Rose's stomach and smiled at her. "Or boy, my darling."

Jonas couldn't believe what he was hearing. "For real? You're pregnant, Mara?"

"I didn't want to steal Dakota's thunder, and I really wasn't sure when the best time was to say," Rose said, feigning nervousness.

"Well, it's a surprise, that's for sure," said Jonas. Surprise was an understatement. There had been no clue, no signs that Mara was pregnant. Just when it seemed he was getting to know them, they threw out another curveball.

"It came as quite a surprise to me, too, when I found out," said Javier. He had no idea what Rose was doing, stirring things up, but he had no choice but to go along with it.

"Congratulations, I guess," said Jonas. "Mara, maybe you can talk to Dakota. You have a lot in common, and maybe you can help each other out? She'd appreciate any advice you can give her."

"Sure, I'll go talk to her. We can start talking baby names," said Rose as she disappeared to find Dakota. "I'm *so* excited."

There was something surreal about it all, and Jonas felt like he was being thrown around on a ship at sea. What were the odds of there being two pregnant women in the group? It was almost like a bad joke, but there was no way Mara would make up something like that. They would just find a way to deal with it. The sooner they got to Janey's the better. She had three kids and would know what to do.

"You remember where you were when it started?" asked Javier.

"What?"

"When the zombies first hit the news? The outbreak, where were you?" asked Javier.

Jonas was still trying to come to terms with Mara's news, and now this?

"I was at a funeral. Look, I don't really want to talk about it, Gabe. Maybe we should go help…"

"It's like the JFK thing, or 9/11, you know? Everyone knows where they were when they first heard about the dead walking. It's not something you can forget."

"No matter how hard you try," muttered Jonas.

"We were shopping," said Javier. "We were in a baby store looking for a cot."

Jonas remembered all too vividly where he was when it started. He could still feel the coolness of the church, the slippery, leathery feel of his dead father's skin as he held him down, and the burning smell in the air when Mrs. Danick put a bullet in his father's head. He remembered how Erik had saved him and Dakota at the church, and he didn't appreciate Gabe churning up bad memories. Everyone had their own stories, each unique and disgusting and upsetting, and Jonas sensed that he was about to hear Gabe's. Everyone had to get it off their chest, tell the others how it had started for them. It united them all. Really they were strangers, yet this was the one thing they had in common, and it gave them a sense of something shared. Like telling tales around a campfire, telling everyone where you were when the dead started rising was cathartic. It brought everyone together and united strangers who had nothing else in common except having to live through a waking nightmare.

"It was a beautiful day," said Javier quietly. "I wanted to buy a cot, even though we weren't sure if Mara was even pregnant at the time. I just knew it was going to happen for us. Anyway, the store was pretty empty, just a typical day really. The assistant was showing us some piece of Chinese crap when she was called away to answer the phone, and then there was a banging on the window. You know how those stores have massive windows at the front to display all their shit? I can see it so clearly. This man was… well, he was dead, no two ways about it. My guess was he had been run over. His neck was twisted so his head was practically facing the wrong way, and his clothes were covered in blood."

Jonas rubbed his dirty hands over his face. He knew it was selfish, but all he really wanted to be was on his own. He didn't need to hear anymore. He had heard a dozen stories like it, and he already knew the ending. Still, he let Gabe go on.

"He was shouting something, but nothing that made sense, just grunting noises really. He kept banging on the window, and I thought he was going to smash it in. The store assistant came back and told us we had to leave as they were closing. I told her there was no way we were going out there with that madman on the street, but she insisted. I should've made her let us stay, but I didn't. I'm a pushover really, just sweetness and light. I don't like confrontation, so I let her go. She went to open the door, and the guy rushed her. He just flew through the door and took her down, like he was running the line for the Broncos or something. He started ripping into her like a dog. Her face looked awful after, and he bit off quite a few fingers when she tried to stop him. I didn't even think about what I was doing. I just grabbed the nearest thing to hand, and I hit him. Turned out that strollers aren't that great at stopping zombies, and he left the young girl to attack me. I was aware of Mara screaming behind me, but all I could think of was how this asshole had ruined my day. All I wanted to do was buy something for my unborn baby, and this motherfucker had upset my wife, damn near killed the shop girl, and now he was coming after *me*? I pushed him back, grabbed the stroller, and pinned him down. I beat him over the head with it until one of the legs came free. I jammed it through his skull until he finally quit. He didn't get up after that."

"And the shop girl?" asked Jonas.

Javier shook his head and pretended to choke up. "Dead. I checked her over. She wasn't breathing. He'd torn her throat out. We called for an ambulance, but we couldn't get through. When the girl got back up, we ran."

A grieving silence fell between the two of them. No two stories about that day were the same, yet they were all filled with sadness. Inevitably somebody died. That was how it always started. Someone's partner, someone's friend or colleague died and came back. What had happened on that spring day to cause it? Rarely did Jonas bother himself with thinking about it, but occasionally the question surfaced. There was no rhyme or reason to it. It wasn't Halloween, the Son of God hadn't returned to Earth, unemployment was up, the Cardinals had just lost, again, and gas prices were rocketing. It was just another day in the good old US of A - except that morning had turned out to be the beginning of the end. Jonas kept wondering when he was going to wake up.

"It was like someone flicked a switch, don't you think?" asked Jonas. "One minute we were fine, the next…"

"You don't have to get bit to turn either. Anyone who was already dead back then came back too. You die, you come back," said Javier calmly. "At least we know where we stand."

Jonas felt for his axe, and remembered it was in the van along with the Pulaski he had found. It was undeniably reassuring to have them so close, but he intended to sleep with at least one of them by his side tonight. It wasn't that he distrusted his friends or Gabe and Mara, but he needed them. Like a young child needs a blanket to sleep, Jonas couldn't imagine being apart from his axe now. They were like extensions of his hands. One day he would probably lose one or both, and that would be that. Until they were ripped from his dying hands, he would fight to the end.

"I think I need to get some sleep," said Jonas. No good would come of trying to talk when they were as exhausted as they were. Their heads weren't in the right place, and neither was his. He needed some space. He needed to make sure Dakota was all right, get some food, and get some rest. They still had to organize who was going to take what shift on lookout overnight, and it was likely that it was not going to be a restful night. Jonas took two steps away from the fence and then turned back.

"Gabe? Thanks. Thanks for everything. You've helped us no end. You're a good friend." Jonas left Javier by the fence, and headed to the van to retrieve his ax before joining the small camp the others had made underneath the old oak tree.

Javier turned back to the valley and smiled. God, Hamsikker was an idiot. They were all so gullible. They still thought they would make it, as if they were somehow better equipped to deal with the zombies than the millions of others who had already died.

The only ones who made it through this were the strong ones; the ones who would do whatever it took to survive. Javier knew he and Rose were going to make it. They would use Hamsikker and his pathetic group until they didn't need them anymore. That was what it took to survive. It was all about putting yourself first. Anything else was suicide.

Javier ran through a mental checklist of what weapons they had left. It didn't take long. He knew that he held the last gun, with a couple of rounds left, and then there was Jonas with his axes. There was a rusted hammer in the van, but since Jonas had left the chainsaw behind, there was nothing else. Javier had the power now, and he knew it. He had given Jonas a sob story to make sure his spirits were low. The real story of where he was when he had first encountered a zombie was not too dissimilar to the one he had just told, but there was certainly no baby store involved. There was a gas station, him holding a gun to some stupid kid who was handing over the contents of the register, and a dead cop in the doorway. The cop didn't stay dead long, and that was when things started to get weird.

When the time came, he hoped Jonas might join him on the road with Rose. He was the only one who offered something. He was strong for sure, and he didn't shy away from confrontation, as he had proved back at the warehouse in Martinsville. Tonight, though, Javier was going to freshen things up and wanted to find time to thin out the group some more. Rose was right. There were too many. It was as if they had taken over a kindergarten, and he wanted to get rid of some of the more annoying babies in the group.

As Javier left the fence, he felt like he was being watched, and looked back at the rows of grapes growing down the valley. He studied them for movement and carefully watched the town, but there was nothing, no movement, not even a zombie, and he joined the others. The town down there was dead, he was sure of it.

* * *

Hamsikker had a sense of déjà vu as he sat staring into the dying embers of the fire. That feeling of hopelessness, the cold air, and the faint rustling of the trees all stirred a vague memory in him. Was this how it was going to be? Sleeping with one eye open? Eating scraps from cans and drinking warm water? It dawned on him that not only did Janey need him, but he needed her. They all did. He looked around at everyone, seeing the same hopelessness he felt in their eyes. There was something else, though, inside of him, a building anger made of resentment, of disappointment, and of revenge. Too many people had died, and if he let the others lose their way, more would die. He needed to make them see that they were in more danger now than ever before.

"We have to start thinking of this as a war. We're in a fight with these creatures, and we can't negotiate a truce. They won't quit until we're all dead. They won't quit, and neither will we. Everywhere we go, every town we enter, every house or yard or garden that we cross, is a battleground. These bastards can hide anywhere. They don't sleep, they don't have remorse, and they don't care who they kill, they just do it. I think it's time we accepted that they're not people anymore.

"Ever since we left Erik's place we've been thinking we would be fine. We keep thinking we're going to stumble across some kind of sanctuary, somewhere like the golf club where we can relax and start over. I'm telling you that it's not like that. It's not going to fall into our laps, and it's not going to be easy. We can pretend we don't know what's going on, or we can get our shit together and fight back. We need to start acting smarter, thinking smarter, and stop letting things just *happen* to us. We're going to take control of our own lives."

"And how do we do that, Hamsikker?" asked Mrs. Danick. "We're exhausted, we have very little food, and…" Mrs. Danick looked at Erik and Pippa, and her eyes sank to the floor. "We've lost too much. This is hard. I'm not sure we have any fight left in us."

Mrs. Danick was one of the strongest people Jonas had ever known, and if she gave up, the sense of futility and listlessness would spread quickly through the others. "That's exactly my point. I'm exhausted too. You think it doesn't tear me up inside knowing Peter's gone? Well, I say no more. Tomorrow we go into that town over the hill, and get some supplies. We get some gas, and we don't stop until we get to Canada. We make a plan, and we stick to it. More than that, we stick together."

"Right on," said Javier.

"I'm sick of running, feeling like I've done something wrong," said Quinn. "I need to feel like I'm doing something, and that we're going somewhere. Let's do it. I don't want to feel like this anymore."

Javier felt a frisson of excitement run through him. If Hamsikker could galvanize the group into action, maybe they could be of use after all. He stoked the embers of the fire with a blackened stick, and dropped it in to burn. "Okay, let's run a sortie tomorrow into town. We need food and water, or we're not going to make it. There's nowhere near as much as I thought there might be in the van. Half of us could go into town, half of us stay here as back-up. You're right, Hamsikker. We can do this."

"We have to," said Erik. His face was cast into deep shadow by the dying fire, and he looked old. Grief had aged him ten years, and his red beard looked faded like his pale skin. "Nothing's bringing my son back, but I'll be fucked if I'm going to sit back and let these things take us all down one by one. The only promise I can make to you all is that I will die before I let them take another one of us. If it's in my power, I'll stop them, no matter what."

Jonas knew his friend was in pain, but nothing he could say or do would change that. Erik needed time. He needed to spend time with Pippa and Freya and help them deal with the loss of Peter.

"Fine, but we don't split up. We all go together," said Jonas as he held Dakota's hand. "Let's try and get some sleep. I'll take first watch with Quinn. We change every hour. Once the sun's up we'll take the van into town and see if we can get some supplies. If it's too dangerous, we'll back off. No more taking risks. But we stick together."

Jonas looked at Freya. She was curled up beside the fire, asleep, and he could see her hands wrapped around the key chain he had given her. It was a cheap piece of garbage, but it meant so much more to her. It was a symbol of trust, of hope, and if he failed her he wouldn't be able to live with himself. He had let too many people down in the past, he could admit that, but he was trying to put things right. He had to make things right with Janey, too, and seeing her and his three nephews again was not just important, but vital. He was going to find her and make a new start. Dakota would love it up there. Janey's house by the lake would be perfect. Even if Thunder Bay had fallen to the dead, even if there was nobody else alive up there, it was still something to aim for. They could make it work. They could fish on the lake, they would have fresh water, and there were plenty of natural barriers between them and the dead cities of North America.

"And then Canada?" asked Quinn. "There ain't no coming back from being dead, Hamsikker. We can't afford to mess this up."

"And then Canada. Quinn, we can do this." Jonas stared into the fire. "We're all on the same side here. We *will* do this."

"I'm turning in," said Mrs. Danick. "It's a long way to Canada, and we're going to need all the rest we can get. Anyone mind if I sleep in the van?"

Erik stood up. "Would you mind if Pippa and Freya slept with you? I'd feel better knowing they were in there. In case, you know…"

"Of course, that's fine."

Pippa picked up Freya and carried her over to the campervan. Mrs. Danick pulled her shawl tight around her shoulders and shivered. "Hamsikker, be careful tonight." She shot Rose and Javier a look that suggested she hadn't bought into their story one bit. "Watch your back, okay? There are monsters out here in the woods."

Javier watched Mrs. Danick turn and head toward the campervan. There was no doubt in his mind now. By this time tomorrow, one way or another, she was going to be in a world of dead.

CHAPTER TEN

Pete Hopper was an insignificant man, just one of many young workers who used to toil away on hot days in the fields and tend to the vines. He had been killed close to the vineyard, and his body still wandered around Utica. There was nothing to draw him away. The legs kept working, and the eyes darted around looking for the living, but it had been months since anything had crossed his path. It was Freya's faint cry that alerted him to the presence of the living. It was so, *so* quiet that it took a long time before he was even heading in the right direction. He stumbled through Utica, down the main street full of dead bodies, and tried to follow the only sound that night that was audible for miles. Through the diminishing moonlight and the quietness the crying sound carried on the breeze, alerting more zombies to the presence of the group. The dead gathered together slowly and began to walk through Utica. The zombies were unaware of the camp at the top of the hill, but if nothing impeded them, it would not be long before they found it. The sound of their dragging footsteps carried even further, and the dead soon began to converge.

Utica had been declared a safe zone, and the residents of nearby Ottawa, Spring Valley, and Oglesby had all been evacuated there soon after the outbreak. Utica's natural population of around 1500 people had swollen to nearly 30000, enticed by the promise of safety. Endless rows of tents had been erected to shelter the homeless refugees, and the small town began to resemble a war-torn city. The National Guard had put up a good resistance, but ultimately they were undone from within. There were several infected within the evacuees, and soon the National Guard had turned on their own. Thousands had died that first day, but as more died, more returned, and the whole evacuation center had very quickly become nothing but yet another place for the dead.

Many of Utica's rapidly expanded population spread out into the surrounding area following the complete collapse of the safety zone, and Illinois was covered in the dead. Like a bad case of chicken pox, its towns and land were covered in festering spots of the dead with pockets of zombies everywhere just waiting for someone living to come along and give them a reason to move. Some wandered the streets, some the fields, and some remained trapped in the buildings where they had died. Eventually, it appeared that the living were wiped out, and after months of inactivity, the zombies in the area fell into a stupor, slumping to the ground or standing inside homes with nothing to draw them out. That was until sunrise, and there was movement at the camp on the top of the hill.

Freya had almost made it through the entire night without crying. She was still plagued by visions and nightmares, but somehow had managed to stay quiet as she slept. It was early morning, and Rose was watching her sleep. She was on lookout with Quinn, and they had separated to cover both sides of the camp. There was little to suggest they would encounter any trouble, and the night had been quiet. Rose saw Freya clench her hands into small fists, and the girl began to murmur. Rose had hoped to get some alone time with Erik in the night and see if he squealed like his son, but the chance had never arisen. Hamsikker had insisted on having two people as a minimum on watch at all times. Rose could tell Javier was annoyed, too, and it meant spending another day with the group of whining losers. They bleated about not feeling safe, about missing Peter, and how things were getting desperate with such little food and water. She hated being so close to the cop, particularly, and keeping up the pretense of being Mara was fun at times, but she longed to be free again. Javier had promised her he would take care of it, but when he was going to man up and do it, she didn't know. She would never tire of Javier, but there was one other man amongst them who intrigued her.

Hamsikker.

She had watched him back at the factory, noticing how effectively and swiftly he dealt with the zombies. The way he handled an axe, the way he kept it under such control, amazed her. It was as if he had been doing it all his life. He was strong, and she couldn't figure out how or why he constantly put up with his wimp of a wife. Dakota seemed like she just drifted through each day, never actually contributing anything, but just content to follow the others and look pretty. Rose wondered if Hamsikker would fuck her like Javier. Was he a gentle lover? Dakota didn't deserve him. Hamsikker wasn't a sheep, he tried to lead, he tried to manage situations, so why was he tying himself to Dakota, just another slutty soccer mom who would grow fat before she grew brains? Women like her used to make Rose feel embarrassed, as if she wasn't good enough. Now she knew that people like that were just zombie-fodder, and she was sure it wouldn't be long before Dakota succumbed too.

Freya screamed, and Rose cried out, shocked.

"Jesus, Freya, keep it down."

Quinn came running up to them both and knelt down beside Freya. "What is it?" asked Quinn. "Is she…"

"She's fine, just a damn nightmare," said Rose. "You watch over Sleeping Beauty for a while, I need to pee."

"Keep on watch, Mara. Don't be long."

"Yes *ma'am*." Rose turned her nose up as she left. She didn't take orders from anyone except Javier, and certainly not from some jumped up colored woman, who should be serving Rose fries instead of ordering her around.

Quinn soothed Freya back to sleep, whispering to Erik that she was fine. Quinn sat down on the ground.

"Can't sleep?"

Erik sighed and shook his head. He reached over to Freya and patted her head gently. "I don't know how she is going to get through this. Peter was her rock. She looked up to him so much."

Erik stopped as Freya murmured again, and then she fell silent.

"You think the dreams will ever stop?" Erik asked.

"One day, Erik," replied Quinn. "Give it time. When you lose someone, there's no getting over it. You just take it one day at a time. Eventually, the pain goes away, even if the memories don't." Quinn recalled seeing Roger eating her mother that horrible hungover morning, and shunted the image to the back of her mind. She couldn't let her mind go there, and she swallowed. "If Hamsikker's right, we could be on to a good thing with Janey's place. I know we're going to get there. She'll be fine, you'll see. We *all* will."

Quinn looked at Erik, and he nodded at her in agreement. She could see he didn't believe they would be fine, but she had to believe it. If she lost hope now, she would return to that dark place where her family was, and it was a place she never wanted to go to again. Quinn sat with Freya and watched the sun rise over the vineyard. The vines were thick and green, full of grapes, and the sunlight shone over them, illuminating a pair of small white buildings at the end of the valley. The sunrise was quite beautiful, and Quinn felt like today was going to be a lot better than the last one. She had been woken up yesterday by Pippa's screaming. Peter's death hadn't seemed real until she had gone out there and seen it for herself. She had fought the zombies and been amazed when Hamsikker had come through it unscathed. Today was going to be different. There was even the sound of a bird overhead sitting in the oak tree, and the air smelt pure and fresh. If Hamsikker and Gabe were happy to share, then she planned on helping to drive, and God willing they would make it to the border long before tomorrow dawned. Roger was her past. This group was her future. They were going to make it, *all* of them, and Quinn smiled.

"Quinn, where's Mara?" asked Jonas.

Quinn looked up at a tired looking face. "Bathroom. She'll be back in a minute."

"We should get going. I want to get on the road as soon as we can."

Jonas went around the camp waking everyone, and soon everyone was in the campervan. Gabe asked him again about how wise it was going into town, but they needed food, and it was more dangerous not going. They were going to need a lot of energy if they were to make it to Canada, and they didn't want to stop any more than they had to. Jonas explained how it was going to work. They would head into the town and look for a drugstore or grocery store they could raid. He and Gabe would go in with Erik right behind them as backup. Quinn would stay at the wheel, and if things turned sour, she was to take off and head back to where they had camped for the night. The priority was the safety of the women and Freya.

Jonas rolled down the windows in the van and sucked fresh air into his lungs as they drove out of the woods and back onto the road. It was good. It felt like more than just another day, more than just another sunrise. It was a fresh start, a chance to make things right, and he was going to make things work. If it was in his power, then he would have them a thousand miles closer to Janey's by the time the moon was up. They just had to get from A to B. The hard part was how.

As they coasted quietly into Utica, Jonas looked around. Where was everyone? He thought they might find some zombies, perhaps wandering the main street, or maybe even chance upon someone living, but the town was curiously deserted.

As luck would have it, they had left the camp at about the same time as the army of zombies had arrived at it. The dead had taken the most direct route to them, through the fields and trees, trampling the grapes into the ground beneath their dead feet. When the van had taken off, the noise had turned them around, and the crowd of dead was right now behind them, heading back into Utica. Of course, not all had been drawn to the noise, and Utica still kept a few secrets amongst its derelict buildings.

"Maybe we can upgrade this thing for an RV. Would be nice to spread out a little," said Terry as he tried to stretch his legs, only to find his knees were wedged into the seat in front of him.

"You see one, you let me know," said Jonas.

"Over there, look." Quinn pointed at a store just ahead of them that had a large blue sign over the door reading 'Brenda's Bakery'. It was sandwiched between a drug store and a nail salon. "There's space out front to pull up. We might find food."

"I want to check out the drug store," said Javier. "There's plenty of stuff we could do with. Headaches are the least of our worries, right, Hamsikker?"

Jonas knew what Gabe meant and had been worrying about Dakota not getting enough vitamins. They might be able to find some supplements that would help with the baby, and he really didn't know the first thing about childbirth. "I'll come with you. Dakota, you stay here with Pippa and Freya."

"Let's go quick. I don't like this. It's too quiet." Erik put his hand to his side as the van rolled to a stop. He felt for his Glock, and then realized it would be useless without ammo. He picked up the hammer from the floor and opened the door. "Terry, you're with me, we'll go check out the bakery. Jonas, Gabe, you hit the drug store. Quinn, I want you behind this wheel. Any sign of trouble, you take off, you got it?"

"And what do I do?" asked Rose. "Sit here and look pretty?"

Erik jumped out of the van. "I'm sure you can manage that, darlin'." He looked up and down the street, but it was quiet. The shops were empty, and there was no sound coming from anywhere. There was a scratching sound emanating from a storm drain, and Erik watched as a skinny rat darted out. It grabbed a piece of crumpled paper in its mouth, and then scurried back into the darkness and security of the drain. He turned back to the van to see Mara with a scowl that had settled across her face. "Look, you can make yourself useful, and keep a look out for us. Stay close to the van. You see anything, yell like there's no tomorrow."

"I'll come with you." Mrs. Danick made to get up, and Jonas pushed her back down. "No way. You're staying put. Pippa, Dakota, and Freya need you here."

"There's a motel over the road," replied Mrs. Danick. "I could take Freya for a walk. Who knows, we might find some bottled water, or…"

"No," said Hamsikker firmly. He jumped out of the van and closed the door. "Stay here. Too many of us start snooping around, and the more of us we put in danger." He nodded at Erik, and then turned to face Quinn. "If we're not back in five minutes, get out of here."

Erik and Terry went quietly into the bakery. They slipped in through the open front door, and Jonas turned to Gabe. "Watch my back, and be quiet."

As Jonas made his way into the store, Javier took the Pulaski from Hamsikker so both of them were armed. He kept the gun hidden, but at hand. He didn't intend to get caught now, and Hamsikker could bark orders any way he wanted. If there was a choice to be made inside, then ultimately Javier was going to be walking out of the drug store alive, one way or another.

It was a small room they entered, with a sole rack down the center of the store and a counter at the end. Jonas could see the racks had been cleared. Evidently the owner had the foresight to clear his stock away before abandoning the place. As he progressed deeper into the store, Jonas's feet swept through a variety of garbage, yet he saw nothing of use. It wasn't easy in the dim light. The store was illuminated by the open doorway, and Jonas scanned the shop. If they were going to find anything of use, they were going to have to search further, go deeper in. There was a closed door in the corner of the room and beyond the counter a door inset into an alcove behind a grill. He turned around and spoke in a whisper.

"Gabe, see if that door over there is open, will you? I'm going to check behind the counter."

Jonas didn't wait for a response but walked towards the counter. The register was open, empty, and he pushed aside the cluttered display of cough sweets and lipglosses. He leant over the counter, expecting to perhaps find a body, but the floor was clean, and there was nobody there. He jumped up, swung his legs over, and dropped to the floor. As he landed, his trailing leg knocked over a can of antiperspirant, and it rolled away from him before he could grab it. It hit the wall with a ding, and Jonas held his breath. The store seemed quiet, but he didn't want to get caught out like he had been before. He slowly counted to five in his head, but the store was silent. He heard Gabe rattling the door handle behind him, but it seemed to be deathly silent ahead. Jonas stood up and approached the grill. The cupboard behind it was locked, and if the owner hadn't cleared it out, it probably held a huge stock of medicine. The only problem was that the grill was secured in place with a padlock. Jonas scanned around looking for the key, but there was nowhere obvious he could find it. He could smash it open with his axe, but he was reluctant to break it, knowing the noise he made could put them in danger.

Jonas raised the axe. They needed supplies, and his unborn child was going to need more than good wishes to survive. Dakota needed help, vitamins, and would more than likely need something to ease the childbirth. He could smash the lock open, grab the drugs, and get out of the store before anything found them.

"Fuck it."

Jonas brought the axe down on the padlock, and it smashed open instantly. There was a tremendous banging sound, but it was over in a second, and he rolled up the grill quickly. The cupboard was locked by a smaller padlock, and Jonas used the axe blade to cleave it open. He pulled apart the cupboard doors and found himself looking at row after row of vials, bottles, and packets of pills.

"Bingo." Jonas smiled and began shoving as much as he could into paper bags that lay nearby. When he had filled as much as he could carry, he went back to the counter. He placed the bags down and noticed the internal door was open. Gabe must've got it open.

"Gabe?" Jonas whispered, and then he realized that with all the noise he'd made, there was little point in whispering anymore. "Gabe?" he called again, louder, but there was no reply.

Jonas jumped over the counter once more, and leaving the drugs safely where they were, he checked out the open door. Jonas found himself staring at a carpeted stairway cloaked in darkness.

"Gabe, come on, let's go." Jonas waited for a reply, but heard nothing. He had a sinking feeling in his stomach as he began to realize something had gone wrong. Surely, Gabe would answer if he could? What if the place hadn't been empty? What if Gabe had found someone up there?

With one foot on the bottom step, Jonas considered his options. Go in and face whatever Gabe had found, or retreat back to the van and get help. There seemed little point in going back to get the others. It would just waste more time, and so Jonas began walking up the stairs. He listened carefully for noises, for a clue as to Gabe's whereabouts, but the building was quiet. The steps creaked as he climbed them, and he gripped the axe in his hands. As he neared the top and saw another open door, he broke out in a cold sweat. There was that unmistakable odor as he neared the upper floor, the smell of foulness, evil, and death that everyone had grown accustomed to recently.

The stairway led into a hallway, and Jonas made out four doors in the darkness. The upper floor was furnished with pictures of birds on the walls, and a small side table with a vase full of brown, dead flowers. As Jonas ventured further into the house, he had no idea which room to try first. Gabe could be anywhere. Every step he took was agony as the silence was replaced with the creaking of an old floorboard.

Something fluttered in his face, and he brushed it away, aware that his breathing was becoming more rapid. It's just a moth, he told himself, and he waved his hand in front of his face to clear the stale air. He told himself to cool it, to focus on finding Gabe, and not panic. Jonas peered into the first doorway and could make out the shape of a toilet. The room was small, containing nothing more than a toilet and a hand basin. Clearly Gabe wasn't there, so Jonas continued on. He paused by the side-table. Brittle petals from the dead flowers crunched under his feet, and he noticed a photograph on the wall showing a young couple on their wedding day. They were happy, kissing, and drenched in sunlight. Jonas took the frame in his hand and placed it back on the table facedown. Those times were over.

The second door was wide open, and Jonas stopped, looking at the double bed that lay beyond. Two figures lay on the bedspread, and Jonas gripped his axe, ready to strike should they rise. Flies hummed above them, and as Jonas took a step into the room, the figures lay perfectly still. They were dead. Their skin was drawn tight around their stiff bodies, and flowing hair draped itself around their heads. The figure on the left wore a suit and tie, and it looked as if the person to the right wore a wedding dress. It was a faded cream color, and there was a bouquet of crisp long-stemmed roses atop the woman's chest. Jonas noticed that they were holding hands, inseparable even in death, and he let his axe fall to his side. God, what had happened here that had made them do this? Why would they not run? Why would they not at least try? Jonas felt anger rising up inside him again. He was *not* going to let this beat him. He was *not* going to end up like them, giving up. He had too much fight left in him, and he turned back to the hallway.

"Gabe, where in hell are you?"

Jonas stormed angrily from the bedroom and pushed back the third door to find an empty room. It was an office cum spare room, full of cobwebs and clutter, but no Gabe. Moving on, Jonas entered the final room. Shrouded in darkness, he saw Gabe at last, standing over something in the middle of the room.

"Gabe, what is it?"

Javier shook his head, but could say nothing.

Jonas could sense something was wrong, and he joined Gabe. When he saw what Gabe was looking at his anger subsided, and suddenly he understood why those people had done what they had done. There were two wooden cribs before him, their headboards decorated with painted animals and stuffed toys. One crib had a smiling tiger holding a sign that read 'Jon,' and the other an elephant with its trunk curled around a board that read 'Matthew.' Inside the cribs, beneath white and cream blankets, lay two small, still bodies. Tiny hands poked above the sheets, perfectly formed, yet blue and rigid. Jon and Matthew's eyes were closed, and they looked peaceful, as if they were still asleep. It was clear they were dead, and their shrunken bodies were almost as small as the stuffed animals that surrounded them.

Jonas put a hand on Gabe's shoulder. "Let's go."

"They never stood a chance." Javier rested his hands on Jon's crib. "I wish I could've been here sooner. Maybe then I could've done something, could've helped. Maybe…"

Jonas remembered that Gabe was looking for his brother, and these two poor boys were probably a stark reminder that the line between life and death was thin.

"Let's go," said Jonas again. "There's nothing we can do for them now." The house was just a dead-end. Jonas would rather be facing an army of zombies than looking so closely at the death of innocents.

Javier trudged from the room with Jonas behind him. Seeing those boys abandoned like that, not even given a decent funeral, was disgusting. He was glad the parents were dead. If they weren't, he would've made them pay. Men and women got together, fucked, married, divorced, remarried, and tried all sorts of rituals to make them prove to themselves that they were close, *together forever*. The truth is, they were strangers trying to avoid loneliness. The real closeness, that real understanding, could only come from blood, from being sisters or brothers. Diego was so close, yet so far away. Seeing those two little babies, never given a chance at life, never given an opportunity to get to know one another, was cruel. Javier was more determined than ever to find Diego now. To hell with the others. They had wasted enough time in this town, and they hadn't got anything to show for it. It was more than past time to hit the road.

"Hamsikker, we should… Shit, where's the van?"

They left the house of death and ventured back outside into the sunlight, only to find the campervan gone.

"What the hell is going on?" asked Javier. He thought he could trust Rose to take care of things while he was inside, but it seemed he had taken her for granted too.

"There," said Jonas, pointing across the street. The van was parked on the other side of the road, in the shade of the canopy of the hotel.

"What are they doing? Why the hell did they move?" Javier began jogging over to the van, aware that they wouldn't have moved without good reason.

As they got closer, Jonas saw Dakota, and whilst he was relieved to see she was okay, there was concern spread over her face. Quinn was pacing up and down and looking worried. Erik and Terry had beaten them back and were deep in conversation with Pippa.

"Hamsikker, we've got trouble," said Erik.

"Where's Mara?" Javier looked around the van, but she wasn't there. She wouldn't have upped and left him, so where the hell was she?

"Mrs. Danick decided she wanted to check out this hotel," said Pippa. She looked back at the hotel, its open doorway looking like an invitation into hell. It was dark inside, and there was a dead body in the doorway. Blood was splashed over the sidewalk outside the entrance. "Rose tried to stop her, we all did, but she was adamant she had time to check it out before you would be back."

"And you let her go?" asked Jonas. He dropped the bags of medication he had picked up in the store into the van.

"We didn't just let her go. There really was no way of stopping her short of tying her up and throwing her in the van." Dakota looked at Jonas. She was pushing her hair behind her ears, her fingers shaking nervously. "Jonas, we have to find her."

"How long's she been gone?" Jonas looked at the hotel. It was no Hilton, but it was big enough for someone to get lost in very quickly, especially in the dark.

"Where is Mara?" asked Javier again slowly and loudly. He approached the hotel doorway, sizing it up. Mrs. Danick was welcome to go off exploring on her own. He would happily leave her behind given the chance, and if he could find Rose, that's exactly what they were going to do. He fingered his gun nervously. He was over this. Too many things were going wrong. Diego was his little brother, and these morons were holding him back. He had been wrong to think he could control them.

"She went in almost as soon as you left us," said Pippa. "She said she would be back in five minutes, tops, but it's been way longer than that. Erik, what if something's happened to her? Like with Peter? What if…"

Pippa began crying, and she looked like she was about to faint. Erik caught her and gently lowered her to the sidewalk. "Sit here. We'll get her, okay? She'll be fine."

"There's something else," said Quinn.

"Jesus fucking Christ, where is Mara? Are you all deaf?" Javier marched up to Dakota. "Where is she, or so help me God…"

"I don't know where she is," replied Dakota calmly. She looked at Gabe and spoke with a weary resignation in her voice. "She went in after Mrs. Danick. She said she would bring her back."

"Fuck. And you've not seen anything since they went in?"

"Hey, Gabe, calm down, there's no need to take this out on Dakota."

Javier stared at Hamsikker. It would be so easy to end it now. The Pulaski felt good in his hands, and it would be so easy to take Hamsikker's head off with one blow. It would be over quickly. He could shoot the others, get Rose, and leave them all to die in this Godforsaken town. No, he was going to need help finding Rose if she was in that hotel somewhere. He bit his cheek, drew in a breath, and lowered his voice. He had forgotten that Gabe was supposed to be easy-going. If he was going to ask for their help one last time, he was going to have to be sweet old Gabe for just a little longer.

"I'm sorry. I'm just so worried about Mara. Hamsikker, we're going to have to go in there. We can't sit around here waiting for them. What if they're in trouble, or trapped? I couldn't live with myself if anything happened to Mrs. Danick."

"Guys, whatever we do, we need to do it fast." Quinn stood in the road and pointed south, to where they had driven into town from. "They're coming."

Jonas looked and couldn't believe what he was seeing. Hundreds, if not thousands of zombies were all heading into town. They were no more than a mile away. So many outstretched arms, so many faces contorted by death, all attached to shuffling bodies with mouths hanging open, blood dripping over swollen, black tongues.

There was a scream from inside the hotel and then two short bangs. Jonas peered at the doorway of the hotel, and from the dry shadows that enveloped the main doors, a figure slowly emerged. A zombie stumbled out into the sunlight, and Pippa screamed. The man was dressed in black pants with a white shirt, and his curly black hair was matted with dried blood. Pippa screamed again as the dead man lunged for her, and Erik batted him away with the hammer. The blow knocked the zombie sideways into the side of the campervan, and Jonas watched as Freya jumped out.

"Freya, get inside, now!" Erik shouted at his daughter as he lunged for the zombie once again, armed with the rusty hammer and a belly full of hate.

Erik grabbed the zombie, and pounded his hammer into the man's temple, smashing the skull in until the man was still.

"Pippa, Erik, you okay?" Jonas rushed back, his axe poised for action, but the zombie was down.

"Yeah, I just..." Erik looked around at the sidewalk, his eyes wide with fear. "Pippa, where's Freya?"

"She's with you, isn't she? In the van?"

Jonas knew Freya wasn't in the van, nor was she on the road. "Quinn, Dakota, you see her?" He looked at their faces but was met with bewilderment and confusion.

"In there." Javier raised his gun, and pointed toward the hotel before speaking. "She ran inside, just like you told her."

Erik raised his hammer, fresh blood dripping from the end. "And you just fucking let her?"

Javier felt like smiling, but he had antagonized Erik enough. He knew he could only push it so far. Still, when Freya had darted into the hotel, nobody else had seen her, and Javier was pleased that the group was splintering. Javier had just about had enough of the lot of them. Now the pig was going to suffer, and Javier hadn't had to lift a finger.

"Freya? Freya!" Erik stood in the doorway, calling for her, but there was no reply.

"Freya, come on back," shouted Terry. "Erik, I'm sorry, I should've been watching her, but with all the commotion, I just…"

"Forget it, Terry. She's probably scared. We'll get her," said Jonas. "She can't have gone far."

"Look, maybe we should think about going," said Javier.

Jonas was incredulous that Gabe would even contemplate it. "What about Freya? Mrs. Danick? *Your wife*? You want to just take off?"

"Well, maybe we could draw the zombies away, and give them a fighting chance. If we stay here and we don't get them out of the hotel in the next three minutes, then we're going to have thousands of zombies on our tails. Then none of us are getting out of here." Javier was half-serious. He knew they would never go for it, but it was going to be interesting to see how they reacted.

Jonas stared at Gabe. One minute he was his best friend, the next minute he was coming out with crazy shit like that. "We're not going anywhere. You want a time out, you feel free. I'm through trying to help you. We've tried, really we have, and I thought maybe you were on our side. I don't get you, Gabe."

"Quinn, I want you to take Dakota and Pippa in the van. Circle back around, try to lure as many of the dead away as possible. Just try to give us a little more time, okay?"

Dakota jumped into the van with Quinn, and Pippa stood mournfully looking at the hotel.

"Go with them, honey," said Erik. "I'll get Freya, I promise."

Pippa reluctantly got into the van, and Quinn instantly roared off, heading for the army of zombies on the edge of town.

Jonas clenched his axe and looked at Erik's hammer. It would have to do. "Gabe, give Terry the axe. We all need to be armed if we're going in there. I know you don't have bullets left, but you can beat the hell out of something with that gun of yours if it comes to it."

Terry took the Pulaski from Gabe, and the four men stared into the darkness beyond.

"I'll go with Erik and head upstairs. Terry and Gabe, I want you to check out the ground floor." Jonas felt the weight of the axe in his hands. He wasn't sure what lay waiting for them inside, but there was no putting it off any longer. "Be as quick as you can, but don't leave any rooms unchecked. Right, let's move."

All four of them ran into the dark hotel, wondering what they were going to find, hoping they would at least find someone alive. Javier was only concerned with looking for Rose, but the others were focused on finding Freya.

As they crossed the threshold of the hotel their shadows were swallowed up, and the odor of death hit them. No sooner had they stepped inside, than the screaming started again.

CHAPTER ELEVEN

The hotel was glum, and even if they needed a bed for the night, Jonas wouldn't have wanted to stay there. It was depressing to see how badly kept the place was. Fifty years ago it had probably been a nice stop on the way north or south, a comfortable, cozy place attended to by friendly staff; a place you could stay for the night in true comfort to experience some true small-town hospitality. Now that the zombies had taken over, it seemed appropriate somehow that the dead were in charge. The walls were coated in greasy paint that had been badly applied, leaving track marks down the walls and painted different colors in places. The skirting boards were chipped, and the numbers on the doors hung lopsided.

At the top of the staircase lay a body. So much of it had been eaten away that there was little left on the bones to identify if it had been a man or a woman, and Jonas and Erik sidestepped it quickly. Tattered pieces of rotten flesh still clung to the yellow bones, and the carpet around the body was sticky. As soon as they had passed by the body, they looked ahead at the row of doors facing them, and it became apparent they weren't alone. Soft thumping noises came from within the hotel, and they looked at each other.

"I guess we go door to door, right?" Jonas asked Erik.

Erik nodded sagely. "Don't try to second guess what we're up against. We do this smart, and everyone comes out alive. I have to get my daughter back, Hamsikker, I *have* to."

Jonas nodded. He understood what this meant. Erik and Pippa had already lost Peter. If they lost Freya, too, it would be over for them.

"Follow my lead," said Erik.

The door to room nineteen was closed, and Erik pressed his ear against it. He looked at Jonas and shrugged, as if to say he wasn't sure if the room was empty or not. As Erik pushed the door open, Jonas stepped inside with his axe held out in front of him. Nothing rushed out to grab him, and so he continued inside, quickly checking the bathroom before proceeding into the bedroom. The drapes were open, and light streamed into the room.

"Clear," said Jonas.

"Freya, you in here?" Erik threw open the wardrobe doors, and pulled back the bed covers, but there was no reply to his question.

"Erik, she's not here. Let's go to the next room."

Needing no invitation, Erik jogged from the room, and paused by the next door as he waited for Jonas to catch up.

Jonas assumed Erik had already listened for any sign of the room being occupied, or not. "You hear any…"

Erik ignored Jonas, threw the door open, and charged inside. To Jonas the hammer in Erik's hands looked far too small and feeble to defend himself with should he be attacked. He followed his friend inside, and this time the room was dark, making it difficult to see much. Erik ran straight into the bedroom.

"Freya? You here, honey? Come out, it's Daddy." Erik pulled open the curtains, and began scanning the room.

"Jesus Christ," said Jonas quietly. On the double bed lay the remains of a woman. She wore a long, yellow sundress that exposed her slim legs, although the skin on them was sallow and blistered. Small bite marks ran the length of her left leg up to her thigh, and Jonas turned away, sickened by what he saw. From the waste up, the woman had been eaten. Her ribcage stuck out, but the meat had been picked clean off it, and the only clue she had ever had arms were the remains of the bones that lay by the side of her body. Her head was gone, and scraps of blonde hair lay nestled on the pillows alongside clumps of meat.

A clatter came from the bathroom as something fell to the tiled floor. Instantly, Jonas bristled, aware they weren't alone.

"Erik, did you check the…"

Jonas watched as Erik ran to the bathroom and flung open the door.

"Freya!"

A small figure emerged from the bathroom and ran to Erik. The face was smeared with blood, and the sunlight exposed the girl's pale face. Her blond hair bobbed around her face as she ran to Erik, and Jonas was both elated and frightened at the same time. There was something in the girl's dead hands - something metallic that swung freely as she ran, reflecting the sunlight and temporarily blinding Jonas. It looked suspiciously like the edge of a key chain.

"No, please God, no." Jonas was filled with horror. How had it ended like this? Days ago Freya had been playing with her brother, laughing, and crying. Freya was nine years old, and on those rare occasions that she smiled, Jonas could see her mother in those blue eyes. Erik was going to be devastated. They all were.

"Erik, it's…"

Erik could tell it wasn't his daughter the second he saw her, and he swung his hammer at the girl. He caught her on the side of the head, and the girl dropped to the floor. She groaned, and he hit her again, causing her to let go of the jawbone she held in her hand. Erik's hammer came away with bloodied blonde hair caught in it, and he punched the wall in frustration.

"God damn it, Hamsikker, where is she? Where the fuck is she?"

Erik charged out of the room like a stampeding bull, and Jonas approached the dead girl. Her brains oozed slowly from the crack in her skull that Erik had given her, and her eyes weren't blue, but deep brown. Jonas looked at the jawbone in her hand, the teeth still buried deep into the gum. The metal fillings sparkled, and he knew for sure then it wasn't Freya. He hoped she still had the key chain he had given her. She kept it on her day and night as she had done since getting it from him, and he knew she thought of it as more than what it was. Freya was dear to him, and if only one person made it out of the hotel alive, it *had* to be her.

A thump came from the wall behind him, and then more, as if people were fighting. Erik.

"Erik, wait for me!"

Jonas ran into the next room to find Erik battering a zombie to death. Tears streamed down Erik's face as he continued to bash the old man's head in, even though he was clearly dead. The old man's brains were so deeply mushed into the carpet that they were never going to come out.

"Erik, stop this." Jonas grabbed Erik's arm, just as Erik raised the hammer to aim another blow at the old man.

"Where is she? I told her to get inside the van, didn't I? I told her, Hamsikker, I told her to…"

Erik shrugged Jonas off and stood up, suddenly calm. He wiped the blood from his face and made for the exit. "She's not here. Next room."

Jonas stood in the doorway and refused to move. "Erik, stop. We'll find her. But you said to me yourself that we have to do this right. If you go charging from room to room, eventually you're going to end up in trouble, and if you wind up dead who's going to take care of Freya then? What would Pippa think if she saw you like this? Stop acting crazy, and together we'll…"

"Get lost, Hamsikker, you don't know what it's like. You don't have any children, so how can you? You play the role of a caring uncle very well, but ultimately she's not your responsibility. She's not your flesh and blood. Why don't you just take off? Hm? Leave like you left me in Jeffersontown. Leave, like you left Janey. You always ran away with things got tough, so it hardly surprises me you didn't have kids. You're chicken shit. So get out of my way, and let me find my daughter."

Jonas stared at Erik. So this was it; the truth that Erik had been holding back all those years, the resentment that he had left him behind had finally come out.

"You know what, Erik, I'm not going to get in your way. Have I made mistakes in the past? Yes, I'll admit that, but who hasn't? You don't know what Janey and I went through when you went home. You don't know what our father was really like. So don't try and guilt me into feeling bad, because none of this is any of my fault. I know exactly what it's like to lose someone you love and for someone to feel pain. Your own flesh and blood, that's what you said. You think I left Janey behind? None of your Goddamn business. You could've protected her, but you didn't. I know about you too. She would've loved you if you'd only ask, so don't accuse me of being chicken shit. You abandoned her just as much as I did."

"Anything else?" Erik eyeballed Jonas, and raised his hammer. "You have precisely ten seconds to get out of my way, or I'll make you."

Jonas smiled. "I lost it once. Remember? Remember Jeffersontown, back in that bus, when you saved me from that girl? Remember the farm where Tyler died, and that stupid fight we had? Well, even though you are a *complete* asshole, I am standing here right now because like it or not, I still have your back. I will follow you into hell if that's what it takes to get Freya back. So I recommend you do what you told me to do once, wind your head in, and focus. You can't push me away, Erik."

Erik's face visibly softened, but he kept his hammer raised.

"Let's go," said Jonas, and he lifted his axe. "Let me take the next room."

Without waiting for a response, Jonas walked across the corridor to the next room. The door was open, and he walked straight in.

Empty.

He crossed over to the next room and walked in, aware that Erik was quietly following him.

Empty again.

There were noises coming from all over the hotel now. There were so many thumps and bangs and groans that it was impossible to tell where they were coming from.

"Jonas, I…"

"Save it, Erik. We're here to find Freya."

Jonas trudged to the next door. Room 23 was closed, but there were clear noises from the other side, and moans too.

"Freya?" Jonas called out, and heard muffled voices replying, calling for help.

It was hard to tell what was being said over the din. It was as if the darkness swallowed up their words, but Jonas thought he heard Mrs. Danick calling out for help.

"Ready?" asked Jonas. Erik looked like a man lost. Jonas knew he was still coming to terms with Peter's death, and if any harm came to Freya it would kill him.

"Do it," said Erik.

Jonas pushed the door open and found himself face to face with three zombies. All three were battering on the bathroom door, and when Jonas appeared, they turned as one to him. Jonas saw three hungry mouths dripping with blood, their rotting bodies swaying unsteadily as they appeared dumbstruck momentarily, as if trying to decide whether to continue bashing down the door or eat Jonas.

"Allow me to make your minds up for you."

Jonas swung his axe into the chest of the first zombie, an obese man wearing a dirty gown. It swung open as the man attacked, and Jonas let him come. Using the axe handle as a guide, he pulled the man out of the room into the corridor. Spinning the zombie around, he pinned him back against the wall, sending a framed picture of Mickey Mouse crashing to the floor.

"Erik, go!" Jonas wrenched the axe free, pulling out much of the large man's guts, and breaking half a dozen ribs in the process. He brought the axe around again, and swung it through the man's neck. The axe head buried itself in the wall, and the obese man's body fell to the floor, leaving his severed head perched atop the axe.

Jonas pulled the axe free and spat on the decapitated corpse. He turned on his heels quickly to see how Erik was getting on. There were screams and cries now coming from the bathroom, and it was evident at least one of the three people they were looking for was in there. Erik was laying into the next zombie, punching it with his fists, and Jonas saw why. The hammer was buried inside the dead man's head, right up to the hilt, sticking out like a comical hat. It would be difficult for any man to retrieve, even Erik with all his strength. The third zombie was trying to get past the second one to Erik, but was trapped in the narrow hallway between the bathroom and the bedroom.

"Erik, bring them out here where I can get them."

Jonas had no sooner spoken than Erik was backtracking, and the zombies spilled out of the room after him. The one fighting Erik continued struggling with him whilst the third ran straight for Jonas.

A runner, thought Jonas, and before he had time to hit it, the zombie had knocked him off his feet. They crashed into the wall together, and Jonas was surprised by how much strength the zombie had. Its foul stench made him want to vomit, but he pushed back, using his strength to overpower it. The zombie rolled to the floor, bringing Jonas down on top of it, and he tried to pin it down whilst he searched for his axe. It had fallen out of reach when the runner had hit him, and the zombie grabbed Jonas's shirt, ripping the sleeve as it tried to bite him.

"Erik?"

Jonas could hear the fight continuing behind him, and he tried to see how Erik was getting on, but he couldn't risk turning away from the zombie pinned beneath him. It was full of energy, and its deadly teeth kept snapping away at him.

"I got this," said a woman's voice, and suddenly the zombie beneath him stopped moving. Jonas saw his axe swing down and obliterate the zombie's head, splattering him with blood and gore. Rose reached down a hand and helped Jonas up. She smiled at him, her eyes bright, and her hand cool to the touch.

"Are you okay?" asked Jonas as he stood up. "Shit, Erik!"

Erik was still fighting with the other zombie, repelling it with punch after punch, but it wasn't going down, and Erik was tiring. Jonas grabbed the axe from Rose and shouted at Erik to stand clear. When the zombie was dead, its head split in half, Jonas faced Rose again.

"Mara, you should've helped Erik first. I mean, thanks, but…"

Rose shrugged, and just smiled at Hamsikker. She walked up to him and embraced him.

"I wanted to save *you*," she whispered in his ear.

Jonas pushed her away. What was her deal? Just as he was about to ask her what she meant by that, he noticed Mrs. Danick was coming from the bathroom.

"Mrs. D, you're okay?"

"Of course, I am. I'm sorry I led you on a wild goose chase in here, but I truly thought I could do more help by looking for supplies than sitting waiting in the van. I'm sorry. I left my bag in the van, or I would've been able to do something about those three chaps that were after us."

"Sure you would. Maybe you could knit them a nice cardigan to keep them warm while they ate us alive," said Rose, her voice full of spite. "If it wasn't for me, you'd be dead."

"And if it wasn't for Hamsikker and Erik, we'd *both* be dead," replied Mrs. Danick. "At least if I went first, I'd like to think I'd have enough class not to eat your skinny ass."

Rose put her hands on her hips. "Skinny? Is that why Hamsikker can't keep his eyes off me? Is that why Peter wanted to fuck me? Your time's over, grandma, and it's time you realized that."

"All right, all right, enough you two," said Jonas. He wasn't looking for gratitude, but he could do without them sniping at each other. There was enough to deal with looking for Freya without having to keep Mrs. Danick and Mara separated.

Erik ran into the bathroom and came out instantly. He grabbed Mrs. Danick's hands. "Where is she? Where's Freya?"

"I'm sorry, Erik, we haven't seen her. I didn't bring her in here. We left her in the van."

"Oh Jesus, this isn't happening." Erik bent down to one of the zombies and put his feet on its neck. He pulled the hammer free and ran to the next room.

"Freya's in here?" asked Rose. The smile disappeared from her face. "What the hell?"

"I'll explain later. If you're up to it, though, can you help us search these last few rooms? You, too, Mrs. Danick?"

"Of course. I'd rather be wandering the corridors of a zombie-infested hotel, than be stuck in that bathroom with *her* for one more minute."

Mrs. Danick's face told Jonas everything he needed to know. They were never going to get on, no matter how much time they spent together.

"Well, I'm glad you two ladies had some time to get to know each other. You can tell me about how you became best friends later, but right now we have to find Freya."

Jonas joined Erik as they searched the last few rooms, but all they found were more dead bodies and empty rooms.

Erik began rattling the emergency exit door, but it was locked. There was no getting it open, and no way could Freya have gotten herself through.

"Let's check downstairs again," suggested Jonas. "Maybe Gabe had more luck than us. For all we know, she's safely back in Pippa's arms right now.

"Gabe's in here?" asked Rose.

"Yeah, he's searching downstairs with Terry," said Jonas.

"Then I hope Terry's watching his back," said Mrs. Danick.

"Just what is that supposed to mean?" Rose glared at Mrs. Danick. "You're the one that's dragging the group down. You should do us all a favor, and just go and have a heart attack."

"For the love of…Mara, will you just give it a rest?" Jonas brushed her shoulder and frowned at her. They reached the top of the stairs, and they stopped.

"You should listen to her, Hamsikker, she's too much. All I want to do is help, and she…" Rose began to cry, and she put her head on Jonas's shoulder. They were crocodile tears, but they had the desired effect.

"Look, I'm sorry for snapping, but you need to relax. We're all on the same side here." Jonas put an arm around her. "We'll get through this."

Erik pushed ahead of them and began descending the stairs. "I'm going to find Freya. You can catch up with me when you're ready."

Mrs. Danick followed him. "Don't let her fool you, Hamsikker. Don't let her drive a wedge between us."

Jonas waved her off and pushed Mara away. "You okay?"

Rose wiped her eyes, drying the imaginary tears on her sleeve. "Yeah, I'm just worried I guess. Gabe's down there, and well, you're so brave. You came looking for me. If it wasn't for you…"

Rose leant forward and planted a kiss on Jonas's lips. She pressed herself against him firmly, making sure he could feel her body against his and kissed him harder.

"Mm, no, stop it," said Jonas, pushing her away again. He was so shocked that at first he had been unable to do anything, surprised at what she was doing. She was undeniably attractive, but this wasn't what he wanted. He wanted Dakota. He wanted a child. He wanted Janey to be okay. He wanted a family.

"Let's pretend this never happened, Mara," said Jonas as he started down the stairs. He didn't look back as he spoke. He didn't know if Mara was playing games, but he had no intention of starting anything with her. Perhaps Mrs. Danick was right not to trust her. Had he been wrong all this time? "Let's go get Freya, and get the hell out of here."

Rose followed Jonas down the stairs, staring at his back. How could he reject her like that? Nobody rejected her. It was only a bit of fun. She thought it was about time she had some more fun. She hadn't played her favorite game in a while. Stick, or twist, would be fun with Hamsikker.

* * *

"Ladies first," said Javier, as he held the door open for Terry. They had crossed the foyer effortlessly and were in a carpeted hallway that stretched out until it reached a fire door. The doors on either side were all open, but there was no sound. The air was murky, and it was difficult to see. Without the lights, the only way to see was from the minimal sunlight that came in sporadic bursts through the occasional open window.

Terry licked his lips, gripping the axe in both hands. He was thirsty, nervous, and not relishing the task ahead. He desperately wanted to get Freya back, though, and stepped into the first room ahead of Javier. The screaming they had heard had stopped so quickly it had been impossible to work out from where in the hotel it came, and so they were searching room to room.

"Freya, honey, it's Terry. Come on out."

Terry's eyes scanned the room for any sign of her, for any clue she might be hiding, but even in the gloom he could tell it was empty. He poked his head into a bathroom, and then advanced further into the room. The bed was still made up, and there was an unopened envelope on one pillow addressed to a Mr. Fuller. The hotel was tired, and it wasn't just the stale air and darkness. There was an aura of sadness about the place. The carpets were thin, and the faded wallpaper was peeling back from each corner of the room where the damp had curled it up. The lightshades looked like they hadn't been dusted since the Fifties, and the televisions were huge, old box sets that had long since outlived their use.

"She's not in here," said Terry plainly. "Next room."

Javier tried the next room, but it was exactly the same. They took it in turns to go into the rooms first, and it was a process they repeated until they reached room seven.

When Terry pushed the door back and called for Freya, he heard a sound come from within the room. He paused and looked at Gabe. Raising his finger to his lips indicating that they should be quiet, he walked carefully into the room. The noise came again, a faint knocking sound, and raising the Pulaski, Terry stepped quickly into the bedroom.

Empty.

There was an open suitcase on the bed, and clothes were scattered about the room all over the floor. The telephone and lamp on the bedside table had been knocked over, and the television was in pieces. It looked like there had been a struggle.

"Freya?"

"She's not here," said Javier, getting tired of Terry's theatrics. The man was not a leader. He was barely a man. As far as Javier could make out, all he had done for the group was babysit Freya, and look how that had turned out.

"In there," whispered Terry pointing to the bathroom.

Javier stepped back, allowing Terry to take the lead once more. It seemed fairly obvious that it wasn't Freya in the bathroom. She would've answered or come out. Whoever was in there was probably incapable of speaking, and Javier had no intention of finding out who it was.

Terry put his hands on the bathroom door handle. In the dimness he tried to catch Gabe's eyes, wanting to know he had his back, but in the darkness all he could see were two dark spots where Gabe's eyes should be. "One, two, three…"

Terry threw back the door, and it banged loudly against the wall. The creamy floor tiles were covered in blood, and there was a body in the bathtub. It struggled to get out, twisting around and around as Terry studied it. Red water sloshed around the body, and the smell was foul. The zombie's hands and feet had been tied together, and it had rotted away in the cold water, causing the room to smell awful.

"Happy now? Next room," said Javier.

"We can't leave them like this," said Terry. "It's not right."

"Not right?" Javier began to think it wouldn't be such a terrible thing if Terry had an accident in the hotel. "So finish it off then, and let's get a move on."

Javier watched Terry take a step closer to the bath. He raised the axe above his head, and then stopped. The body kept twisting and turning, unable to get out, and a clump of hair slipped from its scalp. It floated on the top of the turgid bath water, and Terry stepped back.

"I can't. I can't do it anymore."

"Jesus, give me strength." Javier snatched the axe from Terry's hands and buried it into the zombie's head. It stopped moving instantly, and Javier plucked the axe from the dead man's skull. *"Next room."*

Terry held out his hands for the axe, but Javier kept hold of it. "We don't have time for this, Terry."

"Yeah, but I need that. You can't expect me to go into these rooms unarmed."

"That's exactly what I expect you to do," said Javier. He walked out of the room, aware that Terry was following him like a lost puppy. Javier stood by room eight. The door was closed.

"Well?"

"Terry, stop whining, grow some balls, and get in there," hissed Javier. "If anything goes wrong, I've got your back. It's clear you don't have the stomach for this anymore, so let me keep a hold of the axe. You can have it back outside. Right now we have to focus on finding the others. Standing around talking about it is only slowing us down. So…"

"So?"

Javier swung open the door. "So fucking get in there, and do what we're here to do."

Javier couldn't tell if Terry was afraid or trying to summon up the courage to argue back, but either way, Terry began to walk into the room. Terry had lost the will to fight, that much was clear. It was as if he had lost the belief in himself, and if that was the case, then he was of no use.

"Freya, are you…"

Terry stopped when he saw two figures standing on the far side of the room. The drapes were open, but the window backed onto the rear of the property, and there was nothing outside but a dumpster and an empty vehicle. The two figures had their backs to Terry and were looking out of the window.

"Mara? Mrs. Danick. Thank God," said Terry. "We thought…"

The two figures turned around, and Terry's relief was replaced by confusion. They weren't who he thought they were. They were women, but they were black and dressed in white maids uniforms. One had crimson stains all down her front and a ragged hole in her cheek that exposed her upper jawbone. The other, a plump woman, had a gaping hole in her neck, and Terry held his breath. He was frozen with fear, and his brain was deciding whether to fight or flee. When one of the women started advancing toward him, he made up his mind.

"Gabe," he whispered, "give me the axe."

"Not today, buddy."

Terry swiveled on his feet to see Gabe behind him in the doorway, smiling. It looked like he was about to break out in laughter.

"What? Give it to me, quick!"

"This?" Javier held up the axe and shook his head. "Not a chance. Oh, and if you try to get it from me, I'll shoot you," he said, whipping out his gun. "I'll only pop your kneecaps, that way these two hungry ladies will still get a good meal. How's that sound? Anyway, good luck. This should be entertaining." Javier saw that one of the zombies was about to take a chunk out of Terry. This was going to be a lot of fun. "Oh, and Terry, I'd turn around if I were you."

"What? But…" Terry turned in horror and yelled, putting up his hands as the first zombie leered over him. Its teeth were poised, its mouth wide open. The dead woman was ready to take a bite out of Terry's neck, and there was nothing he could do about it.

CHAPTER TWELVE

Terry felt the first bite on his shoulder, and he screamed in pain as one of the maids took a chunk out of him. He whirled around, and tried to throw the woman back, but she had a good hold on him, and all he could do was crab-walk with her as she continued to bite him. He pushed her back, and they fell onto the bed together. The other woman joined them on the bed, and Terry held out his arm to block the other woman's attack. Instead of her teeth sinking into his face though, they simply sunk into his forearm, and he cried out in pain again. Blood splashed onto the clean linen, and Terry started to thrash and buck, trying to throw off his attackers.

"Gabe? Please, help me. Please…"

The fat maid straddled Terry, and her rotting face buried itself in his abdomen. She clawed her way past his shirt, and then sank her teeth into his skin, ripping it apart until she found his juicy, warm innards. Terry kicked and fought, but she was too heavy to throw off, and the second woman kept nipping at his hands and arms as he tried to repel her.

Javier chuckled quietly as he watched them rip Terry apart. Eventually Terry began to struggle less, and when the fat maid began chewing on his neck, Terry went limp. His head rolled to the side, and Javier could sense Terry was looking at him as he passed. Terry feebly reached out an arm toward him, his hand open, tears rolling from his glassy eyes, and then he was gone.

Satisfied that the two cleaning maids had done his work for him, Javier retreated from the room and silently closed the door. All he could hear from within the room was the sound of wet lips smacking together and the cracking sound of bones being broken. It was a noise he was comfortable with, something that had become part of the new world. There were lots of things that he had grown used to over time, and one of those things was Rose. He would give her another couple of minutes, but if she hadn't surfaced by then, it might be time to call it quits. There was a growing army out there, and he wasn't about to let it, or anything else, come between him and Diego.

Javier yawned and realized there was only one more room left on the ground floor they hadn't checked. He looked at the axe that he now carried, the one that Hamsikker had told them was a Pulaski, and admired the weight in his hand. The blade was still exceptionally sharp, and it would do the job just fine. Javier strolled confidently down the dim corridor.

"Rose, you here? Rose?"

Javier kicked open the last door, but the room was empty. Javier sat down on the bed and bent down to open the mini fridge beneath the rickety wooden desk. It had no power, and the contents were cold, but it was still stocked, and he pulled out a green and gold can. As he sat on the bed sipping the warm beer, he listened. There were faint noises coming from within the building above him, probably the others wandering around. Maybe he should call it quits. The beer, though warm, was good, and he hadn't been able to relax in a while. It was all getting too messy. He had thought he could control them all, fashion them into some sort of cohesive unit who would fight for him, but in reality he despised them. He was already fed up of wasting his time on them, and now he was running around a deserted hotel looking for a kid and an old woman?

As he sat there contemplating his next move, the valance beneath his feet began to stir, and he spread his feet apart. He watched curiously as a snake came out from under the bed, slowly drifting across the floor, and it wound its way around Javier's feet. Its body was thin, perhaps a foot in length, and covered in light brown scales. Javier wasn't too familiar with snakes, but he figured it was probably just hungry, and it was best not to take a chance. He bent down and scooped it up, grasping it behind the head carefully.

The Eastern Milk snake eyed him cautiously.

"You lost too?" Javier looked into the snake's dark eyes, seeing himself reflected there. "You're not going to find much to eat in here, buddy, unless you like peanuts and warm beer."

He could snap the snake's neck, but the snake wasn't doing any harm. It was on its own, just looking for food, perhaps trying to find a mate or a nest.

Javier placed the snake carefully back on the floor, and it slithered back under the bed instantly.

"Good luck." Javier crushed the empty can in his hands and threw it aside.

"Fuck it," he said, and he left the room, heading back down the corridor to the entrance. There was no point heading upstairs. Hamsikker and Erik had that covered, but there were still a couple of doors on the other side of the lobby he needed to check. If they were empty, he was going to call it a day.

As he crossed the lobby, he glanced outside. He could hear the sound of an engine in the distance, and the road was clear. Obviously Quinn had managed to keep them away for now, but she wouldn't be able to fool them for long. Eventually something would find them, maybe hear the screaming, or just stumble upon them by chance. Either way, Javier would be a long way away by then, and Rose had two minutes to appear, or she would be left behind with the others.

"Rose?" Javier called out loudly, but got no response.

He approached a door at the back of the lobby, behind the reception area, and pushed it open with the axe. The door swung back, revealing little. There was no source of light in the room, and Javier squinted. He could make out a maid's cart full of toilet rolls and tiny tubes of toothpaste, and row after row of clean pressed sheets. The utility room was otherwise empty, and he pressed on. The next room was an office with papers spread out over its dark grey floor. Splashes of blood dripped from the walls, and clearly there had been a fight in here at some point. The blood was dried though, and there was no sign that anyone had been here recently. Javier walked down the narrow corridor and turned a corner to see a zombie pushing itself against a closed door. It had its back to him and didn't hear Javier approaching. It kept pushing on the door, scrambling to get in, but the door wasn't budging.

Javier strolled right up behind it, fascinated. It had no idea he was there. All its focus was on that door and whatever lay behind it. The dead woman had probably been a guest, dressed in knee-length shorts, a pleated blouse, and white tennis shoes.

"Hey, bitch."

As the zombie turned around, Javier swung the axe neatly at its head, severing it from the body. The legs stumbled forward, and then the body fell to the floor. In the darkness Javier could see the woman's head roll away, and yet the teeth still clacked together. The jaw continued to work, and the eyes rolled up to look at Javier menacingly. Javier brought the axe down on the head, cleaving the skull in half, and the woman finally was dead.

"You in there? It's me." Javier knocked on the door three times. "Come on, open up."

He heard scraping noises coming from the other side, the sound of a bolt being slid back, and then the door opened. Javier held up his axe, just in case, and a figure rushed out at him. It took a moment in the darkness to realize who it was, and he almost took Freya's head off. She ran up to him and grabbed his leg.

"Hey, Freya, don't worry, Uncle Gabe's got you now. You okay, honey?"

Freya didn't speak, but held onto him tightly, and he bent down to her. He looked her over, looking for a sign or clue that she might have been bitten. He ran his hands through her curly blonde hair and checked her clothes. Nothing was torn, and she appeared to be fine. He stared into her blue eyes, impressed. Yes she was scared, but she still had it together. Even Terry had crumbled quickly, but she had managed to hide, to stay alive.

"All right then. You're safe now. I've got you, Freya."

Javier stood up and found Freya reaching for his hand. Her small fingers slipped into his, and he wasn't quite sure how to respond. He looked down at the little girl, beginning to understand what Rose saw in her. The girl was the prodigy of a cop, but there was still time to save her. She was naïve, weak, yet undeniably cute, and she was strong too. After everything they had been through, after the loss of her brother and being surrounded by ineptitude and death, she was still here.

"Freya, did you see anyone else? Like Mrs. Danick or Mara?"

Freya looked up at him blankly. She shook her head from side to side quickly, and then cast her eyes down at the floor. She shoved a key chain into her pocket, and then thrust two fingers into her mouth. She began to suck on them as they walked down the corridor back to the lobby.

Well then, thought Javier, let's hope Hamsikker has more luck upstairs, or Rose is going to be pissed when she realizes I've left her behind.

Back in the lobby Javier thought about venturing upstairs. Had Hamsikker found Rose, or was he still searching? Freya squeezed his hand, and he looked down at her. Her eyes were wide, and she was staring at the outside.

Javier looked, but the van was gone. "Come on then, let's see what gives." He took Freya out of the hotel and didn't have to wait long to see what was going down. The mob of zombies had almost reached them, but there was no sign of Quinn or the campervan.

"Gabe, over here!"

Javier turned to see Hamsikker waving at him from behind a pillar. Beside him were Mrs. Danick and Erik. From behind them a figure emerged into the sunlight, and he couldn't help but crack a smile when he saw Rose.

"I'll be damned," he said as she ran up to him. They embraced, and Javier felt Freya's fingers slip from his. "Rose, are you okay?"

"I'm fine, just fine," she replied as she kissed his neck.

"Is Freya…?"

"She's fine too." Javier looked at Rose. He thought he could almost detect a teardrop in her eye. Was she really that upset? He had begun to believe they were drifting apart, but perhaps he was wrong. They said stressful events could bring people together, so maybe she was beginning to realize she was better off with him than without him.

"Gabe, I can't begin to thank you enough," said Erik approaching him. Freya was in his arms, her wet fingers back in her mouth, and her blue eyes looking up at him with a look that Javier couldn't understand. Was it relief? Trust? It was a look he wasn't familiar with. There was an understanding, a bond between them that he had never experienced. Javier remembered how she had took his hand after he'd found her and was suddenly curious.

"Looks like a fair trade to me, partner. You got your girl, and I got mine." Javier put his arm around Rose. "Freya here was really brave. Weren't you, honey?" He reached out a hand and patted her cheek.

"She's something else. If I'd lost her, I…well, anyway, I didn't. So you need anything at all, Gabe, you just let me know."

"Hate to break up the reunion, but we have to move," said Hamsikker.

Javier nodded. "So where's our ride?"

"That's what I'm trying to figure out," said Hamsikker. "We can't hang around here waiting though." There was an unspoken question hanging in the air, one that he didn't want to ask, but he knew he had to. Erik was so preoccupied with holding onto Freya and making sure she was okay that he had clean forgotten about Terry.

"Gabe." Hamsikker licked his lips. "Gabe, what happened in there? Is Terry..?"

Javier shook his head. He lowered his eyes to the ground, and let a vacant gaze fall across his face. When he thought about how Terry had died, about how those two zombies had ripped him open while he drew his last breath, Javier had to stifle a chuckle. He had to play it straight for now and keep up the pretense.

"I'm sorry. I tried to stop him, but he was so desperate to find Freya that he got ahead of me. When I caught up to him, it was too late."

So they had lost another. Hamsikker clenched his axe. It wasn't right, and it definitely wasn't fair, but Terry had known the risks. If He had deemed Terry's sacrifice enough to send them Freya back, then so be it.

"Truly, I wish I could've done more, but it was over quick for him." Javier looked at Rose and winked. "He didn't suffer."

Nobody else saw the wink he gave to Rose, and it was enough for Rose to know he had taken care of Terry. She was quite sure it wouldn't have been quick either.

"Runner!"

Mrs. Danick's urgent tone demanded attention, and they turned as one to the horde coming down the main road.

The body of Pete Hopper reached them, and he stretched out a hand. Finally, *finally* he had found them: the living. He opened his mouth ready to taste them, so ready to let their warm blood fill his mouth. He didn't care which one; all his body knew was that it had to get to them.

Hamsikker swung his axe, took off the runner's head, and watched as the body took a few more steps before collapsing. With a soft thud the head rolled away into the gutter. Its eyes looked back at him, and Pete Hopper couldn't understand what had happened. Something wasn't right. Something...

Hamsikker swung his axe down on the decapitated head, and the zombie that had once been young Peter Hopper was no more. The head split open like a melon, and dead brains spewed out into the clogged gutter.

"There's more," said Erik. He pointed at the dead army coming their way. "We have to move."

He began to walk down the road with Freya in his arms.

"He's right," said Hamsikker. "Let's go. Quinn will be here any second, I'm sure of it. We just have to give her a chance."

He took Mrs. Danick's hand and raced after Erik.

"Kill him," said Rose as they followed.

"What?" Javier looked at her, waiting for the punchline, but her face was set deadly serious.

"*Kill him*. Kill Hamsikker next. I want him gone."

"Keep your voice down, *Mara*." Javier glanced over his shoulder to make sure nothing was about to sneak up on them and take a bite out of them. "What's got into you?"

"Kill them all. That stupid fucking old woman, that pig, those two boring soccer moms, and that black cunt who thinks she's a fucking ninja. Leave me the girl, but please can we just get this over with. Most of all, *kill Hamsikker*."

Javier wasn't sure what to make of Rose's outburst. They weren't exactly in a position to do anything at that moment, and certainly not able to discuss anything with the others so close.

"Mara..."

Rose shoved Javier away. "Just kill him," she hissed, and then she raced ahead to join the others.

Javier stood in the road watching Rose walk away. Talk about split personality. One minute she was all over him, the next she was acting insane. What was it about Hamsikker that had gotten her so worked up? Had something happened in the hotel that he didn't know about? He had no problem killing the others. In fact, he was quite looking forward to it, especially the cop, but

Hamsikker could still be useful. He was the only one that Javier wondered if he could be saved. He could still be converted, recruited to the cause. He wanted to get to Canada as much as Javier did, and if they worked together they could really achieve something. Did Rose know something he didn't?

"Gabe, watch your back!" shouted Hamsikker. He could see a runner break ahead of the pack. The bony carcass was covered in tatters, and it looked like a ghost as it ran toward them.

Javier spun around. He wished he could pull his gun out, but that would give away he still had some ammo. Using the axe, he hit the runner as it reached him. At first he just clipped the zombie's shoulder, sending it off balance. The next blow took off its head, and the runner fell to the ground.

"You okay?" asked Jonas.

"Of course," said Javier. He was beginning to tire of these games, and wanted to get well away from Utica. "So where's our ride?"

"She'll be here. Quinn wouldn't leave. She'll have a good reason for not being here." Jonas felt uncomfortable. Gabe was looking at him strangely, as if he had done something wrong. Gabe's eyes were studying him, analyzing him, and Jonas wanted to say something to break the tension. "Look, she'll be here. Quinn's one of the most reliable…"

"Whatever," said Javier, and he left Jonas standing on the street alone.

"Freak," muttered Jonas. Every moment they spent together it felt like a tension was building. It was as if the group was on a knife-edge, and Gabe and Mara were not fitting in. Jonas wanted to get to Janey, *needed* to get to her, but perhaps Gabe wasn't going to be able to help. He was seriously considering splitting away. It might be best for everyone if they broke up.

Jonas found the others crouched behind a bus shelter. Mrs. Danick, Erik, Freya and Mara were hidden behind an advertisement for a crunchy new cereal. The poster featured a smiling mother looking on as her fair-haired son tucked into a bowl of the new breakfast food, his teeth pearly white, and the father was standing behind them laughing. The picture was so ridiculous that Jonas wanted to rip it down. Families like that didn't exist except in the movies and advertisements. The only family that you had now was the people you survived with, the people you ate with, slept with, and killed with.

"Hamsikker, we can't wait any longer. We need to find a way out of here, or at least somewhere safer to hide than this damn bus shelter." Mrs. Danick peered out from behind the hoarding, looking on worryingly. Hundreds of dead bodies were ambling down the main street of Utica, their groaning filling the air. They surged forward in waves, like football crowds leaving a stadium, drunk and giddy, euphoric with success. Success for the zombies, though, meant death for the living, and Mrs. Danick had seen enough death to last her a lifetime.

"We can't stay here," said Javier. "Utica is a ghost town; we stay, we die. We need to move. Find our own vehicle. The others are gone. Fuck 'em. They've fucked us over, so we deal with this my way now."

"Hold on a second, Gabe," said Jonas as he sat down on the seat in the shelter. "We just need to give Quinn time. She'll be here. Stop trying to take over. There's no need for this macho bullshit. We're all friends here, so let's stick together. We have a far better chance of making it that way, don't you think?"

Javier glared at Hamsikker. Rose was right. He fingered his gun, and thought about doing it here. He could shoot Hamsikker in the gut, and leave him screaming in pain on the road. That should give the zombies something to think about and give him time to get away with Rose.

"We can discuss this later," said Erik. "They're here. Let's move it."

Erik took off with Freya still in his arms, and he broke into a jog. The others swiftly followed, and Jonas knew they didn't have much time. He could smell the dead behind them, hear their groans, and feel their eyes burning into his back as he ran. There was no fighting them. If he stopped, they would overwhelm him instantly. There were hundreds of them, far too many to take on. As much as he hated to admit it, Gabe did have a point: where was Quinn?

"This way." Erik charged down a side road, trying to find a way off the main road, away from the dead. Sweat poured down his back. The day was heating up, and he already felt tired from running and carrying Freya. There was no way he was stopping though. He would die first before he gave up Freya again.

Jonas looked behind him and realized they had a moment. The dead hadn't yet caught up with them, and this was their chance to hide. He looked at the buildings on either side of the road, but was reluctant to venture into any of them. Their closed doors and dark windows were forbidding, and he was reminded of the hotel. Though it was small, it had held many dangers, and so might these other buildings. He saw bookstores, a salon, a few offices, and a postal office. He didn't see anything that looked particularly safe. Between them they had two axes, a hammer, and an empty gun. It wouldn't be enough.

"Hamsikker, over here." Erik had pulled open the door to a caravan that was parked up beside a dress shop. It had been adapted to sell food, and the outside was plastered with adverts for hot dogs and burgers, cold cans, iced tea, and hot coffee.

As Erik jumped inside, Jonas watched the others follow, and he joined them, hoping they hadn't been seen.

Rose slammed the door shut, and they all fell silent. As Jonas looked around the grubby van, he began to think they had a chance. There were drapes pulled across the windows, and if they kept silent, they might just make it. The place smelt of rotten meat, and he noticed Mrs. Danick pull open a fridge door, only to shut it again quickly with a look of disgust on her face.

"Down! Everyone, get down," whispered Jonas, as he heard the first footsteps outside.

They all crouched down on the sticky unwashed floor of the van. It smelt of food, too, and as they lay waiting a cockroach crawled across from underneath the stove in front of Jonas. He watched it dart across the floor, and back again, before it stopped. It paused before scuttling back from where it had come, obviously deciding the strangers in its home weren't worth worrying about.

Outside the van, the moaning sound grew louder. They heard more and more bangs and knocks on the side of the van as the dead crashed into it, and it seemed like it would never end. The door began to rattle, and suddenly the handle turned. Jonas jumped up and grabbed it before it could be pulled open. The small latch that held it in place would soon break if a hundred zombies pulled on it, and he looked at Erik.

"Check it out," he whispered. He wasn't sure if one of the dead had got lucky and was playing with the door handle, or if they had been discovered.

Erik drew back one of the drapes carefully, just an inch, so he could see through it. His eyes were squinting, but when he looked outside he opened them wide. "Mother fuckers," he exclaimed loudly. "Gabe, they know we're here. Help Hamsikker secure that door, quickly!"

Javier wrapped his hands around Jonas's over the door handle just as the door lurched violently and was wrenched from Jonas's grasp. Startled, Jonas watched as the door was pulled open, and he looked out at a hundred dead faces all staring back at him. They moaned in unison, and he reached out to pull the door back in.

"Help me, God damn it!"

Javier pulled on the door, but one zombie had already got himself wedged in the frame.

"I can't get it shut." Jonas pulled desperately on the door, but the zombie at his feet was blocking it. If they got in, they were all dead.

"Kill it!" shouted Jonas as he danced from side to side, trying to avoid the snapping jaws of the dead man lying between his legs.

Rose grabbed the hammer from Erik, and bashed in the zombie's head before dragging it into the van. She held the hammer over it as if afraid it might still move, and stepped back.

"Amen," said Mrs. Danick.

As the body was cleared of the frame, Jonas and Javier got the door shut. They kept their hands wrapped tightly around the handle, but the effort to keep it closed was a drain on what little energy they had. With sweat pouring down his face, Javier looked at Jonas.

"What now, Hamsikker?" he growled. He should've killed him back at the bus stop. He should've killed them all and taken off with Rose. "I'd love to know how we're getting out of this one. Thanks to you and your friends, we are now totally fucked."

CHAPTER THIRTEEN

Jonas quickly cast his eyes around the van. He hoped he might see something for inspiration, but there was nothing. All he saw were dirty pots and pans, an old blue bucket full of greasy utensils, a table covered in menus, and five faces staring back at him looking for an answer.

"I don't...I don't know, just let me think, okay? Just..."

Jonas didn't know what the answer was. The door threatened to explode open at any second, and as much as he and Gabe had it under control, it wouldn't be long before it was opened. Next time they wouldn't get it shut, and the prospect of being torn limb from limb was terrifying. He looked at Mrs. Danick, and saw for the first time how old and frail she was. She had the attitude and fight of a twenty year old, but her body was letting her down. He couldn't keep putting her through this. He was supposed to be protecting her, protecting all of them, yet it was harder than he thought it might be. Mara was staring at the dead body that lay on the floor with its brains seeping out as if she had never seen a dead body before. Freya was curled up in her father's arms, her eyes screwed shut, and her hand clutching the key chain Jonas had given her.

"Well?" asked Javier. His eyes bored into Hamsikker's. He wanted him to crumble. He wanted to see Hamsikker suffer. There was a time he thought they could make it work, but it clearly wasn't going to work out. If they could get through this, it would be time to end this fragile relationship once and for all.

"You wanted to be in charge, you think of something." Jonas had had enough. "If you're not part of the solution, you're part of the problem. Ever heard that one before, Gabe?"

"I once heard, Hamsikker, that all you need for happiness is a good gun, a good horse, and a good wife. Right now, we don't have any of those things. You know what I think?"

Javier let go of the door, and Hamsikker felt the pressure on it increase tenfold. "Jesus, what are you doing?"

Javier could let the door open, let them take Hamsikker, and get the door closed as they feasted on his body. It might just buy them enough time to think of a way out of this mess.

"Get your hands back on that door, Gabe." Erik passed Freya to Mrs. Danick. "Now."

Javier ignored Erik. "I think, Hamsikker, that what we need is a diversion. We need to give those folks outside something to play with while we come up with a way out of this dead end."

"Gabe, so help me, you'd better cut this shit out, right now." Erik stepped toward the door, unable to get past the others, and reluctant to leave Freya.

Javier put his hands back over Jonas's on the handle. There was a glint in his eye as he began to squeeze.

"Stop being an ass, Gabe. Look, we can get out through there." Mrs. Danick pointed up to a skylight in the roof. It was narrow, and would take some effort getting the top off, but it was the only feasible way out.

Javier relaxed his grip, and glanced at Rose. He couldn't work out what she was thinking. Did she want him to do it now, to push Hamsikker out to a certain death, or did she want to carry on?

"Nice one, Mrs. D." Erik clambered up onto the stovetop and began to unscrew the latch holding it in place. In less than a minute he had it open, and he poked his head through.

"The road is packed out there. No way through. I think we're close enough to be able to get onto the roof of that store we're parked up against though. We should get moving."

"Go. I'll hold this door as long as I can," said Hamsikker. "When you get up there, don't hang around. Get straight on over to the roof. If we mess around too long they'll see what we're up to, and if they surge toward the van I'm not going to be able to hold them back."

He watched Erik give Mrs. Danick and Freya a lift up, followed by Mara.

"Erik, give Gabe a boost up next. I want you up last. Get ready to lift me up. The second I let go of this door they're going to be in, and I don't want to be here for that. Take my axe with you." He didn't trust Gabe would help him up and wanted Erik to be the last one through. Something inside Gabe had switched, and Jonas no longer trusted him. When they were back with Quinn, safely away from Utica, he would tell him it was time to split up.

"Got it, buddy."

Javier said nothing and followed Rose up through the skylight. Erik disappeared next, and Jonas heard him call back to come up.

Now or never, he thought, and he let go of the door handle. The door whipped back, and he was greeted with a cacophony of sounds, the utterances of the undead, and a wave of sickening smells that made him recoil. He jumped up onto the stove quickly, just as the first zombie crashed inside the van. It looked wild, and focused on Jonas.

"Grab my hand!"

Jonas looked up at Erik and took his hands. He jumped from the stove and felt Erik lifting him through the air to safety. As his head disappeared up outside of the van, he felt the zombie below grab his feet.

"Erik, pull me up, quick!" Jonas felt frantic, and kicked out with both legs, trying to free himself of the zombie's grasp, desperate to make sure he wasn't bitten.

"Quit moving around like that," said Erik as he struggled to lift Jonas up.

Jonas could imagine the teeth of the creature below sinking into his calves, ripping his legs open as he dangled there like a fish on a hook. He would probably die of blood loss before he became one of them. It would really fucking hurt, though, and he kicked again, sure he had connected with the thing's head that time.

"Nrgh," shouted Erik, and he heaved Jonas up onto the roof of the van. Mrs. Danick helped pull him up, and they collapsed into a pile together.

Jonas looked down at his legs. Nothing. He hadn't been bitten. Erik had pulled him up just in time.

"You okay?" asked Mrs. Danick.

"Yeah," said Jonas breathlessly. "Yeah, I am. Thanks, both of you."

He looked across at the roof of the nearby store at Gabe. He was staring at the crowd of dead around them. From the way he had been behaving lately, he hadn't really expected Gabe to help. Mara either. They were both acting oddly.

"We can chat later. Right now, we have to run." Erik pulled Jonas to his feet, and they all jumped over to the roof. The gap between the store and the van was mere inches, and the transition was easy, even for Mrs. Danick.

"Freya, come here, honey," said Erik.

"It's okay, I've got her." Rose smiled. "I'll look after her for you."

"Thanks. You be good, Freya. I just need to help Uncle Hamsikker, but I'm right here. You let me know if you want anything." Erik ruffled his daughter's curly hair, and felt bad about leaving her with Mara, but he knew he was going to be needed, and carrying Freya was going to slow him down. They weren't out of the woods yet.

"I think I see Quinn," said Javier pointing west.

"What the hell is she doing way over there?" asked Mrs. Danick.

"My guess is she got stuck. She must've drawn the zombies away enough to give us time to get out of the hotel but then not been able to swing around to pick us up. You can see how many there are."

Jonas looked at the dead below them. Hundreds of them filled the immediate road, and it looked like a wild party was going on. They jostled and pushed each other, all trying to get to the van. None had worked out how to climb up, of course, so for the moment, Jonas knew they were safe. He peered at the van in the distance. It was Quinn all right.

"She's probably had to drive halfway across town to find a way back to us." Jonas tried to work out her route. There was a major artery running southwest along the edge of town that looked clear. From there, a smaller road would lead Quinn right to them. It would also lead her right into the masses of dead walking the streets.

"That way. Look, see where she's heading? We need to get over the other side of the street where it's clearer. If we can do it quietly without attracting their attention, we could make it."

"Could," said Javier. "*Could.*"

"I don't see any other option." Erik looked at Freya. He had to get her out of here. He looked at the roof they stood on. It was flat, but veered upward as it reached the center of the store. "Here's what we do. We use the roofs to get around. If we stay quiet, they won't be able to tell what we're doing. I figure we're only around the corner from the hotel, right? So over the other side of this building there's what, another one or two buildings before we reach the hotel? We can do this. We're not going to find any zombies up here."

"Quinn will be here soon. We should go." Jonas looked at Mrs. Danick who was nodding in agreement.

"I can do that," she said. "Just promise me you'll give me a foot rub later," she said winking at Erik.

"We get out of this, I'll rub whatever you want," said Erik.

"Gabe? Mara? You with us?" Jonas had to ask. They had said little. Mara was cooing over Freya, whispering in her ear and stroking her cheeks. Gabe was just looking at the swarming dead below them.

"Yeah, we're with you," said Javier. For now, he thought. He needed that van Quinn was driving. There was no other way out of town, so they were going to have to stick together just a little longer.

"Right then. Follow my lead. Be quiet." Jonas picked up his axe, and Erik took Freya back from Mara. They then set off up the roof carefully.

Jonas scrambled up the incline as fast as he dared. He didn't want to slip, fall down, and break a leg. The flat aspect of the roof was asphalt, but the incline was tiled, and it was difficult to grip without the tiles coming loose. In places, they were covered with dry moss that crumbled away in his hands. Soon he was at the apex, and he held out a hand for Erik who was immediately behind him. He helped Erik over, and watched him slide down the other side with Freya hanging onto his back. The roof ended abruptly, but the building was buttressed up against the next one, and the alley that split the buildings was no more than three or four feet across.

Jonas helped the others over and noticed that Mara refused to make eye contact with him. Was she still annoyed that he had rejected her back at the hotel?

As Javier climbed over the summit of the roof, he sat astride the tiles and looked at Hamsikker. "You'd better be right about this. If Quinn abandons us…"

"She won't." Jonas was tired of defending her. He was tired of justifying everything to Gabe. "Back in the van - when you said we needed a diversion - what did you mean? You weren't going to help me pull the door closed were you? You were going to push it open."

Javier smiled, said nothing, and slid off the roof after Mara.

"Dick," muttered Jonas, and he joined them at the edge of the building.

Erik and Freya were already across, and Mara jumped over next.

"This isn't over," Jonas said to Gabe as he looked at the alley below. "We need to talk."

"Sure thing. You know me. I'm all sweetness and light." Javier jumped across the void, leaving Jonas to bring up the rear.

The next roof was flat too, populated by an air conditioning unit and more skylights. Jonas couldn't help but look down as they passed, and he realized they must be walking across the roof of a café. Inside were tables and chairs. A figure flitted across his vision, running somewhere inside, but he wasn't interested in looking too closely. Their footsteps on the rooftop would probably make a lot of noise to any zombie still trapped inside.

As they neared the edge of the building, Jonas could see the hotel in front of them blocking out the sunlight like some monument to a false God. It was only four stories high, and they were coming out at the side of it near the car park. He could hear Quinn getting closer. The engine noise was faint but unmistakable. Erik was looking down at the yard beneath them.

"It's a long drop, Hamsikker." Erik could tell it was too far to jump. It had to be twenty feet up, and the concrete ground was far from welcoming.

"We could use that to get down," said Rose.

Jonas saw what she was looking at. Around the corner of the café was a delivery truck. It was close enough that they could drop onto the hood and get down safely.

"Smart," muttered Jonas. "Everyone follow Mara. Get moving."

One by one they dropped silently onto the truck and then to the ground. Jonas helped Freya down into Erik's waiting hands. As he passed the downstairs window, Jonas thought he sensed movement again from inside the café. There was a net curtain hanging over the small window, yellowing and stained from being exposed to the sun over the years, and it moved faintly.

"Leave it," said Mrs. Danick. "I saw it too. Whoever's in there is long gone."

They ran to the front of the hotel and were relieved to find the street clear. The zombie horde had followed them right around the corner, and left the street in front of the hotel clear. Suddenly Quinn came around the corner, the tires screeching as she raced up to them.

"Finally," said Javier. He fingered the gun that lay quietly waiting by his waist.

As he watched Quinn come to a halt in front of them, Jonas thought he heard a cry and turned back to the café. He couldn't see anyone, but he swore it sounded like a voice. It almost sounded like someone asking for help, but he was sure he was mistaking it for something else, perhaps a door swinging shut or an animal cornered by the dead, whimpering for its life. The hotel loomed ominously over them, and he remembered that Terry was inside. There was no way they could help him now, and as much as Jonas wished he could afford to give him a decent burial, it was just too hard. It would only be a few seconds until the dead heard the engine noise and found them again.

"Oh my God, are you okay? We tried to turn back for you, but the streets were too thick with them." Quinn jumped out of the van, leaving the engine running. "We had to circle around the whole damn town." She opened the van's side door and helped Mrs. Danick inside.

Dakota and Pippa jumped out of the van, too, and ran up to their respective husbands.

Jonas saw Pippa embrace both Erik and Freya. They were a true family, united by not just grief for Peter, but a love that he barely knew. He loved Dakota more than anything, but it felt sometimes as if something was missing. Maybe the baby would change all that and bring them closer.

Dakota held him tightly. "I was so worried. Are you sure you're okay?"

"Yeah, I'm fine. It was getting hairy back there, but we got through it together."

"Jonas, where's Terry?" Quinn watched as Erik, Pippa and Freya clambered into the back of the van, and only then did she realize they were one short.

Jonas simply shook his head.

"Oh honey." Dakota held him tight again. "When will it end? I want to get to Janey's too. I just want to get somewhere safe," she said.

"I know." Jonas whispered and held Dakota close. He could hear the dead coming, smell them, but he wanted that moment to last. He never wanted to let her go. She was his everything. Despite their bickering and their differences, she had always stuck by him.

"I'll give him kudos for one thing, he put up a good fight," said Javier as he ushered Rose into the passenger seat.

"What's that?" asked Quinn.

"Oh, I was just talking about Terry. Those two zombies made short work of him. Probably still chowing down on his bony ass right now, but he put up a good fight. I watched him, but I wasn't about to waste a bullet on him."

Quinn looked at Gabe with her mouth open. She was about to tell him to get in the back, when she stopped. It almost sounded like he was proud of it, proud that he had seen Terry die.

"What?" Jonas told Dakota to get in the van. "Gabe, I don't think we need to hear this. Terry was a good man. He's been with us a long time, so show the man a little respect, will you?"

Javier began to walk around to the driver's seat.

"Hey, what do you think you're doing?" Quinn followed him. "I'm driving. I'm perfectly capable. Get in the back."

"I'm driving from now on. In fact, I'm doing the driving, the decision-making, and whatever else needs to be done from here on in. So *you* get in the back. You're not Rosa Parks, so hush down, and sit in the back like a good little woman."

"Hamsikker, are you hearing this?" Quinn was furious, and she looked at Jonas for support.

Jonas could see the dead coming now. They had discovered that their prey had given them the slip, but the noise of the engine had brought them right back. He walked up to Gabe who was standing beside the open driver's door.

"Gabe, you started pulling this shit back there, but it's time to stop. Quinn is a better driver than any of us. I don't know what goes through your head sometimes. Come on, just get in back, and…"

"Please."

"Say what?" Jonas could see that Gabe was enjoying this. It was as if he wanted to fight. Jonas held his axe down by his leg, making sure he kept it there. If he got riled up he was liable to take off Gabe's head.

"Please. It was the last thing Terry said before I let him die. He pleaded with me for help, but really, why would I waste my time saving an old man?" Javier took a step toward Hamsikker so they were almost nose-to-nose. Their eyes were locked together, and Javier could smell the stale sweat on Hamsikker.

"Gabe, this isn't going to work out. I've tried, we all have, and I really hoped we could make a go of it. When I think back to Saint Paul's and how you helped me, well, we're forever in your debt for that. But maybe it would be best for us to go our different ways. You and Mara seem to be coping well enough on your own, and I'm not sure hanging out with us is the best option for you right now." Jonas thought it was worth a shot. Maybe Gabe would reason with diplomacy, see that there was no need for all this animosity.

Javier laughed. He couldn't help it. It sounded like Jonas was dumping his high-school sweetheart. "I'm sorry, go on."

"It's just that we all have our own issues to deal with, and it feels like we're not on the same wavelength, you know? I think we should make a break now. We'll split up what we have. I'm not looking at taking anything that isn't ours. I'm sure you probably feel the same way, right?"

Javier rubbed his eyes and began laughing again. He exhaled slowly, trying to get himself under control. "Sorry, honestly, I didn't mean to…"

Jonas had expected a reaction from Gabe, but not laughter.

"You see, I can see your lips moving, and you stand there looking all forlorn as if you just accidentally drove over a little puppy, but the fact of the matter is all I hear is shit pouring out of your mouth." Javier regained his composure. "You still don't get it, do you? You're trying to be all sympathetic, but you don't have to play nice anymore, Hamsikker. Those days are gone. You know what you should've done? Hm?"

Jonas was taken aback. Gabe wasn't laughing anymore. Suddenly he seemed very confident and not at all surprised at Jonas's suggestion that they split up. "What's that?"

"You should've killed me. You should've fucked my girl, killed me, and taken my gun when you had the chance. Then you and your little gang would've been fine."

Jonas sensed the heat rising through his cheeks. He felt like he was being scolded. His father used to berate him like that all the time, always telling him what he should do, what he shouldn't do, what he should've done. At least he only used words. Janey suffered far worse. "Listen, Gabe, before you say something you regret, why don't you and Mara just leave. We'll manage from here. No harm, no foul, right?"

"Did I ever tell you about my dog, Tucker?" asked Javier. "He was a stray, but I tamed him, made him my own. I taught him everything I could about living on the street."

It seemed to Jonas that Gabe was trying to wind them up. Why else would he behaving like this? Maybe the hotel had gotten to him. Maybe he was just scared, and this was all an act. It was self-defense.

"I'm sure it's a very sweet story, but I'm really not interested." Jonas was aware that the dead were getting closer. He could see in the mirror behind Gabe that they were advancing menacingly. Some were almost close enough to see the whites of their eyes.

Javier smiled and slapped Jonas on the back. "Sure thing, buddy. I guess I can fill you in on what happened to Tucker later. Why don't you hop in back with Quinn?"

Jonas watched as Javier slid in behind the wheel, tucking the Pulaski beneath the driver's seat. Jonas walked back around to Quinn. Her face was a mixture of shock and fury.

"Just what the fuck is he doing? Hamsikker, I don't like this. What was he saying about Terry? Is he for real?"

"I know, I know. I think he's lost it. Just get in will you? Let's go along with it for now. I don't know what's eating him, but we can't afford to hang around here discussing it any longer. Those things are getting way too close for comfort. If he wants to drive, just let him. When we're clear of town, we'll reassess."

"Hurry up, Hamsikker. I'm not waiting all day."

Jonas heard Gabe's order and bristled. The man had truly lost it. Jonas helped Quinn in and jumped in alongside her. The van backed up to the street as Javier prepared to turn them around. The way ahead was blocked, and they were going to have to retreat from Utica the way they had come in.

"Runners. Step on it, Gabe." Annoyed as he was, he didn't feel like being eaten alive, and Hamsikker saw three runners break away from the pack. They were running straight for the van.

As the van pulled away, Jonas heard the same voice he had heard earlier, only this time much louder.

"Stop. Wait. Please!"

The voice was female and sounded desperate. The words came out in between harsh breaths, and Hamsikker thought he was imagining it. Everyone was inside the van, so who was it? He leant out of the still open side door, and looked back at the hotel. He saw a young woman come running out from the café next door. Long dark hair flew behind her as she ran, her face pale, and her eyes red.

"Gabe, stop the van," yelled Jonas. The woman had emerged from the café and was sprinting after them. As she got closer, Jonas saw her face. She was so young, no more than fifteen or sixteen, that he couldn't believe what he was seeing. How long had she been in there, hiding away from the world?

The van began to speed up, and the girl cried for help, realizing they were going to leave her behind.

"Gabe, for fuck's sake, slow down. We can help her," said Erik. He was powerless to intervene, sandwiched into the back of the van beside his wife and daughter, but even he could see they had the time to stop and pick the girl up.

"Slow down, you idiot." Mrs. Danick reached forward and tapped Gabe on the shoulder. "Can't you see what's going on?"

They began to slow, and Jonas reached out a hand. He leant out of the van as far as he could, with his other hand gripping a seatbelt so he didn't fall.

"Run!" shouted Jonas. "We'll help you, but you've got to hurry!"

Behind the girl were three runners, and they were closing in on her. The girl was crying now, tears pouring down her face, but Jonas could see she was going to make it. She was getting closer, and he urged her on. He smiled, trying to reassure her that she would make it. He held out his hand.

"Don't look back. Just run. Come on, you can do it."

The girl reached him, and her hand briefly touched his. Her skin was cold and clammy despite the heat. Jonas could see she was in pain. The running had sapped her energy, and who knew how long she had gone without a decent meal. She must've been locked away in that café for months, living on whatever she could scrape together.

"That's it. I've got you." Jonas leant out and grabbed the girl's hand. Her dark hair stuck to her face that was covered in sweat. The burning sun had all but drained every last ounce of her energy, and Jonas urged her on. Just one final push, and he could get her in. The runners were close now, right on their tail, and he could see them snapping at the girl's heels, their arms trying to grab her.

"Jump!"

Jonas grabbed the girl's arm as she leapt into the van. At that precise moment, Javier put his foot on the accelerator. He had been watching them in the mirror, keeping a close eye on how the girl was getting on. Jonas was doing all he could, but it would never be enough. Javier stepped on the gas, and just as the girl put a foot inside the van, it lurched forward sending her tumbling backwards.

"*NO!*"

Jonas tried to grab her, and he snatched at thin air as she was pulled out of his grasp. He was agonizingly close to reaching her, and his fingers brushed her hand once more as she desperately tried to reach for him, but all he could do was watch her fall away from him.

Jonas knew that the terror in that girl's eyes would fill his nightmares for as long as he lived. Her face, so young, was etched with a fear he had often thought of, yet never experienced as fully as her. They both knew this was it for her. There would be no second chance. She was going to die now, and Jonas could do nothing to stop it. Everything seemed to happen in slow motion. The engine roared louder, and he heard himself shouting for Gabe to stop, but he knew the van was not going to stop or slow down. Jonas didn't need to look at Gabe to know this was no accident. He had sped up on purpose.

The girl landed on her back on the road, and her body bounced once. Her head was thrown back onto the tarmac, and Jonas was quite sure he heard her skull crack open. He caught one last glimpse of her eyes. They were bloodshot, and instead of terror or anger, there was confusion and sadness. She held up one arm, and the other hung limply at her side, broken in two places.

"I'm sorry," whispered Jonas.

Then they were on her.

The runners were first. Four zombies grabbed the girl, and began to feed, biting her all over. Two held her arms while the third ravaged her neck. The other dug its fingers into her eye sockets and pulled her head back. The girl's body jerked as the zombie began to rip her face from her skull, tearing the skin like rice paper, and Jonas heard a faint scream, but it soon ended. The horde of zombies engulfed her, drowning out her cries, and quickly he could see nothing of her at all. Jonas knew she would suffer. However long it took for her to die, he knew that every second would be filled with terror and agony. She had been so close. He had her in his hands, and then she had been taken away from him.

Gabe.

Jonas drew the side door closed. The van was quiet. Pippa was crying, and the horror of what had just happened settled over everyone. They had let her die. They had driven off and left a young girl to die horribly.

That bastard Gabe.

Jonas was more than angry. Any apology would be pointless. He wanted answers. Gabe had let her die, and he wanted to know why. Jonas's fingers curled around his axe. He should've taken the sadistic fucker's head off when he had the chance. Gabe probably had let Terry die, just as he'd said. Who was he? Who was this psycho? If he could do that to Terry, to a young girl, what was he capable of really? Were any of them safe?

"Gabe. Stop the van," said Jonas.

The van continued to speed up, and nobody said anything.

"Gabe. I'm not asking you. I'm telling you, stop. You saw what just happened, right?"

"Hm? Oh, yes, that. No harm, no foul, right? No, I'm not stopping. We have a plan to stick to, or had you forgotten about Canada?"

Jonas looked at Gabe. He was smiling. He was actually smiling.

"Gabe, just what are you doing? When you stop this van, I'm going to kill you."

CHAPTER FOURTEEN

"You son of a bitch, have you forgotten what's going on? Seems you're confusing right and wrong. You'd be dead if it wasn't for me, and this is how you repay us?" Jonas remembered his promise to Dakota. As much as he wanted to, he just couldn't kill Gabe. But he could cut him off. Send him packing and resume control of the group. They didn't leave people to die, that wasn't their style. Gabe was different. He lived by his own rules, and he wasn't fitting in with the group anymore.

"Really?" Javier passed Rose the gun, and told her to point it at Hamsikker. "Say that again. You were going to, what, kill me?"

Jonas looked at the gun. "Gabe, I know it's not loaded, so stop playing games. This is ridiculous." Jonas wasn't afraid. He didn't believe even if it was loaded that Mara would shoot him. "Mara, don't be a fool. Gabe's lost it. Surely you can see that? He may as well have killed that girl with his own hands. I had her. *I had her*. Look, we've got no beef with you. You can stay with us. We can help you. We can protect you."

Rose stroked a hand across Javier's cheek and cocked the gun.

"You're going to protect me?" Rose sneered. "Don't make me laugh."

"Now listen up," said Mrs. Danick. "I've just about had enough of you. Put down that gun you silly girl, and…"

Rose pulled the trigger, and the sound of the gun firing was deafening. Blood splattered Jonas's face. Screams and shouting erupted around the van, and Jonas looked around. He hadn't been hit. By rights, he should be dead, but then he saw blood pouring over Mrs. Danick, and her face had gone a deathly white.

"Put…it…" Mrs. Danick passed out, and Dakota screamed as Rose began to giggle.

"Mara, put that gun down." Jonas wiped Mrs. Danick's blood from his face. Quinn and Dakota were tending to her. Something terrible was happening, and before things got any more out of control, he had to make Mara see sense. "Listen, I know you didn't mean that. It was an accident, right? You didn't know there was a bullet left in the chamber."

"Sure. An accident." Rose couldn't stop smiling. "Trust me, I've plenty more bullets where that came from. Keep pushing, Hamsikker, and you'll find out exactly how many." Finally she had the power. Finally, she would be in charge. Javier had trusted her with the gun, and…

Rose flinched away as she caught sight of Javier's hand coming at her from the side of her eye, but she was too late. The back of his hand swept across her face with a sharp sting, and the shock of it took her breath away.

"I told you to take the gun, not to start shooting the place up. What *was* that?"

Rose was shaking. She had been so exhilarated when she'd shot Mrs. Danick, and she thought Javier would be proud of her. She looked at him, but he wasn't smiling. He looked angry. He looked angrier than she'd seen in a long time.

"I thought…I just thought I…"

Javier hit her again, and Rose fought back the tears. Her breaths came in short, sharp gasps. "I just thought…"

Javier hit her a third time. Her cheeks were glowing bright red, and her eyes were watery. She wouldn't cry, no matter what. She had messed up. She could see that now.

"I'm sorry," she said quietly. Slowly she reached out a hand to touch Javier. Her fingers brushed his shoulder before tenderly rubbing the warm back of his neck. "I'm sorry."

"Now, for once, just do what I ask. Don't start your shit up again. I'm not in the mood."

Javier swung the van around a corner in the road, and they were free of Utica.

"What a backwater shithole that place was," said Javier. "Okay, here's the deal. From now on, you guys keep quiet. I don't want to hear a peep from any of you unless I speak to you."

"What should I do?" asked Rose.

"Keep the gun on them. Just try not to shoot anyone else. If you do have to shoot anyone, make sure it's a head shot. The last thing we need is a zombie slipping around inside this damn van."

"Jonas, we need to stop. If we don't do something she's going to bleed out." Dakota was pressing a dirty rag onto Mrs. Danick's shoulder, but blood was still seeping through.

Jonas felt like he had slipped into a parallel universe, a warped version of reality which was already freaky enough without adding a couple of psychos into the mix. Gabe and Mara were acting like Mickey and Mallory. It wasn't real. They had to see what they were doing was crazy. Jonas could see Mrs. Danick sat behind him, with her blood all over Dakota. Her eyes were closed, and it looked as if she was dead. This couldn't be real. This couldn't be happening.

"Jonas, she's been hit in the shoulder. She's still alive, but we need to do something quickly."

Jonas could see Dakota was serious. Her eyes were full of fear, not for herself, but for Mrs. Danick. Jonas looked at Quinn. She looked scared. He looked at Erik who was holding his wife and daughter. There were no answers, just questions. What was going on?

Erik looked angry, and he leant forward. "You get the chance, you kill them," he whispered.

"No talking. You think I don't know you're planning something back there," said Rose. "One more word out of you, and I'll blow your brains out."

Jonas stared ahead, trying to figure things out. He kept wondering when things had gone wrong. What had happened to make Gabe flip out like this? Whatever it was, he sure had Mara convinced too. Why would she put up with him beating her like that?

"Mara, talk to me," said Jonas. He kept his voice low, and his eyes fixed on her. He thought maybe he could make her see sense. He tried to take on a soothing tone. He didn't want to come across as threatening. "Mara, we look out for each other, that's what we do. There's really no need for this. Whatever it is you want, or Gabe wants, we can help. We can…"

"Shut the fuck up. Seriously, just, like, listen to me, and shut up. I need to think. Jesus." Javier hit the driving wheel, and looked across at Rose. "One more word out of Hamsikker, and you have my permission to shoot him."

Jonas sighed. For now, he was going to have to do things their way. He still thought there was time to retrieve the situation. Gabe might come round. Mara was following his every word, but that didn't mean she would follow his every order.

Jonas looked back at Dakota. Mrs. Danick's breathing was shallow, but she was still alive. How long would she be able to hold on? There was little they could do right now, and Jonas hoped that Gabe would hurry up with what whatever it was that he was thinking about.

The land around them changed, and as they left Utica behind, Jonas saw less chance of finding any other survivors. That poor girl had been the only one lately who had even come close to living. She had been so scared when she'd fallen. She offered no threat, so why had Gabe cast her aside like that? The cracking sound of her head breaking still reverberated around his head. He could see her being pulled apart, still fighting for her life even as the zombies ripped her body open. Gabe had to answer for that. It wasn't fair. The girl had probably been squirrelled away all summer, waiting for an opportunity, waiting for the right moment to escape. And just when it seemed like she had made it, just when she thought she could relax, and she felt the touch of another human, the warmth in Jonas's hands, salvation had been snatched away from her. Her death echoed around Jonas's head, and the pictures of her last moments of agony refused to die.

They drove past fields full of dead corn and dried up wheat that no longer served any purpose. Now and again a zombie stumbled into the road, and sometimes Jonas saw small groups of them, pockets of the dead on street corners or scavenging in the fields. He saw a whole herd of slaughtered pigs, their skin flayed from their bodies, and zombies munching on the pigs' carcasses with relish. He kept looking, hoping he might see some sign of life, but all he found were the dead. The zombies ruled the world now.

He tried to think if they had anything left with which to overpower Gabe and Mara, but they had precious little. He still had his axe, and Erik the hammer, but he was quite sure that was all. Evidently Gabe had been holding onto the gun with good reason, hiding the fact he still had some ammo; wrestling it from Mara was out of the question. He couldn't afford to take the risk and get someone else shot. Quite what Gabe's motives were, Jonas didn't know, but at some point they would have to stop. Gabe wouldn't be able to drive them all the way to Canada, and when they stopped he would take his chance.

"How far from the border are we?" asked Gabe.

Erik sighed. "A long way. Couple of day's drive easily. Depends on a lot of things, but we haven't even reached the Mississippi yet. I assume you're trying to get to the Interstate?"

"None of your business. Not yet." Javier slammed on the brakes, and they came skidding to a halt. "Shit a brick."

"What's up?" asked Rose.

"Road-block." Javier sighed and unbuckled. "Nothing we can't handle. Right, Hamsikker?" Javier turned around and looked at Jonas with a glint in his eye. "You've still got that precious axe of yours, right? So get your ass out here, and help me."

Javier jumped out of the van and pulled the Pulaski out from under his seat. He pointed at Rose. "Stay here. Hamsikker's coming with me. Anyone else moves, kill them."

Jonas slid the van door back. Dakota squeezed his shoulder as he picked up the axe, and he got out of the van.

"I'll be fine. Whatever it is, I'm sure we can handle it. Stay here."

He hated leaving her, but there was no point arguing. Plus there may be an opportunity to take Gabe down. That was something he was not going to miss.

"What's going on?" asked Quinn. "This is such a crock. Just let us out. Mara? Are you listening to me?"

Rose frowned. She could shoot Quinn now, but it was too simple. She wanted to take her time. There wasn't really enough time to do anything now, not with Javier absent. She was going to have to bide her time. Rose raised a finger to her lips.

"Shush." Rose drew her gun from left to right across the van and watched as they all recoiled when the gun was trained on them. Quinn, Dakota, Erik, and Pippa: they all flinched when she pointed it at them. Finally, she left the gun in her hand pointed at Freya. The girl was the last person she'd shoot, but the others didn't know that. "We wait here. No talking. One word, and Freya bites a bullet."

"Animal," muttered Erik. He pulled Freya into him, trying to shield her from Mara, but knowing there was little he could do to stop a bullet should she shoot.

* * *

"I hope you've got a plan," said Jonas. He was looking at the road ahead of them, with Javier at his side.

They'd stopped at a bridge that crossed the Illinois River. It had to be twenty or thirty feet across and was full of zombies. An overturned garbage truck at one end barred their way, and a pile up at the other meant they were trapped.

"There's no way round," said Javier plainly. "I'm not backtracking. It could cost us hours looking for the next bridge. Plus, we're way too close to Chicago. If we get stuck on the wrong road and head east, we're going to find exactly the same thing except a hundred times bigger. We're best to clear this now."

"Even if we take all the zombies down, which isn't going to be easy, by the way, we still have to get around the vehicles. You think we can squeeze past them?"

"At a push. There's room if we use the sidewalk. The zombies are too stupid to figure it out. But we're going to have to take it slow, and with all those zombies in there, they could easily overwhelm us. Too many get in front of the van, and we'd be stuck. No, our best option is to kill as many as we can, get back to the van, and mosey along."

Jonas reckoned there to be over fifty zombies. The cars that littered the bridge should spread them out thinly, giving them enough time to take them on. It evened up the odds a little. Still, armed with just one axe, it was daunting having to face so many.

"You know, we'd be able to so this a lot quicker if we used the gun. I'll take both axes, you use the gun, and…"

"Oh, please, I'm not stupid, Hamsikker. I give you this axe, and you'll start getting ideas above your station. No, we do this my way. One weapon each. You go ahead, and I'll follow."

"Oh, yeah, well I'm not stupid either, Gabe." Jonas knew full well that Gabe would leave him hanging and had no intention of going out there first. He didn't doubt any longer that Gabe had let Terry die. The man had flipped out. "We clear this together. Side by side."

"Need I remind you who's in charge here? Get out there, Hamsikker, and stop delaying. Those crispy zombies are waiting."

"Gabe, I'm not going out there alone."

"Hamsikker," said Javier quietly. "I didn't want to bring this up, but, you know, I kind of feel like you're forcing my hand here."

Jonas could hear the dead banging on the vehicles ahead, walking into them, trying to find a way out. The longer they delayed this, the more chance they would bring more of the dead with the noise they made. "What are you talking about? Look, we need to..."

"I know what you think. Back off. Run away. But if we go back, then we end up losing yet more time. I can't do that. I *won't* do that."

"If you think I'm going to stroll up there and start taking them on without any support, you're even crazier than I thought. You want me to do this? Well I'm telling you we need to do it together." Jonas was exasperated.

"What do you think, this is fucking Disneyland?" asked Javier. "Get out there and slaughter some fucking zombies. You know what, Hamsikker, back at Saint Paul's when we were opening the gate, there was a zombie. Remember?"

"Sure I do." Jonas was trying to figure out if there was a way he could convince Gabe that what they were doing was near suicidal. It didn't seem like there was any reasoning with him anymore. Jonas was also worried about Mara. He couldn't trust her, and while she had that gun anything could happen. Every second they waited was a second they were closer to danger.

"I saved your ass. I put a bullet in its head before it took you down. Now, I'm asking you to return the favor. We had a deal, Hamsikker. That's how you survive when you're part of a team. I scratched your back..."

Jonas remembered it differently. They had worked together in killing that zombie, and if anything, it had been Jonas who had saved Gabe's life. The deal was getting to Canada together, not taking on an army of the dead.

"Deal's off, Gabe, I'm not going out there. I like to think we've got each other's back, or at least we used to, but this? This is insane. Find another route."

Javier appeared to think it over. Jonas could see something ticking over in the man's mind.

"You know, what, I can't force you. Let's go back to the van."

Javier turned toward the van, and Jonas followed him, surprised that Gabe had caved.

"Goodbyes are hard, that's what my Mom used to say," said Javier. "Of course, she was a drug addict whore, so what did she know? Personally, I find saying goodbye quite easy. Do you?"

"Huh?"

"Am I speaking French? I said, do you find saying goodbye hard? I was just wondering how hard it was going to be for you to say goodbye to your wife."

"Gabe, what are you talking about?"

"Well, as soon as we get back to the van, I'm going to kill Dakota. I'm going to drag her out onto the road and chop her up into pieces while you watch. Then, when I'm done, I'm going to start on your friends. Of course, you won't be able to stop me, not with my girl holding a gun to your head."

"Gabe, stop it. Stop this."

"I think I'll save Freya 'til last. Should be interesting to see how she copes with seeing her parents chopped up. Maybe I'll leave enough of her Mom to reanimate. Now *that* would be interesting."

"Enough!" Jonas stopped and raised his axe. "Fine. I get it. I'll go."

Javier smiled and pointed toward the amassed zombies on the bridge. "Ladies first."

As Jonas walked toward the pile of broken cars and trucks, the zombies spilling from the sides of them like ants scurrying around their nest, he knew he was unlikely to get back to Dakota if Gabe had his way. He would sell him down the river, just like he had Terry. If he was going to make it through this, he was going to have to do it his own way. To hell with Gabe, the man was certifiable. He seemed to have Mara under his spell too.

The first zombie Jonas took down was easy. A thin woman, slow on her feet, took the axe through her jaw and fell like a stone. The next was a little harder: an old man, his body shriveled and withered, his skin pale and greasy, took two blows to go down. After that it became increasingly difficult. They came at him in quick succession. Men and women, black and white, all of them waving their arms, all of them grinding their teeth, and all of them focused solely on him. He tried to use the vehicles for cover, keeping his back pressed up against them so he couldn't be snuck up on. He kept the zombies in his line of sight so he could pick them off one or two at a time. He didn't need any surprises, and had to contain his rage, to maintain a cool head as he fought. He didn't think beyond the next zombie. If he thought about how many there were, about how insurmountable it was, he would feel overwhelmed. Instead, he locked his eyes on the next zombie, raised his axe, and killed it.

When one pocket was done, he moved on, and trod carefully. So many body parts and pieces of metal from smashed cars littered the road that he didn't want to trip and find his face buried in a zombie's grasp. Jonas swiveled on his feet and ventured forward, knowing there was no going back. Gabe was somewhere behind him, but Jonas knew that the coward wasn't putting himself in harm's way. Gabe would stay well back. Jonas just hoped that Gabe wasn't getting back in the van and driving off.

"Like having my own soldier," said Javier as he watched Hamsikker fight. He stayed on the road, just outside of the crash zone, ready to pick off any stragglers. If any zombies got past Hamsikker, he didn't want them getting to the van.

One zombie that had been caught under a vehicle heard Javier's voice and crawled out. Its body was emaciated, weathered by being out in the open for so long, and deep cuts and gashes were evident from head to toe. The extended belly had blown out, spilling entrails and intestines which waved around its knees and legs like a hula skirt. Javier saw it coming and wondered how it had got past Hamsikker.

"Tut tut, Hamsikker. You missed one." Javier let it get up close, so close he could feel the stench of death wash over him, and then he smashed it. The Pulaski's blade sank through the zombie's brittle bones like a sharp knife through warm butter, and when the zombie was dead, Javier yawned. Killing was too easy. This world had taken all the fun out of it.

Jonas wiped the sweat from his brow. His arms were trembling, but he couldn't stop. He couldn't go back to Gabe without having finished off the dead. Swathes of them were cut down, line after line tumbling like dominoes. To Jonas it resembled something out of a war movie, with dozens of soldiers climbing from their damp trenches only to be mown down before they had a chance to fight. The dead came at Jonas constantly, wave after wave of them. There had to be even more than they'd thought.

"Gabe, where are you? I could use some help," panted Jonas.

He and Erik should've been more prepared. They had thought the threat from Gabe and Mara was minimal, so they'd given up their weapons and risked everything. He hoped the others were still waiting. He hadn't heard the van's engine, but he couldn't be sure of anything. His face was covered in blood, and the air was full of terrible groaning sounds as more of the dead attacked him.

If they had left, then what? Erik would do what he could to protect the group. He would fight, kill if he had to. But they were at a disadvantage, and Gabe knew it. Gabe had the upper hand, and Jonas couldn't figure out how he was going to get out of this.

"Gabe!" The zombies seemed to be spurred on by something, and another wave of them crashed into him like a long line of bugs, all following the leader. Jonas swung his axe, dismembering arms and heads from their owners, leaving chunks of meat lying in pools of blood on the road. One tore his shirt, ripping off several buttons, and another almost succeeded in biting his flesh, but Jonas ducked and weaved, dodging them like a boxer, remaining light on his feet. Slowly, slowly, their numbers began to drop.

All of a sudden, they stopped. As he took the last zombie down, a small boy with fair hair and blue eyes, they ceased completely. Jonas sank to his knees. He looked up at the road ahead. It was clear. He had done it. He had fought them all, and won.

Gabe.

The man hadn't lifted a finger, hadn't helped at all. Jonas got to his feet wearily. He was drenched in blood, and spat out thick saliva. Was this some sort of joke? A test? Jonas glanced around him, hoping he might see something in one of the cars he could take. If only he could stumble across a gun, he could regain the advantage. As he looked around, he heard a noise. A faint rumbling that grew louder as he walked amongst the smashed cars. He shook his head, and the van pulled up slowly on the sidewalk.

The side door slid open, and Mara was sat there pointing the gun at him, grinning from ear to ear.

"Need a lift?"

CHAPTER FIFTEEN

"How's she doing?" asked Jonas as he hopped into the van. It was warm inside, and he was aware that he was covered in blood. Mrs. Danick looked terrible and was still unconscious.

"I really don't know," said Dakota. "I've tried to stop the bleeding, but she really needs proper medical attention. Maybe if we…"

"All right, cut it out." Javier brought the van back onto the road with a bump, and they began to speed up, leaving the grisly carnage behind them. "See what happens when we work together?"

"I'd hardly call that working together," said Jonas as he wiped his face. "You stood and watched me do all the hard graft."

"It's called delegation, Hamsikker. No point in me getting my hands dirty when I've got you to do it for me."

"So that's how this is going to work? You kidnap us and force us to kill as many zombies as we can, just so you can go on a wild goose chase to find your brother?"

"Something like that. You can dress it up however you like." Javier found himself coming up onto the Interstate and smiled. "Now we're getting somewhere. Finally."

"Nice work, honey." Rose waved the gun around, enjoying watching the rest of the group in the back squirm. "So from here on in, not a peep. Understand?"

They drove on silently for a few minutes, and the road opened out before them. There were precious few cars around, and they managed to pick up some speed.

Erik nudged Jonas in the back, and pointed out of the left window. He whispered into Jonas's ear. "That's the regional airport. We're not heading north. That idiot's going to lead us into Princeton. That's several thousand zombies just waiting for us, man. We've got to do something."

Jonas could hear the worry in Erik's voice. "You sure?" he asked.

"Sure as I know Gabe's done a deal with the devil. He took a wrong turn back there and brought us up onto I80 instead of I39. We passed La Salle five minute ago."

"Uh, Mara, can I say something?" Jonas leant forward. "I hate to tell you this, but you're going the wrong way."

"Sure we are. I guess you want us to head on back to Jeffersontown." She turned to Javier. "You want me to snag him?"

"I'm not kidding here. Jesus, just listen to me. We need to get off this road, quick."

Jonas saw a small airport disappearing fast behind them and the van whistled past a golf course. Stooping figures shambled across the greens, slowly pursuing the van, but they had no chance of reaching it. Jonas saw two zombies fall into a sandpit, and then he looked up to see a large road sign announcing Princeton was 21 miles away.

"Gabe, get us off…"

Suddenly a gas tanker loomed up ahead of them in the road, its front end a crumpled mess, tangled up with the highway barriers and a delivery van. Javier saw the exit just in time, and took them off the Interstate. Following the curve of the road, he slowed down, and the road narrowed into a straight line.

Pleased they were finally heading away from Princeton, Erik realized they were now heading south, which was really no better. They were going to find themselves in a dead-end when they met the Illinois River, and he had to somehow convince Gabe to get them back heading the right way. He didn't want them to end up driving in circles. "Gabe, take a left. We can cut through Spring Valley, and go back to…"

"I'm not going *back*." Javier swung the van round a hard right corner, jolting everyone out of their seats.

"Slow down a little, honey, or you're going to get us all killed," said Rose. "Please?"

Javier slowed down a little. "I don't need everyone telling me what to do or how to drive. Got it?" The town of De Pue came up to greet them, and Javier saw the burning buildings in the distance. He had to admit he was frustrated. It felt like Diego was only getting further away, and he knew he had to stop and check what direction to go. He didn't want that cop telling him what to do, but maybe he could find a map and check.

Javier swung the van to the left before they reached the town center and travelled down the road a short way. He brought the van to a screeching halt. At the end of the road he could see the Illinois River. If only he could jump in a boat and sail up to Canada. The choice now was simple: east or west. Javier was so confused that he turned the engine off and waited for inspiration. It was a mess, he knew that.

"Everyone out."

With his feet planted on the dusty ground, Javier looked around at where they were. Another dead-end town that was dying long before the zombies turned up. Laid out just before the sluggish river lay some unused rail tracks; weeds grew on the line, and the iron had rusted. A skink darted across the ground, and Javier could swear he heard the whistle of a train. It seemed to float on the wind, and he knew he was imagining things. There couldn't have been a train pass by here in months, at least. From the look of the tracks, it had probably been years.

The air was hot, and he could feel beads of sweat snaking their way down his back. Wiping his brow, Javier watched the others file out of the van one by one. Quinn and Hamsikker gently placed Mrs. Danick on the ground, propping her up with her back against the van in the shade. The old woman still held onto her handbag, but a makeup mirror and empty purse couldn't help her now. She had regained consciousness and was looking around with a frown on her face, obviously disorientated. Her eyes wore the tired look of someone who knew they were defeated.

"What do you think?" asked Rose quietly.

Her face was still red from where he'd hit her, and he stroked her cheek with his fingers. "I think we need to thin out our numbers. They're throwing me off. We need to get back on track."

Rose drew a long knife from her boots. "Can I go first?"

Javier simply nodded, and they walked back around the van to where the others were sat on the ground, sheltering in the meager shade that the van offered.

"Have you come to your senses? Are you going to find some help?" asked Jonas. He looked from Gabe to Mara, searching for humanity, but finding nothing but evil.

"We're going to play a little game," said Javier crossing his arms. He wanted to kill Erik, but it was too soon. Javier had plans for Erik. The cop still had his uses. "I'll let Mara explain. No need to get trigger happy, just do your thing, sweetheart."

Pippa clutched Freya to her. "I'm not letting you harm my daughter. I don't know what you people did to my boy, but if you so much as look at my daughter the wrong way I'll kill you. You hear me? Just leave us alone!"

Javier walked across to Pippa, reached down, and grabbed Freya's arm. He pulled her easily from Pippa's weak grip.

"No!" Pippa fell to the ground and began sobbing.

Erik kept his head bowed and spoke clearly. "Gabe, if you harm my daughter..."

"You'll what? Arrest me?" Javier tossed Freya to Rose. "Put her in the van. She's coming with us."

Freya looked back at her mother, but was too weak to resist. Jonas could see the pain etched onto Erik's face and didn't know how the man managed to resist the urge to attack Gabe, even with a gun in his face.

Rose effortlessly picked the girl up, and put her gently in the back of the van. "Don't worry, cupcake, we're going to look after you."

Jonas thought Freya was going to speak, but all she did was look sorrowfully out of the window as Rose slammed the side door shut. The girl couldn't possibly understand what was going on. Hell, Jonas didn't know if he understood what was happening. Gabe and Mara were on a different planet. What did they think they hoped to achieve by kidnapping Freya and abandoning the others in the desert?

"Gabe, I'm warning you," said Erik. He lifted his face and looked calm. Jonas could see he was seething, but he realized that if he attacked Gabe he would likely be shot, and then he would never be able to help his daughter. "You need to stop this now, before it goes too far. Just talk to me, okay, buddy? Let's just talk this out."

Suddenly Pippa jumped up and screamed. "Leave my daughter alone!"

Pippa raced towards Javier, and before anyone had time to react, Rose fired three rounds off, hitting Pippa twice in the stomach and putting one into the shoulder. Pippa crashed to the ground, kicking up a dust storm as her body cartwheeled. Jonas felt like he was watching it in slow motion. One minute Pippa was running, the next she was on the ground with the life bleeding out of her.

Erik jumped to his feet, and Rose pointed the gun at him. "Don't."

Jonas became aware that Dakota was crying, and he looked at Erik, who was eyeballing Gabe. Jonas didn't doubt for one second that Erik was not about to stand there and wait whilst his wife died.

"You'd better have enough bullets for all of us. If I get my hands on you…" Quinn was tensed up, her arms and legs ready to fight, her body poised like a cat about to jump on its prey.

"Gabe, I'm going to my wife. You want to stop me, you better put a bullet in me right now," announced Erik.

Erik walked over to Pippa and knelt over her. Jonas couldn't see Pippa moving, and he knew he was unlikely to see her move again. Was this real? Was he having another bad dream? The heat on his neck told him this was real, but he couldn't believe Gabe was doing this.

"Rose, come here."

Rose walked sheepishly across to Javier. He smiled at her, and then slapped her face so hard that she stumbled backwards and tripped, ending up with her ass in the dirt.

"*Don't* do that again. Please?" Javier looked at Rose with disdain. He was tiring of all of them, and her inability to follow his simple instructions was beginning to grate.

"Rose?" asked Jonas. "What are you talking about, Gabe?" Was Gabe suffering from some sort of delirium? Had he flipped out so badly that he didn't know who he was or where he was anymore?

"I'm sorry, Javier, but she was going to take her away from me," said Rose. "I'm sorry, honey," she said as she rubbed her face. Her cheek was cut, and a thin line of blood splashed across her face. She held up the gun as if it were a peace offering.

"Later." Javier snatched it from her. "You and I are going to have a little talk. Understand?"

Rose nodded, all too aware what that meant. Javier did his talking with his hands. It was something she had grown accustomed too. He wasn't the first man to beat her, and it was better than being alone.

"Javier?" As if he had been doused in cold water, suddenly Jonas understood. Mrs. Danick had been right all along. "Your name's not Gabe, is it? You and Rose killed him. Mara, too, I'm guessing. Jesus, how could I have been so stupid. All this time…"

"What?" Dakota's tears were falling into the dust, and her voice was faint. "What's happening?"

"These two were never high school sweethearts. They're just a couple of common thugs." Mrs. Danick sighed. "I didn't have the convictions of my beliefs to follow it through, but I knew something was up. Something about their story just never rang true."

"Just who are you freaks? What the hell are you doing?" Quinn was aching to get up and fight. She was beginning to think she might be able to reach Javier before he could shoot.

Jonas watched Javier's face as they talked. The man never looked shocked, concerned, or angry; he was calm and cold and waiting for his time to speak. He almost looked amused, as if this was all some game.

Javier pointed his gun into the air and fired. The gunshot rang out around the valley, and everyone stopped talking. "Now that we are clear on that, it's time to get a few others things cleared up," he said. "Firstly, I am Javier, and this is Rose. I appreciate you must be a little confused, but it's really down to your own stupidity. I mean, who trusts a complete stranger nowadays?"

Rose giggled, and Jonas noticed she was looking longingly at the van, at Freya. The girl had her face buried in her hands. Had she even seen what had happened to her mother? Erik was still cradling Pippa, and Jonas had no idea if she was even still alive.

"We needed help in getting this far, and I hadn't intended to cut the journey short this early, but you were just *so* annoying." Javier stooped to give Rose a hand up. She clung onto him as he helped her up, and they held each other for a moment.

"You killed Cliff because he was a threat, right?" Dakota whispered in Jonas's ear.

"No. I mean yes, he was a threat, and that's why I told myself that what I did was okay, but..." Jonas looked at Dakota and hoped that what he said next wouldn't drive a wedge between them. "I killed him because he deserved it. Call it revenge, getting even, call it what you want, I don't care. He deserved it."

"I've changed my mind," said Dakota. She pulled Jonas closer, and wiped his face.

"What's that?"

"Remember when I told you to promise me you wouldn't kill again, that you wouldn't take another life?"

Jonas nodded.

Dakota looked at Javier. "I want you to kill that bastard."

Jonas looked at Dakota. She wasn't joking. Her face was full of worry.

"Rose too. If you don't, I will. Javier fooled us all. He tricked his way into our lives. Cliff was a thug and an idiot, but Javier is a manipulative son-of-a-bitch. They're killers. Despite everything, we were a group, a family, and we stuck together. He's ruined all of that. I don't doubt he killed Terry; probably Peter too. Look at Pippa. Oh Jesus, I can't believe this. Jonas, if we give them time, they'll kill us all. Kill him, Jonas. I want him dead."

"So where were we? I hope you're not plotting anything." Javier waved the gun menacingly. "That would be a *bad* idea."

"She's slipping away," said Erik. He slumped back, and Jonas could see what he meant. Pippa's face was pale, and her eyes closed. It was only going to be a matter of time before she passed.

"Moving on, Rose is going to play a little game with Quinn." Javier couldn't care less about Pippa. Quinn was dispensable, too, and Rose was caressing her knife with such eagerness Javier knew he couldn't hold her back any longer.

"Stick, or twist, Quinn?" Rose licked her lips, and sunlight glinted off the knife as she approached Quinn.

The sound of the gun left a ringing noise in Jonas's ears, and at first he didn't realize what had happened. He knew for a fact that

Javier hadn't fired. Rose had been walking toward them, undoubtedly ready to kill Quinn, when she spun away from them. Her face was torn apart by the first bullet, and the next ripped open her chest. A cascade of blood fell to the ground as she collapsed, dead before she hit the ground.

"Fuck you," said Mrs. Danick. She had pulled the gun from her handbag when Javier and Rose had been arguing, unaware what she had been doing. Everyone had forgotten she had it, so discreetly tucked away in her handbag was it, and even she hadn't been sure if it was still loaded. She turned the gun on Javier, pleased to see the surprise in his face. The shock that had embraced Javier spread to an ice-cold fear as he stared at Mrs. Danick. The old woman. That was how Rose died? That was how *he* died?

Mrs. Danick pulled the trigger, and her gun clicked empty. She pulled the trigger again, and again, but she knew her luck had run out.

Javier looked down at Rose's dead body. She had been knocked down so many times in her life that he still expected her to get up. He half expected her to get up and laugh, to give him a kiss, and carry on where she had left off. But her head was in pieces, and dark red blood poured from her chest where the bullet had ripped her open. She would never be getting up again.

"You." Javier angrily spat out the word, and pointed the gun at Mrs. Danick. He fired twice at close range, killing her instantly. He put both rounds straight through her skull, and Dakota screamed.

Quinn scrambled away from the van, and Jonas dragged Dakota away, too, trying to get away from the firing.

"Stop!" Javier swung the gun around. "Nobody move."

Dakota was trembling, horrified, unable to comprehend what she was witnessing. "What did you just do? What did you just do?" She kept repeating it over and over as her brain tried to absorb what had just happened.

Jonas pushed Dakota behind him and stood up. He walked toward Javier, no longer thinking of the consequences, just wanting to put a stop to the madness.

"Jonas, don't!" screamed Dakota.

Jonas didn't even hear her as he marched toward Javier. He ignored the bodies of Pippa, Rose, and Mrs. Danick, and looked at Javier's eyes. The man showed no remorse, and Jonas knew if he didn't do something now, he wouldn't stop. The lazy heat surrounded him, and he heard the whispering moans of the dead carrying over the wind. The sound of the gunshots had carried far and wide, alerting the zombies to their presence. The sun had dried out the crusty earth, and every step he took seemed to crackle with energy. He had to end this now.

"Javier…"

Javier punched Jonas square on the side of the jaw, sending him reeling backwards. Dakota screamed, and there were gasps of horror from Quinn and Erik as blood spurted from Jonas's broken nose. Blood fell to the dusty ground in great big globs.

Jonas was caught off guard, and he tumbled backward. Tripping over his heels, he crashed to the ground painfully.

Erik jumped up, and Javier whipped out his gun. He pointed it at Erik's head.

"I don't think so. Back off, big guy."

"Javier, stop this. Please. Like Hamsikker said, we go our own ways. Let's call it a day. Nobody's going to stop you. Just let Freya out, take the van, and go."

Jonas got back on his feet and clenched his fists. Javier could see that both Hamsikker and Erik were ready to take him on. The cop had plenty of practice taking down armed criminals, and Javier knew better than to try to play this out. Erik would keep him talking, try to make him see sense, whereas Jonas would simply try and fight. It was a fight that Javier would be happy to engage in, knowing Hamsikker would never win.

"Get down on your knees. All of you," ordered Javier. "Now."

"You can't be serious," said Hamsikker. "You're kidding, right? You're going to execute all of us?"

Javier pointed the gun at Hamsikker. He looked at Rose's inanimate body and felt the pain burning in his chest. "I despise you, all of you. To me you're just cockroaches and rats, scavenging what you can from the rotten debris of humanity. Everything you do, everything you say, you're pathetic. All you think about is yourself; what can *I* get out this. Oh, what's the point? I thought I could convince you to see things my way, but I'm not going to waste my breath."

Javier pulled the trigger, and the gunshot echoed across the Illinois River.

Jonas could feel the wetness of his own blood begin to seep through his shirt. He hadn't felt any pain when the bullet entered his body, just a slight pinch of the skin, as if a bee had stung him. It was all over in a split second. There was no pain, just a sense of lightness, of the world falling away beneath his feet, and then he fell. The clear blue sky cartwheeled above him, and he felt the hard ground rush up to meet his body.

Dakota rushed to her husband on her hands and knees, ignoring the stones and gravel that cut her hands.

"Jonas, talk to me." She could see Jonas's eyelids fluttering as he struggled to maintain consciousness. She ran her hands over his chest, trying to find where the bullet had entered his body. "God damn it, Jonas, stay with me."

CHAPTER SIXTEEN

Javier was watching Dakota, wondering who to shoot next. With Hamsikker out of the way, he thought he should probably finish off the family line and take out Dakota. That was when Erik took his chance. He lunged at Javier, and both men tumbled to the ground. Erik threw a succession of quick punches, some of which hit their mark, some of which missed. He knew he had scored some good hits, though, and was sure he felt Javier's nose break. He had motivation in spades, and kept Javier's arms out of reach, ensuring the gun was well away. Erik used his stronger right arm to pound Javier's side, causing him to drop the gun. Erik was just about to lay into Javier, to let him know how he really felt, when he sensed a stinging in the side of his head.

"Umph."

Javier curled his hand around the rock, and struck Erik again, knocking him off balance. The skin around Erik's temple split open, and Javier pushed the dazed man off him. He grabbed his gun, and kicked Erik in the stomach.

Seeing Quinn running at him from the corner of his eye, Javier whirled around and pointed the gun straight at her. Quinn skidded to a halt and stared him down.

"Playtime's over," said Javier, coughing. He spat out a stringy, gooey lump of phlegm and blood as the pain from the beating Erik had given him started to kick in. The contusions around his jaw were forming into black and blue shapes, and the blood in his mouth was warm and sweet.

"What happened to sweetness and light? What happened to trust?" asked Quinn.

Javier laughed. "Sweetness and light? Don't make me laugh. You guys are living in cuckoo land. That shit went out about the same time as all the lights. This is a land of darkness now. You need guts, guile, and a fucking steady hand to get through this. You don't need friends or someone to hold your hair back when you puke, you just need a big fucking gun and even bigger balls. Sweetness and light? You crack me up."

"Why don't you just leave us?" Dakota helped Jonas up. Despite her protestations, he refused to stay down. "Just go."

Javier was surprised to see Hamsikker standing. His arm was covered in blood, and Dakota had ripped off the bottom of her shirt to use it as a makeshift tourniquet.

"Looks like my aim is a little off," said Javier.

Jonas's left arm hung limply at his side, but he knew he was lucky to be alive. Three inches to the side, and he would be stone cold dead. Erik had given it his best shot, but Jonas could see he was beaten. His wife lay dying in the sun, and his daughter was trapped. Erik was curled up on the ground, nursing his aching head, and Jonas tried one last plea. "Just go, Javier. You've had your fun."

"Oh, no. After what you did to my Rose, I'm only just getting started." Javier looked at Rose. It was such an odd sensation, seeing her like that. She really had brought it upon herself. He wasn't about to make the same mistake though. It wasn't the end he'd wanted for her, but that was her reality, not his.

"What makes you think you have the right to tell any of us what to do? Just who died and put you in charge?" asked Jonas.

"Hell is the absence of God." Dakota's shoulders slumped. "We're in Hell," she whispered to herself. Despite the strong overhead sun, she was cold, and found herself longing to feel a warm pair of arms around her. How could she bring a baby into this world, into this Hell?

Javier strode up to Jonas, smiling. "Who put *me* in charge? I would've thought that was quite obvious. Your God has forsaken you. Any more questions?"

"Yeah," said Jonas. "I got one."

Javier looked at Hamsikker, studying him. Even though he'd been shot and his friends were dying all around him, he was strangely calm, not like the others. When Javier spoke most people looked away, scared to catch his eye, all too aware of the inherent violence that always threatened to erupt, but Hamsikker stared back at him.

"What is it?" Javier noticed the groaning sounds of the dead coming from apparently all around them. He was going to have to wind this up. "Well?"

"How long do you think you'll take to die once I take that gun from you?"

Javier's smile briefly faltered. Hamsikker was serious, Javier was certain of that, but he cast aside any thoughts of defeat. No, Rose had made a mistake, a deadly one, and he wouldn't do the same. Hamsikker really thought he could take Javier down, but he was mistaken.

"Dream on, Hamsikker. You're a relic. Cops and cowboys don't exist no more. Jugheads like you couldn't catch me even when you had real power. You're a nobody, Hamsikker, so keep on dreaming about how you're going to kill me. What we're doing, what we're trying to achieve here - you know we could've helped each other out. We're in the same predicament, and for a while there I almost believed we could be like...brothers. I thought underneath it all that we might be the same. Instead, you get all preachy on me, and you just bitch like the rest of your sorry group."

"We are *nothing* alike, Javier. The difference between you and me is a chasm, *almost* large enough to squeeze your ego into. The difference is that I kill to survive. I know what's right and wrong. You have no idea of morals, selflessness, or survival. Everything you do is just leading you closer to death."

"Is that so?" asked Javier. His face was stinging from the blows he and Erik had traded, and his broken nose stung. It would probably stay crooked from now on, but he was past caring. He looked to either side of the van and could see them coming. So many zombies, so many of the dead coming from both east and west that the only way to escape would be the way they came in. He would have to backtrack to get back onto the Interstate. He couldn't use the sun as a guide to find his way. It was directly overhead, cooking those dead bodies that were slowly shuffling toward them from Du Pue, Utica, and Spring Valley.

"So what's to stop me shooting you now? If I'm no more than a killer, with no regard for anyone or anything, then I should just blow your kneecaps off and feed you to those zombies, right?"

"You tell me. What *are* you waiting for?" Jonas knew this was the end. Either Javier was going to shoot him again, or there would be some sort of trade-off. Javier must want something, or they would all be dead by now. "Take away the bravado and the gun in your hand, and you're just like all the other little boys out there, running around thinking they're real men. Try looking out for someone else for once. Try fighting for something that counts, like a family. Try literally having to beat zombies to death with your bare hands, knowing if you don't your family is going to die. You could've stopped Rose, but you didn't. You let her die. You're pathetic. You're nothing but a pantomime villain."

"Me? I'm the fucking hero!" Javier launched a fist at Jonas's face, and connected sweetly with his jaw. Jonas fell back, and rolled to the ground.

"Stop it!" screamed Dakota, but Javier had seen red. Nothing was going to stop him now.

Javier aimed a boot at Jonas's head and kicked it like a football. Jonas rolled away as blood spurted from the fresh wound on his head, a cut erupting above his left eye. Another boot landed squarely on his back, and then another planted itself on the back of his head, making him see stars. He tried to scramble away, but the blows kept coming, thick and fast, and soon his face was covered in cuts and bruises. In the background he heard Dakota screaming at Javier to stop, but it was futile. Pain spread throughout his body, and he wasn't even sure if he was still conscious. He was aware of a dull thudding which was the sound of Javier's feet kicking his head. Jonas ran his tongue around his mouth, and realized he'd lost a couple of teeth. His left eye had swollen shut, and he knew there was nothing anyone could do to stop Javier. As another boot split open his lip, he rolled onto his back and looked up at the blue sky from his one open eye.

Javier watched Jonas try to get up from the ground, but the man was weak and dizzy. "You accuse me of being pathetic? Look at you. Crawling around in the dirt like a fucking pig. I don't need a gun to finish you."

Javier wiped the blood from his mouth. He felt strong. He had Jonas just where he wanted him.

"Stop it, stop it, stop it." Dakota rushed toward Javier, her salty tears stinging her eyes.

As she ran toward him, Javier screwed up his hand into a fist and planted it on the side of Dakota's face. His fist collided with her cheekbone with a smack, and with one blow he knocked Dakota out cold. Her body fell to the ground and lay in the dirt next to Jonas.

"Javier, stop this." Quinn was disgusted with Javier, yet also with herself for not stopping it sooner. She couldn't stand by and watch this anymore, just waiting for her turn. She walked toward him, her hands up defensively. "If not for us, then for yourself."

Javier looked at her, hoping she would come at him too. He was really in the mood now, and he didn't need her interfering in this. He wanted to finish Hamsikker.

"In about thirty seconds there's going to be a million zombies here. Look. You've run out of time." Quinn was barely a foot away from Javier now, and she could see Erik curled up in the fetal position beside Pippa. He had given up. Quinn was the last one who could do anything to stop this. She knew she had to stop it, and was going to have to start playing Javier at his own game. The man was a compulsive liar, and she had told enough in her time to know she could pull it off. When she had been with Roger, her whole life had been a lie. Now she was going to have to go back there and bring the old Quinn back. "Javier, let me help you. Look at you. You're in no state to drive. I can get you out of here."

Javier had to admit his strength was fading fast. The dead were getting mighty close too. He wouldn't trust Quinn for a second with his life, but he did need a driver. Maybe he could turn this situation to his advantage. "Get in the van. Take Erik with you. He's coming with us."

"What about Hamsikker? And Dakota, right? I'm not leaving them here," said Quinn folding her arms.

Javier pointed the gun at Quinn. "*Get in the van.* If you want to live to see the next sunrise, then you'll do as I say. Get Erik. Get in the van, and wait for me. You even think about driving off, and I'll put a bullet in Hamsikker and Dakota's heads."

"You're going to do that anyway, so why should I listen to you?"

Javier chuckled. Quinn had guts, he had to admit. "Fine. You promise not to drive off without me, and I promise not to kill them. Deal?"

Quinn hesitated, but she knew she couldn't argue any more. Javier would surely shoot her dead, and she reassured herself that she had at least bought them some more time. She reached down and pulled Erik to his feet. He was like a big baby and followed her unquestioningly. Quinn opened the van's side door and pushed Erik inside, where he wrapped his arms around Freya. Quinn closed the door, went around to the driver's side, and got behind the wheel. She started the engine, and tapped impatiently on the wheel.

"Come on, Hamsikker, come on," she muttered.

Jonas got to his knees and looked up. Both his eyes were almost swollen shut now, and blood caressed the side of his face, mingling with the dirt that had stuck to his cheeks. He could see Dakota next to him, unconscious, and he wished he had the energy to get up and fight Javier, but he was spent. Jonas looked at the van, at Erik and Freya tucked in the back, and he guessed it was Quinn sitting in the driver's seat.

"Well, Hamsikker, it's been fun, and credit where credit's due, you put up a fight, but it's over."

Javier kicked out once more, catching Jonas full in the face. Jonas's nose shattered, and blood squished out as he fell onto his back. Javier sank to his knees and straddled Jonas's prostrate body. He leant over his victim.

"What's that, I can't hear you," said Javier grinning. "Are you still breathing, boy?" Javier put his ear down over Jonas's mouth, and heard a faint breath escape his lips.

"Please…" Jonas heard Javier talking, but his head was fizzing, and he knew the blackness was coming to take him.

"Still hanging in there, huh? Listen up. I've got something to tell you," said Javier with delight.

The group that had survived for so long in Jeffersontown over the last few months had disintegrated over just a couple of days. Javier felt proud, knowing he had used them to the fullest. It was a shame about Rose, but he could always find another woman if he wanted. There was no time left now to truly enjoy the moment, just enough to dispense with some advice. He smiled, remembering the story he and Rose had told them about how they had arrived at Saint Paul's. The part about Rose being pregnant, and the tale about them being high-school sweethearts was pure gold. Every single one of them had taken it in hook, line, and sinker. Rose had taken on Mara's moniker with ease, and he had been surprised how quickly she had adapted. He had found it difficult to suppress his urges to kill them all, especially that interfering old woman Mrs. Danick, but she had got hers in the end. It had been easy to use Gabe's name. There was a part of him that would always be Gabe now, but it was time for a fresh start. Gabe was dead and gone.

Quinn sounded the horn, alerting Javier to the fact they were out of time. He could smell the dead now, and knew it was time to go.

Javier pulled Jonas close, making sure he could still hear. "You know I'm going to find my brother, but I just thought you'd like to know you've left an impression on me. I'm going on a little trip to Thunder Bay. I think I'll look up your sister while I'm there. Janey, wasn't it? Lives in a little red house by the lake? Yeah, that was it. I'll be sure to say hi from her big brother."

Javier pulled Jonas up by his collar, and punched him again, this time knocking him out. He then strode over to Dakota who was curled up in a ball, whimpering. He kicked her in the stomach, and Dakota cried out, clutching her stomach. Javier swiftly kicked her in the back of the head, and the cries stopped as she passed out.

Javier quickly ran to the van and jumped in. He pointed the gun at Quinn, and grinned. "What? I told you I wouldn't shoot them. Now drive."

Quinn's heart raced, but she knew she had no choice. There was a chance Dakota or Jonas would wake, but deep down she knew it wasn't likely. Javier had left them to die, and she was doing the same. As she turned the van around, she thought about Roger, about how he had killed her parents. She blamed herself for that sorry mess, and she felt the same pangs of guilt as she drove away. With Javier pointing the gun at her as she drove, she didn't feel like she had much choice though. At least if she was alive, she could help Erik and Freya.

"Javier, don't make me leave them." Quinn hated leaving Dakota and Hamsikker to die like that. "Please," she said through gritted teeth.

Javier pressed the muzzle of the gun up against Quinn's cheek. "You want to join them? Get us the fuck out of here."

A tear raced down Quinn's cheek as she drove away. It wasn't fair. This wasn't how things were supposed to go. Had she done all she could? Her mind raced to think of something else she could do, but she drew a blank. It was over. Javier had proved he would willfully shoot them all given half a chance. It was killing her that she was leaving Hamsikker and Dakota behind, but what option did she have?

"Degenerate," she said, not caring if Javier heard her. She didn't know what Javier had planned for them now, but was quite sure it wasn't pleasant, and probably didn't involve them being alive for too long.

Javier watched the deserted train tracks recede behind them, and the Illinois River faded from view. Dakota and Hamsikker were lying where he left them, cloaked in dust and blood. The dead were close, and it would only be a matter of minutes before they were torn limb from limb. He stifled a laugh, wishing he could be there to watch it, but Quinn was right. They had to get moving. He turned to face Erik. The man was clutching his daughter closely, his eyes closed. Freya held onto her father but looked back at Javier.

"Buckle up, girl, we're in for a long ride," said Javier, before instructing Quinn to get them back onto the Interstate headed north.

It was important to keep the girl safe and well. As long as she was alive, Quinn and Erik would do whatever he asked to protect her. She was his little star now that Rose had gone, and he was going to make sure she stayed alive. Rose was gone, that was true, but it was just a hitch. Not everything went to plan, and the truth was he had been running out of patience with her. The way she had taken out Peter was reckless. If their cover had been blown back then, well, they were still outnumbered and outgunned, and who knows who would be sitting behind the wheel of the van? It was for the best.

At some point on their road trip, Quinn was going to have a little accident. He didn't intend to take a back seat in this new relationship. She and Erik would come in useful during the trip north, but when they crossed the border, they were history. He had no use for a young girl and even less use for a cop. Once they arrived at Thunder Bay, he could find Diego, and they would be brothers once more. Diego might be running with a crew to stay alive, so Javier knew he might have to change to fit in with his brother's group. Bringing a little girl with him, well, that would just be weird. He'd have to take care of that once they crossed into Canada. Alone again, he would be free. Free of burden, of looking out for this pathetic group of losers, of feeding and watering the parasites that clung to him like leeches, desperate for attention and someone to hold their hand while the world got fucked.

In the distance he saw a fence panel give way, and a plethora of zombies ran through it onto a field that bordered the road. They churned up the grass and ran straight for van, but they wouldn't make it. The road was reasonably clear, and Quinn had her foot down. They were making good progress. He leant his head against the window, and the soothing vibration passed through his head to his bones. His life was taking a new direction now. Javier was back in control, and soon he would be reunited with Diego. He swore he would keep his promise to look in on Janey though. One Hamsikker in the world was too many, and if there was any chance she was still alive, he would make sure she ended up the same way as her brother. It would be good to get payback for Rose.

"Javier, just where are we going?" asked Quinn. "Don't you think we should…?"

"Shut it, Quinn. You know where we're going. Keep heading north until we reach the border. I'm going to find my brother, and you are going to help me. Thunder Bay is a long way off, but we'll get there." Javier turned around to face Freya again.

"Won't we, sweetheart?"

Freya looked down at the keychain in her hand, noticing the green and yellow paint had become scratched. She was supposed to keep it safe for Uncle Hamsikker. He'd told her he needed her to keep it safe for him while he fought off the monsters. Opening up her small hand, she let it drop to the floor. It bounced off her shoe and landed in a pool of dried blood. Uncle Hamsikker was gone now, just like Peter and Mom. None of them were coming back. There was no point in holding onto the keychain anymore.

The funny man sat next to Quinn was scary. He had saved her in the dark hotel, but she decided he wasn't very nice, not after what he had just done to Mommy.

Freya snuggled up to her father and said nothing. She stared out of the window, wishing she could go home, wishing she could play with Peter again, and wishing that her Mom was there to give her a kiss and a cuddle. Freya knew in her heart that none of those things were going to happen. The funny man had changed everything. She wished he was dead. When they stopped, she was going to make everything all right again and kill him. Daddy had told her never to hurt anyone, but this man wasn't nice. She knew that it was okay to hurt people now. It was okay to kill people. So she would. She looked out of the window at the dust cloud they created as they drove, and she felt beneath her seat.

"Next stop, Thunder Bay," said Javier.

Freya's fingers touched the tip of the hammer that her Daddy had left there. She'd kill the funny man just as soon as they stopped.

EPILOGUE

The Illinois River churned slowly around Du Pue, its dark frigid water like a lazy snake curling its way around the land. Occasionally a fish would bob to the surface, or a dead body would slip beneath the water, dragged under by the current. From the banks and the trees, the birds kept a fearful distance, uncertain of the strange behavior of the people in the neighboring towns. They were not so much ghost towns, as dead towns. Scraps of food were hard to find, yet the air was clearer, and there was a proliferation of flies that kept the Cormorants' bellies full.

A flock of Canadian Geese flapped their large wings and settled beyond the disused train tracks. Their black eyes observed the zombie crowd from a distance, safe in the knowledge they were not the target of the mob. The recent activity had drawn their curiosity, but they were no more concerned with what was happening in Du Pue than they were the rest of America.

Pippa's body stirred, and her fingers clawed at the ground, gouging out furrowed lines and leaving her fingernails thick was dirt. Her arms moved next, the muscles throbbing and pulsing until finally her legs began to twist and turn, and her feet found traction on the stony ground. Slowly, her body pushed itself into an upright position. The cold, hard bullets in her body were still there, and her eyes were glazed over. Pippa turned on her feet unsteadily and grunted. There were more like her, close, but they held no interest. She didn't think anymore, didn't try to rationalize where she was or contemplate her existence. There were no thoughts in her head, just basic impulses driving her body forward, the same as a headless chicken will run around long after it should've died.

Just as the van roared away, Pippa had died. The noise was intriguing, but of far more interest were the two bodies lying on the hot ground close to her. They weren't moving, but they weren't like her. They were breathing. Spurred on by the knowledge the living were at hand, Pippa put one foot in front of the other, and soon found herself standing over one of the bodies. There was so much blood. It covered the man's face and arms, and the breaths coming from his mouth were long and labored. Pippa sank to her knees and reached out for the man. She could feel the warm body beneath her cold hands, and opened her mouth, ready to take the first succulent bite. She lowered her head down to the man's, his warm breath ghosting across her face, and she prepared to sink her teeth into his neck.

Suddenly a gunshot rang out, and Pippa's head exploded. Her blood showered Jonas, but he didn't move, even when Pippa's lifeless body fell on top of him. The top of her skull lay on the ground, and her brains leaked from her head like yolk oozing from a cracked egg.

A murmur came from Dakota. Her eyelids twitched open, and she drew in a quick breath before succumbing to a coughing fit.

Another gunshot rang out, and a runner fell. The leading zombies had almost reached them, and the pack of dead was close.

Dakota murmured again. "J...Jonas?" She rubbed the back of her head and found a lump that was too tender to touch. Quickly she withdrew her fingers, and immediately the pain in her belly blossomed into a white-hot pain.

Another gunshot rang out, and another zombie fell down dead only feet away.

"Give me your hand, little lady. I ain't gonna hurt you."

Dakota offered up a hand and felt blinding pain soar through her body as she tried to stand. Collapsing to the ground, she tried to speak, but her dry mouth was full of grit. She winced as she was suddenly lifted into the air. Hands swept under her, and she became aware of lots of hair beneath her. There was a snorting noise accompanied by heavy breathing, and she patted her fingers against the rump of a horse. God, what had happened? Where was Jonas?

More gunshots.

"Get outta here," yelled the voice that had spoken to her a moment ago. She didn't recognize it, but whoever it was seemed to be helping her. She slumped over the horse, and fell into a state of semi-consciousness.

Through the sunlight Hamsikker saw a hand reaching down to him. Either Javier had come back to finish the job off, or he was about to be devoured by the dead. Pain had no meaning anymore. His head felt like it was twice the size it was supposed to be, and he wasn't sure where he was. Maybe he was already dead, and this was Hell.

The hand was rapidly joined by another, and he felt himself being hauled through the dusty street, out of the sunlight and into the shade. His left eye was swollen shut, and blood had dried over the other, making it difficult to see properly. Arms reached under him, and then abruptly he was lifted up into the air. He felt himself being lowered over a man's broad shoulders.

"Erik?"

Jonas couldn't imagine how Erik had gotten away, but the person carrying him now was definitely a man. Jonas tried to look at whoever was carrying him, but he didn't have the strength to lift his head. He heard boots scuffing across the ground, and then they paused. The ground was speckled with blood. Jonas tried to focus, tried to pick out something he recognized, but as he turned his head all he saw was Rose's dead eyes looking back at him. There was a gunshot close by, evidently fired by the man who now carried him.

"Damn zombies," said the man carrying Jonas.

Jonas found himself being lifted higher, and then he was lowered down onto something soft. The surface was warm, moving, and it felt like he was on a horse. How the hell did Erik get a horse?

Jonas reached out a hand, and he felt a body lying next to him. A woman: a living, breathing, woman. Jonas rolled his eyes painfully around his head and saw who he was lying next to: Dakota.

She was alive.

Jonas felt the world spinning away from him again and knew he was about to black out. He wasn't sure which part of him hurt the most, and as he laid there with surging pain racing from his broken bones to his brain, he passed out.

"Easy, brother."

A grizzled, tanned face, weathered by time and sun with creases around the eyes, looked out at the throng of zombies. There was no way forward through them. Ammo was strictly in limited supply these days, and he had done enough. He knew when it was time to attack and when to retreat.

"Hup," the man said, and his horse responded to his instructions, taking them away from the carnage. The man spat out a flavorless piece of used gum and began at a canter away from Du Pue. As they rode, he talked out loud. He didn't know if his two new companions would hear him or not. Some of the words may sink in, and some may go straight over their heads, but the man was used to talking to himself, and it comforted him as much as it did his horse.

"You've been tucked away in your houses and your homes, away from the real world. Things have changed. This country is what you want it to be, what you make it. I'm making it better. You two got lucky today. Real lucky. Time was I would've passed by. Time was any man would've passed you by. You should be banged to rights, dead on your feet like all those other poor saps. I'm guessing you two folks are married, but it ain't really none of my business. I'm just going to get you back on the mend. Can't do much for you other than give you some shelter, some clean water, and see how you fare. When you pull through, *if* you pull through, I'll set you on the road again. That's the way it is now. No point cussing and fighting about it."

The man felt a hand touch on his thigh.

"Please." Jonas hoped that Dakota wasn't suffering as much as he was. His whole body ached, and he felt like sleeping for a week. This man, though, this strange man who talked to himself was a mystery. It wasn't Erik, that much was for sure. Not that there was much he could do about it, but Jonas wanted to make sure they weren't being dragged from one place simply to die in another. He forced his head up, just enough to catch a look at the stranger who had plucked him and Dakota from the ground. The man wore a brown coat or cape of some sort, and Jonas caught a glimpse of a bright purple shirt poking over the collar. The face looking back at him was old but kind. Short white hair sat atop a dark face, and the man's skin was leathery and wrinkled. "Please." Jonas saw the man smile. "Who are you?"

The man seemed to consider his response, as if worried the wrong words might cause offense. "Well, I'm glad you're still alive, son. I was beginning to think I'd picked up two stiffs."

Jonas lowered his head, unable to keep it up anymore. The splashes of sunlight that filtered through his aching eyes burned his retina, and he just needed to sleep. He wanted to sleep for such a long time.

"The name's Bishop. Nothing else, before you ask, just Bishop. I ain't a man of the cloth, neither. I got my own way."

Bishop patted his side, and Jonas caught a flash of light strike against metal there. A small gun protruded from the stranger's belt, but there was something else. It looked like the man carried some serious protection, something more than just a gun. The shiny metal object was long, silvery, and sheathed in something long. The handle was cross-shaped and adorned with small black crosses. Jonas recognized it was a sword, and just before he passed out again, he wondered what kind of a cowboy carried a sword.

"I sure hope you make it," said Bishop. "You seem like good folk to me." He steered his horse home, contemplating what he might have to do before the sun disappeared behind the mountains for the night. "Still," Bishop said patting his sword, "if you don't, I got ways of dealing with that."

THE END

Acknowledgements

If you have enjoyed reading 'Hamsikker 2,' then look out for the next installment.

As ever, this novel is a work of fiction, though it is set in and around some real places. Don't go looking for the real Javier, you won't find him. Other than perhaps in your nightmares…

As always, I thank my publisher Severed Press for their continued support. You can check them out at www.severedpress.com. Please consider leaving a review, and visit my website www.russwatts.co, or check out my other titles:

The Afflicted
The Grave
Devouring the Dead
Devouring the Dead 2: Nemesis
The Ocean King
Hamsikker

CHECK OUT OTHER GREAT ZOMBIE NOVELS

Z BURBIA
by Jake Bible

Whispering Pines is a classic, quiet, private American subdivision on the edge of Asheville, NC, set in the pristine Blue Ridge Mountains. Which is good since the zombie apocalypse has come to Western North Carolina and really put suburban living to the test!

Surrounded by a sea of the undead, the residents of Whispering Pines have adapted their bucolic life of block parties to scavenging parties, common area groundskeeping to immediate area warfare, neighborhood beautification to neighborhood fortification.

But, even in the best of times, suburban living has its ups and downs what with nosy neighbors, a strict Home Owners' Association, and a property management company that believes the words "strict interpretation" are holy words when applied to the HOA covenants. Now with the zombie apocalypse upon them even those innocuous, daily irritations quickly become dramatic struggles for personal identity, family security, and straight up survival.

ZOMBIE RULES
by David Achord

Zach Gunderson's life sucked and then the zombie apocalypse began.

Rick, an aging Vietnam veteran, alcoholic, and prepper, convinces Zach that the apocalypse is on the horizon. The two of them take refuge at a remote farm. As the zombie plague rages, they face a terrifying fight for survival.

They soon learn however that the walking dead are not the only monsters.

CHECK OUT OTHER GREAT
ZOMBIE NOVELS

900 MILES
by S. Johnathan Davis

John is a killer, but that wasn't his day job before the Apocalypse.

In a harrowing 900 mile race against time to get to his wife just as the dead begin to rise, John, a business man trapped in New York, soon learns that the zombies are the least of his worries, as he sees first-hand the horror of what man is capable of with no rules, no consequences and death at every turn.

Teaming up with an ex-army pilot named Kyle, they escape New York only to stumble across a man who says that he has the key to a rumored underground stronghold called Avalon..... Will they find safety? Will they make it to Johns wife before it's too late?

Get ready to follow John and Kyle in this fast paced thriller that mixes zombie horror with gladiator style arena action!

WHITE FLAG OF THE DEAD
by Joseph Talluto

Millions died when the Enillo Virus swept the earth. Millions more were lost when the victims of the plague refused to stay dead, instead rising to slaughter and feed on those left alive. For survivors like John Talon and his son Jake, they are faced with a choice: Do they submit to the dead, raising the white flag of surrender? Or do they find the will to fight, to try and hang on to the last shreds or humanity?

CHECK OUT OTHER GREAT ZOMBIE NOVELS

VACCINATION
by Phillip Tomasso

What if the H7N9 vaccination wasn't just a preventative measure against swine flu?

It seemed like the flu came out of nowhere and yet, in no time at all the government manufactured a vaccination. Were lab workers diligent, or could the virus itself have been man-made? Chase McKinney works as a dispatcher at 9-1-1. Taking emergency calls, it becomes immediately obvious that the entire city is infected with the walking dead. His first goal is to reach and save his two children.

Could the walls built by the U.S.A. to keep out illegal aliens, and the fact the Mexican government could not afford to vaccinate their citizens against the flu, make the southern border the only plausible destination for safety?

ZOMBIE, INC
by Chris Dougherty

"WELCOME! To Zombie, Inc. The United Five State Republic's leading manufacturer of zombie defense systems! In business since 2027, Zombie, Inc. puts YOU first. YOUR safety is our MAIN GOAL! Our many home defense options - from Ze Fence® to Ze Popper® to Ze Shed® - fit every need and every budget. Use Scan Code "TELL ME MORE!" for your FREE, in-home*, no obligation consultation! *Schedule your appointment with the confidence that you will NEVER HAVE TO LEAVE YOUR HOME! It isn't safe out there and we know it better than most! Our sales staff is FULLY TRAINED to handle any and all adversarial encounters with the living and the undead". Twenty-five years after the deadly plague, the United Five State Republic's most successful company, Zombie, Inc., is in trouble. Will a simple case of dwindling supply and lessening demand be the end of them or will Zombie, Inc. find a way, however unpalatable, to survive?

Printed in Great Britain
by Amazon.co.uk, Ltd.,
Marston Gate.